Double take

Carter backed up, but paused at the top of the steps to look at the monitor again. The image really was very cool, despite it not being what she'd wanted. He could watch all of downtown from there, see everybody—there went Taggart, in fact, and two of the Bakers, and he recognized David Boyd. And he could make out the edge of his office from this vantage point, and if he looked down along the street, he could see—

Huh.

That was odd.

He blinked and looked again.

Nope.

Carter frowned and studied the picture. Was he wrong about the angle, or the distance? No, he was sure of it—he covered that same ground at least twice a day, and often more like three or four times. And yet—

Café Diem wasn't there.

He had no idea what that meant.

But he had a feeling it was something big.

EUReKA

ROAD LESS TRAVELED

CRIS RAMSAY

ACE BOOKS, NEW YORK

THE BERKLEY PUBLISHING GROUP
Published by the Penguin Group
Penguin Group (USA) Inc.
375 Hudson Street, New York, New York 10014, USA
Penguin Group (Canada), 90 Eglinton Avenue East, Suite 700, Toronto, Ontario M4P 2Y3, Canada
(a division of Pearson Penguin Canada Inc.)
Penguin Books Ltd., 80 Strand, London WC2R 0RL, England
Penguin Group Ireland, 25 St. Stephen's Green, Dublin 2, Ireland (a division of Penguin Books Ltd.)
Penguin Group (Australia), 250 Camberwell Road, Camberwell, Victoria 3124, Australia
(a division of Pearson Australia Group Pty. Ltd.)
Penguin Books India Pvt. Ltd., 11 Community Centre, Panchsheel Park, New Delhi—110 017, India
Penguin Group (NZ), 67 Apollo Drive, Rosedale, North Shore 0632, New Zealand
(a division of Pearson New Zealand Ltd.)
Penguin Books (South Africa) (Pty.) Ltd., 24 Sturdee Avenue, Rosebank, Johannesburg 2196,
South Africa

Penguin Books Ltd., Registered Offices: 80 Strand, London WC2R 0RL, England

This is a work of fiction. Names, characters, places, and incidents either are the product of the author's imagination or are used fictitiously, and any resemblance to actual persons, living or dead, business establishments, events, or locales is entirely coincidental. The publisher does not have any control over and does not assume any responsibility for author or third-party websites or their content.

EUREKA: ROAD LESS TRAVELED

An Ace Book / published by arrangement with NBC Universal Television Consumer Products Group

PRINTING HISTORY
Ace mass-market edition / April 2011

Copyright © 2011 Universal City Studios Productions LLLP
Eureka ™ & © Universal Network Television LLC
Cover photographs by Joey Lawrence/Syfy.
Interior text design by Kristin del Rosario.

ISBN: 978-0-441-01902-1

ACE
Ace Books are published by The Berkley Publishing Group,
a division of Penguin Group (USA) Inc.,
375 Hudson Street, New York, New York 10014.
ACE and the "A" design are trademarks of Penguin Group (USA) Inc.

PRINTED IN THE UNITED STATES OF AMERICA

10   9   8   7   6   5   4   3   2   1

Published by arrangement with NBC Universal Television Consumer Products Group

To Aaron Rosenberg—
who is me in another life

ACKNOWLEDGMENTS

- Writers don't exist in a vacuum. Unless they write in outer space. I don't, so I had lots of people around while I was writing this book. And some of them were a huge help! Particularly:

- my Transatlantic Twin, Steve, for playing sounding board and cheerleading squad

- my wonderful wife, for her love and support and advice

- our delightful children, for letting me write and being excited when the books arrive

- my awesome editor, Leis, for making this book sing

- Jaime Paglia, for keeping us true to the show and its characters

- all of my fellow *Eureka* fans, who I hope enjoy reading this book—I certainly enjoyed writing it

CHAPTᵉR 1

Whoop! Whoop! Whoop!

Sheriff Jack Carter almost fell out of his chair, and the whole thing tipped sideways. "What the hell is that?" He managed to get himself upright again and staggered to his feet, glancing around. There were warning lights flashing in every corner of the office, in concert with the blaring alarm.

"Burglar alarm!" Jo Lupo was already halfway to the door. "Come on!"

"We have a burglar alarm? Who'd be stupid enough to try breaking into the sheriff's office?" Carter followed her, as much to get away from the siren as to get answers to his questions. Why, even after all these years in Eureka, were there still things he didn't know about the town? And why did his deputy know most of them, and hadn't bothered to share?

"Not here," she snapped over her shoulder, with that patented "You're an idiot, aren't you?" Lupo charm. "Worse."

"Worse? Of course. Why wouldn't it be worse?" They stepped outside and Carter straightened, sighing in relief as the doors closed behind them and cut off most of the racket. "Okay, where— No, don't tell me. Let me guess." There was only one place in Eureka important enough for someone to install the equivalent of a foghorn in the sheriff's office in case anyone triggered the alarm.

Jo nodded. "GD."

"Great. Just perfect." Carter yanked open the door to his Jeep. "Get in. I'm driving." He had the Jeep in gear before she'd finished fastening her seat belt.

"Do we have any idea what tripped it?" he asked, as he floored it and raced toward Global Dynamics.

"Not a clue," Jo admitted, tugging her long, dark hair back into her customary ponytail. "It isn't Section Five, though—that's got a different alarm."

"Of course it does." Still, the news was a relief. Section Five was Global Dynamics' ultra-high-security wing, which housed its most dangerous projects—and that was saying something, considering GD employed the town's best and brightest, and everyone in the town was a genius of one stripe or another.

Everyone except Carter.

And maybe Jo. But he wasn't willing to bet on that one.

So the fact that whatever had set off the alarm wasn't in Section Five meant it wasn't as heavily classified. It might even be nonmilitary. That didn't mean it wasn't valuable, or dangerous, but at least it probably wasn't a weapon.

Not a deliberate one, anyway.

Carter sighed. He was racing toward the world's top research facility to answer a tripped alarm he knew nothing about, related to some project he didn't know anything about either.

Well, at least it wasn't raining.

"Sheriff! Jo!" Fargo was hovering by GD's front entrance as they pulled up. "Thank god!"

"Fargo!" Carter nodded to the wiry little researcher as he braked, put the car in park, switched off the ignition, and levered himself out of the Jeep. Jo was already several feet from the vehicle. It never failed to amaze him how fast she could move, especially since she could never be described as tall. Lovely, yes. Athletic, certainly. Dangerous, no question. But not tall. "What happened?"

"Anomalous readings," Fargo explained as Carter caught up to him and together they headed after Jo. "A containment field rupture in bio lab twelve-B. The security protocols kicked in automatically, of course, but they couldn't compensate for the shift in pressure or the increased ionics. I'm trying to regulate both using an atmospheric moderation program, equalizing pressure and ambient temperature and static charge by redirecting air from neighboring labs, but so far it's a losing battle. I think I may need to—"

Carter cut him off. "Fargo! What are we looking at? What tripped the alarm?" They were inside GD now, charging up the steps, past the security gates and toward the central lobby. Hallways branched out to both sides, and directly across was the curving glass wall that marked the front of the director's office. Carter wanted to glance over and see if Allison was there, but right now he didn't have time for that. Nor did he have time for Fargo's typical stream of science babble. He just needed to know the basics.

Fargo blinked at him. "I did," he confessed. "I tripped it. The alarm in the lab had been disconnected. Someone's stealing the Thunderbird!"

"Thunderbird. Right." Carter glanced at Jo, who shrugged. "Bio lab twelve-B." That, at least, he understood. He took off in that direction, with Jo right beside him. Fargo followed as best he could.

"What the hell's a thunderbird?" Carter muttered to his deputy as they ran. "Besides an awesome vintage muscle car, which I somehow doubt is what they're working on here." Though at GD, you never knew.

"Native American myth," Jo offered, not even out of breath despite the pace they were maintaining. "Massive bird spirit whose eyes shoot lightning and whose wings create claps of thunder. Ancient and powerful."

"That's what they have in bio lab twelve-B? Remind me to stay well away from this place on Adopt-a-Pet day." He only got a faint groan in reply.

Several minutes later they rounded a bend and skidded to a stop outside the door to bio lab twelve-B. It was closed, but not completely—a crack of light showed between the door's edge and the frame. And there was noise coming from within.

"Sounds like somebody didn't finish the job," Jo whispered, drawing her pistol in one smooth, silent motion. Less like a small-town deputy and more like the Special Forces ranger she had been before coming to Eureka.

Carter was convinced she'd switched jobs because she'd wanted something with a little more excitement.

"Any other entrances to this place?" Carter asked over his shoulder, just as Fargo puffed up beside them.

"None," the researcher replied between gasps. "And Drs. Boggs and Korinko aren't in right now—I checked." GD kept track of all its personnel through the communications devices they all carried, which were like smartphones but far more powerful. Everyone in Eureka had them.

"I take it this is their lab?" Carter asked quietly, moving to one side of the door. Fargo nodded. "What about any assistants?"

"One," Fargo replied, "but she's got the day off. Her communicator shows she's out near the lake, has been all day."

"Okay, so we've got an unauthorized intruder in their lab, messing with their project," Carter clarified. Jo had taken position on the door's other side. "Let's take this nice and easy," he warned as he reached for the door handle. "We don't know who's in there, or how delicate this Thunderbird thing is—or what could happen if something sets it off somehow. We just need to—"

He'd only gotten the door open another few inches when Jo slammed her shoulder into it, shoving it back completely and muscling past Carter into the lab. He now realized the lab was filled with smoke and strange, shifting lights. "This is the police!" Jo shouted, her words sharp, clipped, and loud. "Come out with your hands up!"

"Or," Carter muttered to himself, "we could just barge in instead."

Now that Jo had committed herself, however, he didn't

have much of a choice. He wasn't about to let his deputy face whatever the problem was alone. So he stepped into the lab as well, though he left his pistol in its holster. One loose cannon was probably enough.

"What's with the lights?" he wondered out loud, squinting and glancing around. The constant swirls of color made it impossible to see anything clearly, and the farther across the lab he looked, the worse it got. "Listen, whoever's in here," he called out, "we've got the only exit blocked off. So let's talk this out and see what we can do to resolve whatever's going on."

Nobody answered. He thought he saw someone moving near the far side of the lab, but it was just a haze of vague motion and he couldn't be sure.

"Fargo!" he shouted over his shoulder. "Can we do anything about clearing this fog?"

"Fog? There shouldn't be—" Fargo stuck his head through the doorway and stopped, staring. "Oh, that's not good." He gulped audibly.

Carter sighed. He knew he was probably going to regret this, but he just couldn't stop himself. "What isn't good, Fargo?"

"That's not smoke," the researcher explained quickly. "It's spillage from the containment field. Pressurized gas mixed with sedatives and a few other nasties. And now it's expanding. And spreading."

"Great." Carter shook his head. "Shut it off."

"But I can't just—"

"Shut it off, Fargo!"

"It's not that—"

"Now!"

"Okay, okay! Jeez!" He disappeared back into the hall, though Carter could hear him muttering. There was no guarantee Fargo could actually fix whatever this was, but at least someone was on it. And it kept him out of Carter's hair. Fargo meant well, but he could be a bit . . . irritating.

In much the same way water was a bit wet.

"Can you make anything out?" Carter asked Jo, returning his attention to the matter at hand.

She shook her head. "Nothing certain. I think I can tell where all the tables and benches are, more or less, but I have no idea what's on any of them, or where anyone else might be in this soup."

"Yeah, me either." Carter waved a hand in front his face, but it didn't help. "Well, let's just take it slow. If we sweep the room and keep the exit guarded, whoever's in here with us shouldn't be able to get past."

Jo nodded and they spread out, Jo heading to the left side of the lab and Carter to the right. Then they began walking slowly and carefully toward the far wall. As Carter advanced, more details swam into focus—a vague blob resolved into the edge of a long lab table and the shapes upon it became papers and notepads and beakers and wires. But the door was now blurry around the edges when he glanced back. The room wasn't getting clearer; they were just able to see for a short way around them, taking that bubble of clarity with them as they walked.

The problem was that if they moved much farther from the door, they wouldn't be able to see it properly anymore. And then the intruder would be able to slip right by them and take off before he or she could be identified.

Carter stopped. He was pretty sure Jo was still moving forward. If he hung back where he could still just make out the door, he'd be able to keep anyone from escaping. All he had to do was wait until Jo herded the intruder toward him. He relaxed a little.

Which was when the overhead fans kicked on full force.

Followed by the sprinklers.

"Yes!" someone shouted from somewhere nearby, though Carter didn't think the sound had come from in front of him. Regardless, he had to raise a hand to cover his eyes as the fog flattened, clouds of mist becoming long gray tendrils instead, the water somehow condensing the fog and forcing it into a more manageable form. He had to admit, Fargo was a genius.

Now the room really was clearing and Carter could see Jo on the opposite side. He could also see the rest of the room's tables and benches, its computer monitors and testing arrays, its wire-mesh cages—

—and the still-shadowy figure beside one open cage, holding two large, rounded objects close to its chest.

"All right, freeze!" Carter shouted. The figure started, and almost dropped one of its prizes, but clutched at it frantically and pulled it close again at the last second. For some reason, Carter felt relieved. You never knew what could go wrong at GD when things broke or spilled.

And then the tendrils of flattened, water-infused gas began to whip about wildly, every which way.

And the light show intensified, casting long shadows and brilliant beams of light and color in every direction.

Carter was sure he actually heard a sizzle as one of those beams brushed the figure and then illuminated the object in its right hand.

And the object suddenly exploded with light.

"Whoa!" Carter was glad his hands were empty; he'd probably have dropped whatever he had been carrying just so he could get arms and hands up in front of his face. It was like looking at a miniature sun—something Carter unfortunately had experience with now—only this varied more wildly. One second it was searingly bright and the next it had faded to a manageable glow.

Whatever it was.

"What the hell is happening here?" he demanded of the figure, or of Jo, or of the air in general. He didn't care who answered, as long as he got an answer.

"It's one of the Thunderbird eggs!" The reply came from Fargo, who must have returned to the doorway because he had just shouted through it. "It must have hatched prematurely! Most likely the shift in energy and chemical composition around it set it off!"

"Thunderbird . . . eggs?" Carter stared in the direction of the strobing object. Yeah, it did look kind of like an egg. Which would make the large, awkward bird rising up toward the bio lab's roof, wings flapping furiously and producing tiny sonic booms on each stroke, lightning flickering from its golden eyes and all along its hooked beak—

A Thunderbird.

Great.

Jo responded immediately. Her gun swiveled around, its barrel rising to target the new threat, and then she squeezed off one, two, three rounds—

—and watched as the bullets vaporized inches from the incandescent creature.

It cawed, a sound that echoed strangely, like a miniature thunderclap. Its eyes glowed gold and yellow and green. Energy arced across its talons. It seemed to be glaring at Jo.

And then tiny surges of lightning shot from those eyes, coalescing into a wide, flickering bolt that struck Jo in the chest. The blow threw her into the lab's side wall, and she slumped against it for a second, shaking off the effects. Her hair stood on end and her uniform was charred and smoking slightly across the front, though it seemed the fireproofing woven into the fabric had blocked the worst of it.

Right. No shooting the Thunderbird.

"Nice Thunderbird," Carter cooed softly, shifting a little closer as the creature eyed him warily. "Good Thunderbird. Nice and calm. No reason to get all riled up, hm?" He took a step forward and his belt buckle caught on the edge of the table he was standing beside.

Which gave him an idea.

Slowly, to keep from spooking the thing, Carter undid his belt and slid it free. The belt had several small pouches on it, of course, all of them filled with various tools of the trade.

And it was one particular tool he pulled free and held on to as he coiled the belt loosely around his right hand.

He would have to time this carefully.

"Okay, you big ball of feathers and fluff," Carter whispered, once he was sure he was ready—or at least as ready as he could be, given the fact that he had no idea what he was doing, really. Still, going on instinct seemed to work most of the time. Well, some of the time. "Come and get me."

Then he took a deep breath, squeezed his eyes shut for a second, and shouted, "What kind of lousy excuse for a bird are you, anyway?"

The response was immediate. It spun in his direction and its eyes flashed again, the air between them crackling—

—and Carter tossed his belt directly at the Thunderbird, buckle first.

As it flew from his one hand, his other hand shot up and latched on to the belt's tail end—with the handcuffs he'd pulled from their pouch. The belt was sturdy, standard police issue, with small metal rivets all down its length and wire mesh inside.

An excellent conductor.

And the handcuffs weren't those flimsy-looking hand-ties cops used these days. Nope, these were good old-fashioned handcuffs.

One hundred percent stainless steel.

Carter clamped one end onto the belt and the other onto the leg of the nearest table. Which was also metal. And bolted to the floor.

Hey, if Benjamin Franklin could do it with a kite and a key, why couldn't he use a belt and some handcuffs?

The creature squawked at him and lightning shot from its eyes—and was sucked into the belt buckle, down the belt's length, through the handcuffs, through the table leg, and into the floor.

The rubber floor.

Where it dissipated harmlessly.

"Yes!"

But then Carter realized that it hadn't stopped. The belt was still somehow caught up on the Thunderbird, maybe hooked onto one of its claws. And electricity continued to arc down it. The bird was struggling, but it couldn't seem to pull free, or to stop generating those little bursts of lightning. And each one seemed to leave it smaller and weaker.

It was killing itself.

The Thunderbird dwindled rapidly as Carter stared, unable to do anything to save it. There was one last flash, bright enough to blind him for a second, and when his sight cleared the bird was gone completely.

And so was the shadowy figure that had tried to steal it.

Along with the second globe, which Carter assumed to be a second Thunderbird egg.

He growled slightly and bent down to retrieve his belt and handcuffs, which were hot to the touch. Jo was groaning and shaking her head, still leaning against the wall, though she seemed to be recovering. But the thief was already gone.

And then the sprinklers kicked on again. This time, there wasn't any gas left to absorb the heavy spray.

Carter just stood there, getting drenched.

Perfect.

CHAPTᵉR 2

"Carter? Everything okay in there?"

The question—and the voice—made Carter spin around. The person asking was a lot more welcome than Fargo, which wasn't really saying much. But Allison Blake was one of Carter's favorite people in the whole world, a fact that had given both of them some awkward moments—and some serious thought. Right now, though, he was just happy to see her.

The frown that crossed her pretty face, however, suggested she didn't feel the same.

"What exactly is going on here?" Allison asked as she stepped into the bio lab—or, rather, started to step in, glanced up at the sprinklers, and stopped. She tapped a console set beside the door. "Operations, this is Director Blake. Kill the sprinklers in bio lab twelve-B." Carter could practically hear the technicians leaping to obey. Allison ran GD, and though she was by no means a despot, she did expect her orders to be carried out immediately.

"Um, actually," Fargo interjected behind her, "that's not really something they can do right now. I had to bypass the regular interfaces to activate them manually."

"Why did you—?" Allison stopped herself with visible effort and closed her eyes for a second. "Just shut them off, Fargo. Now."

"Right away." He disappeared again, and a second later the indoor deluge ended. Carter was still sopping wet, of course. And now, without the water to block the building's air-conditioning, he was shivering as well.

Great.

"Okay, what happened?" Allison asked again as Jo carefully made her way toward them. "Where are the Thunderbird eggs?" It didn't surprise Carter at all that she knew what the lab held. She knew everyone in GD and everything they were working on. It was part of what made her so good at her job. The other part was that she knew when to be supportive, when to be patient, and when to be demanding. Now was one of the latter times.

"Somebody broke into the lab and killed the alarms," Carter explained. "Fargo noticed and triggered them manually. We got here, found the door open, and stepped inside, but we couldn't see anything—Fargo said something about a containment field leak, I think. Somebody else was in here, but we couldn't clearly see who it was. He or she had two eggs, though." He winced at the memory. "One of them . . . broke."

"It broke?" Allison was shaking her head. "Do you have any idea how much time and money has gone into this project? Each of those eggs represents several million dollars' worth of research!"

"Makes one hell of an omelet, too," Carter joked. But she just scowled at him. Right, not the time for jokes. "Anyway, the Thunderbird got loose, and—"

"Wait, you saw it?" Now Allison bore a different expression: excitement. Carter tried not to notice how attractive she was with her eyes lit up like that, or her lips slightly parted, or— "What did it look like?"

"A bird made of thunder and lightning and storm clouds," Jo answered. "Maybe the size of an ostrich, a little ungainly, with a raptor beak and long talons."

"Yeah, kind of like a Muppet version of a thunderstorm," Carter added. "With wings."

Allison ignored that. So did Jo. Even Fargo just rolled his eyes. What was it with everyone today?

"What happened to it?" Allison wanted to know. "Was it stable? Did it escape?" She looked around wildly, like she expected to find the Thunderbird hiding behind a cabinet or curled up under one of the tables.

"No, it . . . drained away." Carter held up his belt and handcuffs. "It attacked Jo, and was going after me next. I had to do something."

It only took her a second to realize what he'd done. "You used the belt and handcuffs as a lightning rod. Smart." She shook her head. "And the bird was probably too young for its body to have stabilized completely; it was still mostly energy. That's why the whole Thunderbird dispersed when its lightning fed through the belt and into the floor." She sighed. "I'm not sure Boggs and Korinko will be happy to hear that. The bird's longevity has been one of our major concerns the whole time."

"Why would you even want something like this?" Carter asked. "I mean, it was cool looking and all, but unless you're in the market for a guard dog that doubles as a night-light, I don't see the point."

"Think about it, Carter," Allison admonished, though gently. "These things are living, breathing storms. They generate more than just thunder and lightning—they produce wind and rain as well. Imagine hatching a dozen of these in a desert somewhere. Or over a drought-stricken farmland."

Carter let that thought sink in. These birds could bring water, and therefore crops, to places that had never been able to sustain themselves before—and to ones that hadn't been able to for years. Yeah, he could see the value in that.

Which meant he could also see why somebody would want to steal them.

"How many people knew about the Thunderbird project?" he asked as Allison led them back out of the room. He and Jo squelched as they walked.

"No idea," Allison answered. "It wasn't classified, so Boggs and Korinko were only under the usual nondisclosure agreements and strictures. They could talk about their work with anybody who had sufficient clearance, which is most of GD."

"Great. That's a lot of potential suspects," Carter muttered. Beside him, Jo nodded.

"But whoever did this knew how to bypass the alarms and deactivate the containment fields," Fargo pointed out. "Not everybody could do that."

"You could," Carter answered.

"Hey, I didn't take them!" the little researcher whined immediately. "I'm the one who called you! I was behind you when you got to the lab, remember?"

"You're also the one who let the thief escape," Jo pointed out sharply. She hated to fail at anything, and Carter knew letting the burglar get away definitely counted as a loss in her book. He felt the same way. "If you hadn't activated the sprinklers, the Thunderbird wouldn't have hatched and we could have caught him. Or her."

"You couldn't see three feet in front of your face," Fargo countered. "And it was getting worse instead of better. I was monitoring the readings outside. The containment field was still leaking. You'd have started feeling the effects in another thirty seconds, and you'd have been in no shape to catch anybody!"

"He's right," Allison agreed, though she seemed to do so grudgingly. "I know how those fields work, and what sort of gases they contain. You'd have experienced dizziness, nausea, drowsiness, and shortness of breath." She frowned. "The ratios are carefully maintained, but when the field was torn open the valves must have gotten jammed open somehow. They were continuing to pump those chemicals into the room. You could have asphyxiated if you'd stayed. And then the gas would have spread into the hall and into the neighboring labs, then throughout the building."

"There, you see!" Fargo puffed out his narrow chest. "I saved everyone at GD!"

"Yeah, by letting our burglar escape with a Thunderbird egg!" Jo snapped.

Carter shook his head. Fargo had done the right thing, he realized. The gas had been the immediate threat, and not just to them. Fargo had taken care of that. It wasn't really his fault that the solution had triggered the egg, and that in countering that problem, Carter had then let the burglar get away.

But that was often the case around Fargo. He always meant well, and some of his solutions were brilliant, but they usually had unintentional side effects.

"At least nobody got hurt," Carter reminded them. Jo arched an eyebrow at him, then pointedly glanced down at her blackened, smoking shirtfront. "Much." He sighed and ran a hand over his short, wet hair. "Now we just need to figure out who the burglar is, catch him or her, and retrieve that remaining egg."

"We also need to figure out how they got through the lab's security and took apart the containment field, all without triggering any alarms," Allison reminded. "I'm not real happy that someone can just waltz in and remove projects whenever they want. If they work for GD, they're violating all kinds of regulations. And if they don't, well, then we have a bigger problem."

Carter nodded. "Absolutely. We'll start by—" He was interrupted by the ring of his smartphone. "Hang on a sec." He pulled it from his pocket and raised the slim device to his ear. "Sheriff Carter."

Then he listened. "Uh-huh. Uh-huh. Really? No, I believe you. Yes, I'm sure you do. No, I'm not being condescending. I'll look into it right away. Yes, absolutely."

He hung up and pocketed the device again. Allison, Fargo, and Jo were all watching him, waiting to hear what the call had been about.

"You're not gonna believe this one," he told them, then corrected himself. "Of course, you will. Why not? That was Mrs. Hendricks, over on Albany Court. She said there's a cold front and she wants me to fix it."

Fargo laughed. "Wow, some people have an exaggerated

faith in your abilities, Sheriff! They think you can change the weather?"

"Apparently so." Carter frowned. "The thing is, Mrs. Hendricks says the temperature has dropped twenty-seven degrees in the past six minutes. It's currently thirty-eight degrees in her house, and the heat isn't helping one bit."

"Thirty-eight degrees? It's the middle of April," Jo pointed out. "That shouldn't be possible."

"I know," Carter agreed. "And even if this was some sort of freak cold front, it wouldn't have hit that fast. Or with no warning. Or with her being the only one affected." As if that were a cue, his phone rang again.

"Okay, not just her," he corrected a minute later. "That was David Boyd. He's got the same freak cold snap."

"Isn't he also on Albany Court?" Allison asked. Carter nodded. So did Fargo and Jo. A few months back, Boyd's house had been one of many that had been switched, exchanged for a house from outside Eureka. That had been a nightmare! For obvious reasons, most of the addresses of the houses involved had stuck in their heads.

Carter's phone rang again; this time it was Dan Harlowe on Durbridge Drive, which was one block over from Albany Court. By the time they'd reached GD's main lobby again, Carter had received four more calls, all of them complaints or concerns about the sudden chill. And all of them from the same part of Eureka.

"Something's causing the temperature to plummet, but only in a four-block radius," Jo summed up. "What could do that? A freeze ray?"

"Don't even joke about it," Carter warned. He glanced at Allison, but she shook her head. Good, no freeze ray. That was a relief.

Allison pursed her lips a second later, however. "I think I know what could be the cause, actually." Her gaze settled on Jo. "Albany, Durbridge, Pershing, Restin—Silver Road's right around there, isn't it?" Carter was annoyed for a half second that she'd ask Jo and not him, before he admitted to himself that he would have done the same thing. He knew his way around the town, of course, but Jo seemed to have a perfect map of Eureka imprinted in her brain. She knew every single street, corner, alley, building, streetlight, turn signal, stop sign, and park bench. He knew for certain because a couple times he'd tried quizzing her. That never lasted long.

Right now his deputy was nodding. "It's right between them, actually. Albany and Durbridge cross it; Pershing's on one side and Restin's on the other."

"That's what I thought." Allison grimaced. "Savile."

"Is that another street?" Carter asked her.

"No, it's a name—Steve Savile." Allison led them into her office and tossed him and Jo towels while she talked. He guessed they were there for when she nursed or changed Jenna, her little girl, but right now he was just happy they were clean and dry. "He's one of our researchers. Been working on a portable ambient heat sink. He must have taken it home with him." She shook her head, looking for all the world like a mom dealing with a kid who'd just done something a little silly. Which, come to think of it, probably summed up a lot of her day-to-day interactions with GD's scientists. Far too many of them still acted like little kids. Really, really smart little kids.

"Okay, so this portable any-bent heat sink is going in reverse and freezing the neighborhood instead?" he asked. He could tell from the looks he got that this wasn't the case. Oh well. He was used to it by now.

"A heat sink," Fargo told him, taking on that pompous tone that made him even more annoying, "is a device you attach to a heat source, like a computer. It siphons off the heat and energy so the source can run without overheating. A portable heat sink would be one you could carry around and attach to any device whenever you needed it."

"Exactly," Allison agreed. "But Savile's been working on something a little more universal. An ambient version. You don't have to attach it to anything—it draws the heat from its surroundings, cooling everything down at once. You could set one of these in a computer bank and maintain all of them simultaneously."

"Only he's drawing the heat from his neighbors by mistake, and turning that part of Eureka into Iceland." Carter nodded. "Got it. So I just need to get him to shut the thing down and everyone should thaw out again."

He turned to Jo. "Go back to the lab while I'm dealing with this. See what you can find there. I don't want the trail to get cold. We've got a burglar to catch. Oh, and stop by the infirmary to make sure you're okay." He gestured at the blackened patch where the Thunderbird had zapped her, and she nodded briskly. "And take Mr. Wizard there with you." He jerked a thumb toward Fargo and watched his deputy's eyes narrow.

"Why?" was all she asked, but the way she ground the word out between her teeth made it clear she would have some other, more choice things to say about this suggestion later.

"He knows the containment field, and the lab, and the people, and the project," Carter pointed out. "And he's already involved." He glared at Fargo, deflating the little researcher's sudden preening. "And he's at least partially to blame for the burglar getting away, so the least he can do is help us catch him or her properly."

"Of course, I'm happy to help, Sheriff," Fargo responded, straightening to attention and snapping off a pitiful attempt at a salute. "Come on, Jo." It didn't help that he had a painfully obvious crush on Jo, and had for years. The look Jo shot at Carter as she followed Fargo from the room made him wonder if Savile had left one of those heat sinks here as well. Carter was shivering, and not from his recent rain shower.

"Why don't I come with you?" Allison suggested as Fargo and Jo headed back to the bio lab. "I know Savile, so I can help you talk to him."

"Sounds good." Carter wasn't about to turn down Allison's company. "Let's go." He tossed the towel onto her couch and headed for the door. He hoped Allison wouldn't mind his blasting the heat on the way.

CHAPTᴇR 3

They drove in silence, mainly because Carter was still busy mentally running through possible suspects for the Thunderbird theft. It wasn't doing him much good, though, because while he did know a fair number of people around Eureka by now, there were still plenty more he didn't know. And a lot of those people worked at GD. Plus, he couldn't limit himself to GD employees, or even to Eureka residents. What if some think tank somewhere else had gotten wind of the Thunderbird project and sent someone to steal the notes or whatever else they could find? What if it was ecoterrorists, worried that the Thunderbirds were a threat to the natural order of things? What if it was Greenpeace?

Okay, clearly that was enough of those thoughts.

Still, it was a companionable silence. Carter couldn't help glancing over at Allison a few times as he drove. She was staring out the window, apparently lost in her own thoughts, and didn't notice his quick perusal. Which was probably for the best. Carter knew he had strong feelings for her, and suspected she did for him as well. Sometimes he wanted to pursue that. But she was also one of his best friends, not to mention sort of his boss. A relationship could be awkward. And that was assuming it worked out. So for now they stayed friends, with occasional meaningful looks or comments to remind one another that more potentially lurked beneath the surface.

"Turn left up here on Restin," Allison instructed, breaking the silence when they reached the affected area. Not that Carter needed anyone to tell him they were getting close. He'd noticed a faint crunching sound a few seconds before, and a telltale sheen to the road in front of him. The entire surface was covered in a thin layer of ice. It wasn't glass-slick like black ice, fortunately, and it was so thin his Jeep's tires shattered it at a touch. But it was still creepy. Ice on the road in April? Even up here, that was just wrong.

As he turned onto Restin, Carter felt like he'd taken a wrong turn into Winter Wonderland. Icicles clung to the streetlights and mailboxes and dripped from the edges of roofs. The sidewalk and street glittered. The entire scene had that still, clear quality you only get in the dead of winter, when it's so cold even the air has crystallized.

He drove slowly, just in case the icy road got more treacherous, and a few minutes later he turned again, this time onto Durbridge, then from there onto Silver.

"That's it." Allison was pointing to a modest stucco home painted an improbable pale orange, and Carter maneuvered his Jeep into the driveway. He shut down the engine, and hoped as he did that the system wouldn't freeze over before they returned. That would be a fun one to explain to Henry when they called for a tow.

Opening the car door was like stepping into a meat locker. A blast of ice-cold air struck him full in the face as he stepped out, and he could feel the last little bits of water on his hair, face, and uniform freezing instantly. He took a deep breath, and it burned all the way down to his lungs.

Yep, just wrong.

Allison, however, was twirling around like a little girl, and giggling. Giggling! She was holding both hands up like she expected it to snow at any second. Carter glanced suspiciously up at the sky, but it was clear. A sudden blizzard in a four-block area was all he needed right now. She didn't seem too concerned, however.

"Having fun?" he asked her after a few seconds. He hated to interrupt her when she seemed so happy and carefree, but if it got much colder it could actually pose a serious risk to anyone caught outside without full arctic gear. Including them.

She stopped spinning and flashed him a surprisingly impudent grin, then looked a little shamefaced. But only for a second. "Sorry." She laughed. "I used to love winter days like this when I was a kid. I'd visit my grandparents over the holidays, up in Washington State, and it was sort of magical to go walking in this weather, with everything so still and calm and clear. I miss it sometimes."

Carter nodded. "I used to see my grandparents for the holidays, too," he recounted. "Up in Maine. The snow would get so deep it was over my head. I'd dig a little cave into it and make that my secret fort, and stay out there drinking hot chocolate and reading comic books." He shook his head, chasing the memories back so he could focus on the job at hand. "Not sure we have enough hot chocolate for the entire town, though."

"Vincent might," Allison countered, and Carter had to laugh. Yes, if anyone could supply hot chocolate—in an infinite variety of styles and flavors, no less—to all of Eureka, it would be Vincent. The town's resident chef was known for being able to flawlessly concoct any dish or drink, and for having an endless supply of tasty treats back at the town's sole eating establishment, Café Diem. Still, Allison took the mild rebuke for what it was, and straightened up, leading the way up the frozen path and toward the orange house's sturdy front door.

She was closer to the doorbell, and Carter hung back a step while she pushed it. They waited a second, shivering slightly, but there was no response. So she rang it again.

"Maybe the wires froze," she suggested. But Carter moved closer to the door and leaned in, so his ear was almost touching it. He gestured for her to try again, and she did.

Ding DONG!

"It's working, all right," he replied, straightening up again and putting a little space between him and the door. The last thing he wanted was to have his ear freeze to it. "He's just not home—or not answering." Raising his hand, Carter pounded on the door itself. *Thud thud THUD.*

Nothing.

He tried again.

Still nothing.

"I can bust it down," he said, considering his options out loud. The door looked sturdy but not monstrously so, though of course in Eureka looks could be and often were deceiving. Still, he thought he could batter his way through it. Those years of college ball should count for something.

But Allison put a hand on his shoulder. "That shouldn't be necessary." And she reached into her pocket, pulling out—

—her phone.

"You're going to call the door down?" She gave him a half smile but didn't answer. Instead she was busy dialing.

"Dr. Savile," she said after listening for a second. "This is Allison Blake. I am standing outside your front door with Sheriff Carter. There have been complaints. It's obvious you brought your project home with you and have been working on it here rather than back at GD in your lab." She took a deep breath, and Carter could tell she was working to keep her voice calm. "You are not in trouble, Dr. Savile. Not yet, anyway. But your heat sink is working a little too well. It's drawn all the heat from the other houses on your block, and from the surrounding blocks as well. And I suspect the temperature is still dropping." She was right—Carter was fairly certain it was even colder now than it had been when they'd pulled up.

"You need to shut the heat sink down now," she continued. "Immediately. Otherwise, there will be consequences." She turned off her phone and pocketed it again.

"That's it?" Carter asked her. "Consequences? You didn't even say what they were!"

"I don't have to." The smile she gave him was sweet—and,

under that, a little bit dangerous. Like the smile of a small child seconds away from a massive tantrum.

"Okay, but I—" He stopped midsentence and looked around. "Is it me, or did it just get brighter somehow?" He hadn't even realized it, but the street had been a little dim for a clear early morning. Now he noticed it because the effect was gone, as if someone had cast a thin curtain over the sun and just pulled it back again.

And it felt warmer, too.

He breathed in, and there was only a mild discomfort. Yes, definitely warmer.

"It worked," he marveled. Allison just gave him a smirk before heading back to the Jeep.

As always, Carter was impressed. She was always so calm, so collected. So in control.

Except, apparently, when she was twirling in the cold mountain air, waiting for snow.

"Thanks for coming with me," he told her as he slipped back into the Jeep, started her up, and reversed out of the driveway. "I would've wound up kicking in the door and bullying Savile into shutting the thing down."

"That would have worked, too," Allison agreed, laughing. "But my way there's less cleanup." She leaned back in her seat. "Anyway, you're welcome. It's actually nice to get out for a change, rather than being cooped up in meetings and status reports and presentations all day."

"Is that what you've got lined up when we get back?" Carter chuckled. "Fun!"

"Sometimes it is," she argued. "Actually, one of our researchers thinks she's had a breakthrough with her project, and asked me to stop by for a demonstration. That's one I'm actually looking forward to." She smiled. "Care to join me?"

Carter considered. There weren't any other cases or problems pending right now, except for the Thunderbird theft. He'd left Jo and Fargo to scour the lab, and until he knew what they'd found, he couldn't proceed. So he probably had some time. Plus, wandering around GD with Allison would give him a chance to check on the security systems there, to make sure everyone else's lab was still secure and still wired to report any problems. That wouldn't be a bad thing.

He liked to keep up on what was going on at GD, as much as he could. The projects there had a bad habit of spilling over into the town proper, making messes Carter then had to clean up. If he knew about the projects beforehand, he had a better idea of what had happened and how to stop it or fix it or contain it or do whatever else needed to be done.

And he was always happy to spend more time with Allison.

"Sure," he answered. "Why not?"

"Great!" The smile she gave him was warm and genuine, and did more to combat the recent cold than all the heat lamps in the world.

"So, how's Jenna doing?" Carter asked a few seconds later. "I haven't seen her in days!"

That got a laugh. "You're such a doting godfather!" But Allison was beaming when she said it. "She's doing great, thanks. I think she tried to talk the other day!"

"Of course, she did," Carter agreed. "She's, what, six months old now? She should be writing her dissertation soon!"

"Only if she follows in her big brother's footsteps," Allison joked. Kevin, her son, was a teenager now.

"How's Kevin doing, anyway?" Carter smiled. "No more sidewalk graffiti?" On his first day in Eureka, several years ago now, Carter had seen Kevin drawing with chalk on the sidewalk near the sheriff's office. Drawing an incredibly complex string of mathematical equations.

"He's good," Allison answered. "His new tutor's been wonderful at bringing him out of his shell, though of course the effect is only temporary." Kevin was autistic, and spent most of his time wrapped in his own thoughts. But when he did emerge, those thoughts were often brilliant, even for a place like this. Carter suspected that the lanky teenager might be the smartest person in the entire town, which was an unsettling thought. Fortunately, Kevin was also a sweet, good-natured boy, even if he could be incredibly cryptic on the rare occasions when he chose to interact with the rest of the world.

Carter looked over at Allison again, admiring the way she glowed when she talked about her kids. It hadn't been easy for her, he knew. Her first husband, Kevin's father, had died long ago, and she had basically raised Kevin on her own while working and dealing with his autism. She'd met and married Nathan Stark shortly after moving to town, but that relationship had fallen apart and Nathan had left Eureka. It had been rekindled—much to Carter's chagrin—when Nathan returned, and the two had actually planned to marry again before Nathan gave his life to save Eureka—and in fact the world—from a time-space experiment gone horribly wrong. A few months later Allison had discovered she was pregnant with Nathan's child. Carter had helped as best he could, including being her birthing partner, but she was still a single mother raising two children while balancing an incredibly complex and demanding full-time job. And yet he saw how she doted on both kids, and what a great job she was doing with them. It was truly amazing.

"You know what Kevin needs?" Carter told her. "A pet! You should get him a pet! But not a boring one, like a cat or dog or a turtle. He needs something different. Something more . . . exotic."

"What, like a Thunderbird?" Allison swatted him on the arm. "Yes, because it's not bad enough cleaning up after a teenage boy—even an autistic one—and a toddler; you want me to have a small sentient thunderstorm floating through my house as well! Thanks a lot, Carter!"

But she laughed as she said it, and Carter grinned. This whole little detour to deal with Dr. Savile and his heat sink had been worth it, just to cheer him up.

Too bad they had to go back to GD eventually.

CHAPTᵉR 4

"I don't believe this," Jo grumbled as she marched back down the corridor. "Bad enough I've got to work a case here at GD, and that Carter's going to be counting on me to find something useful. But now I've got to do it with a bloody albatross around my neck?"

"Hey, I resent that!" Fargo was practically jogging to keep pace. Jo sped up. "Sheriff Carter asked me to help because he knows how valuable my input can be."

"Yeah? Valuable like when you gave the thief a smoke-screen so he could get away?" Jo snarled over her shoulder. "Valuable like when your little sprinkler trick hatched one of those eggs in the first place? That sort of valuable? Because I'm not seeing a whole lot of value there—at least, not for us, anyway."

"I had no way of knowing the combination would set off the egg," he protested between breaths. "The egg was less stable than I'd expected. And I had to deal with the containment gases, for everyone's sake."

Jo just growled and gritted her teeth. The worst part was, she knew he was right. He hadn't really done anything wrong;

he had been trying to help. Hell, he *had* helped—she and Carter would have succumbed to those gases otherwise, and who knows how many other people at GD might have been affected? Plus, the thief did escape, but at least with only one Thunderbird egg instead of both. That was something.

But she was still pissed. Pissed that they'd let the thief get away, pissed that they'd needed Fargo's help at all, and pissed that now he had a license to tag along and make annoying comments and puppy dog eyes at her. Great.

Jo much preferred working alone. She wasn't good with partners, even—maybe especially—if they were her friends. Even Carter drove her nuts sometimes, particularly when they shared a case. At least Carter was a trained law enforcement professional. But a civilian like Fargo? She was going to have to devote way too much time, energy, and willpower to not throttling him every time he opened his mouth.

And she could really use her full concentration right now.

She reached the door to bio lab twelve-B just in time to see someone else disappearing into it ahead of her. Damn! She picked up the pace, breaking into a short sprint, and was just shy of the doorway when she heard the shriek from within.

"My lab!"

Okay, so not the thief coming back to snatch anything he'd missed the first time around. Probably.

Jo ducked through the door and studied the figure in front of her. Female, average height or just a bit above—which meant she'd tower over Jo—solid build, glossy black hair.

"Dr. Korinko?" It was a safe bet on Jo's part. She knew the other Thunderbird researcher, Dr. Boggs, was a guy.

"What?" Dr. Korinko turned, saw Jo, took in the uniform, blinked, blinked again, and then twisted around fully, the concern on her face collapsing into relief. "Oh, thank god! Someone's trashed my lab!"

"Yes, I know." Jo gestured behind her. "Why don't we talk in the hall, where it's . . . cleaner?" She backed up, and the researcher followed her. Fargo almost smashed into them as he skidded to a stop in the hall outside.

"I'm sorry, Dr. Korinko, but there was a break-in," Jo explained. She experienced a brief thrill from the statement, which she did her best to hide. It wasn't often that she got to deal with a standard crime. Escaped robots, marauding viruses, mutated experiments, absolutely. But a break-in? Almost never. "Someone broke into your lab and stole one of the Thunderbird eggs."

Dr. Korinko was naturally pale, but now she turned white. "They're gone? Oh, no."

"One of them is," Jo corrected. She took a deep breath. "The other one . . . There was a gas leak when the thief shattered the containment field. The sprinklers took care of the gas, but the combination—"

"—caused the egg to hatch prematurely," Korinko finished. She sighed. "We'd been working on ways to increase stability in order to prevent exactly that situation. So far we haven't found anything without sacrificing viability and other key factors." She glanced around. "What happened to the fledgling?"

"Destroyed," Jo admitted. "It attacked us, and Sheriff Carter was forced to siphon off its energy to prevent that. The entire Thunderbird came apart at the seams."

The doctor was nodding to herself. "Yes, it would," she agreed. "That soon after birth, and especially a premature one, its energy matrix would still be highly unstable, as would its physical cohesion. It was more energy than flesh to begin with, and even more so at that point." She met Jo's eyes. "I'm sure you had no choice. I'm glad no one was hurt." Her gaze flicked to Jo's shirt, then back up, and narrowed. "You didn't get hurt, did you?"

"Not enough to matter." She'd gotten a hefty shock from the blast, but the uniform had absorbed a lot of it. Beyond some intensive hair repair and a clean uniform and maybe some salve for any bruises, she was as good as new.

"Good." Korinko stood. "Does Sean know yet?"

That was Dr. Boggs's first name, Jo remembered. Sean. "Not yet. It only happened an hour ago, and we wanted to inspect the lab before contacting either of you."

"He should be in soon," Korinko mentioned. "But of

course, do what you need to do." Her mouth pursed. "Do you know who did it?"

"Not yet." That's what Jo was hoping to find out from looking around the lab.

"And whoever it was, they got away with the second egg?"

"Yes."

"You'll need to be careful when dealing with it," the researcher warned. "That egg was unstable to begin with, and taking it from its containment field will only make matters worse. It could erupt at any time, especially if subjected to loud noises, heavy vibrations, rapid changes in temperature, or any other altered stimuli."

"Erupt?" Jo didn't like the sound of that.

"Yes. Explode. Hatch." Korinko smiled. "Unfortunately, when you're dealing with a creature that's mostly electricity, one is much the same as the other. When it tears free from its shell there will be a burst of energy that accompanies that escape. Here in the lab we have equipment to absorb most of that discharge, and to shield against it. If the thief doesn't have similar preparations . . ."

Jo nodded. "Things could get messy." She thought about the first egg and its former inhabitant. "What about the Thunderbird itself? If it does hatch, how stable will it be?"

"Very," Korinko replied, "if it has twenty-four hours to stabilize. Before that?" She shrugged. "These two eggs are numbers one forty-eight and one forty-nine in our attempts. So far we've never had one survive more than an hour past birth. Sean and I were hoping these two would be different." She sighed again. "It could disintegrate the second it breaches the shell, or the instant it tries to use its lightning. Or it could survive the next fifty years. There's no way to be sure."

Jo rubbed her stomach. "Well, if the first one's anything to go on, shooting lightning won't kill it." Which didn't necessarily improve matters. In some ways, they'd be better off if the remaining Thunderbird did fall apart the minute it broke free. Then they wouldn't have to worry about a sentient, enraged miniature thunderstorm wandering Eureka, electrocuting anyone who got in its way.

"There is one good thing in all this," Fargo pointed out, and both Jo and Korinko glared at him. He gulped, but continued. "The egg's going to require constant attention. Otherwise, it could hatch early, just like the first one. And whoever stole it wants it for something, or they wouldn't have taken it in the first place. So they're going to be busy monitoring the egg, which should distract them."

Jo hated it when other people noticed something before she did, but she couldn't deny Fargo's logic. The thief obviously knew the egg was valuable, and so he'd want to keep it intact. Which meant he'd be busy watching the thing like a hawk—and would never see her coming.

Assuming she could figure out who he was and where he was hiding, and get to him before he had a chance to sell the egg or whatever else he had planned for it. If he was smart and he was looking to sell the thing, he'd have lined up a buyer first and stolen it second, which didn't give her a whole lot of time. But he may not have counted on having to babysit the thing, and she'd take whatever advantage she could get.

Fargo was watching her closely, clearly waiting for her to acknowledge his contribution, and Jo forced herself to smile and nod. He beamed like he'd just won first prize at the county fair.

Great.

"Any idea how long we have before it hatches, assuming it's cared for correctly?" she asked Dr. Korinko quickly.

The Thunderbird researcher frowned. "Within the week, I'd say," she answered after a moment. "The eggs reached full maturation just a few days ago." She looked torn between tears and rage. "All that work, and we didn't even get to see it hatch!" Her reaction further convinced Jo that Korinko, at least, hadn't had anything to do with the theft.

Which left the glaring question of who did.

The first thing Jo needed to check was the door panel. Every door in GD had one—some required everything from a password and voice match to a retinal scan, while others had a simple OPEN/CLOSE button. But it was the perfect place to look for fingerprints, and it also kept a record of when it was opened and by whom.

But she had to stifle a groan as she turned to the panel and saw instead an array of wires protruding from a gaping hole in the wall.

"Where is the door panel?" she asked softly.

"I had to pull it off to get to the controls," Fargo explained. He glanced around and frowned. "I'm not sure where it went. I set it down somewhere nearby, but I was a little busy with the programming to worry about it. I suppose the janitorial staff may have swept it up already."

Jo closed her eyes, clenched her jaw, and counted to ten. A crucial piece of potential evidence, swept up with the trash because Fargo had tossed it aside like, well, trash. Great. Even if she could find it, any prints would probably be long gone, and no doubt its circuits had been broken or lost as well. The overall security log would have records for the door, but there were ways to bypass those. She'd hoped the actual lock would be more foolproof. She hadn't realized it would also need to be Fargo-proof.

Well, she'd check with the janitorial staff just in case, but most likely the panel was a dead end. At least she still had the lab itself to look over. Preferably alone.

"Fargo, why don't you stay out here and discuss technical details with Dr. Korinko while I inspect the lab," Jo suggested as sweetly as she could. He started to argue, then saw the look on her face and instead nodded quickly. Good. That would keep him out of her hair for a few minutes, anyway.

Leaving the two eggheads to natter on about wavelengths and chemicals and whatever, Jo carefully stepped back through the lab door. The place was a disaster—no wonder Korinko had screamed. Between whatever the thief had done to get in initially, the damage from the containment field's collapse, the additional damage from Fargo's attempts to contain that, the explosion of the Thunderbird hatching, the energy blasts from its attacks, and the detonation when it blew apart, the place looked like . . . well, like it had tried to cage a small but powerful hurricane.

Which, in essence, it had.

That didn't make investigation very easy, though. Jo picked her way through shattered test tubes and fragmented beakers, past blackened, twisted cages and charred, water-logged notes. The tables were still mostly intact, as were some of the chairs and stools, but almost everything else had been destroyed. She assumed Korinko and Boggs had backed up their research, but that could only do so much. They'd probably lost months, if not years, worth of work.

And a lot more than that if Jo couldn't recover the Thunderbird egg.

But even after scouring the room for twenty minutes, Jo had to admit she was coming up empty. There was nothing to go on. Any fingerprints that might have existed had been washed away. Same with any footprints. The security cameras were fried as well, and though she'd call up any recent footage, Fargo had already mentioned that the thief had disengaged the cameras when he'd bypassed the alarms. She might have been able to tell if the door had been forced open, though with all the additional damage during the thief's escape, it would now be impossible to tell which damage had occurred when.

She could try tracking security footage in the hall as well, she realized. Fargo had mentioned that they'd been blanked all the way from the lab to the front entrance, but maybe that was only for as long as the thief thought he would need a clear path. Maybe he'd gotten careless and missed a second on the way in. Still, even if she got that lucky, Jo wasn't sure that a brief glimpse was going to be enough. And this thief had definitely come prepared. All it would take was a scrambler of some sort, or simply learning the cameras' sweep patterns and ranges and pulling on a mask and gloves while standing in a dead zone, and they'd never see anyone suspicious. She might have better luck on the departure, since the thief had exited in a hurry and it would be harder to disguise something the size of the Thunderbird egg. Though it wasn't impossible; she could think of at least three ways to get that egg down the hall and out of GD undetected.

She sighed.

This day was not off to a good start.

And to make matters worse, Fargo was still waiting when she returned to the hallway. His whole face lit up when he saw her, and he trotted over to her at once. Just like a puppy dog. A big, annoying, yappy puppy dog. That kept getting underfoot. And chewing your favorite slippers.

Wonderful.

CHAPTᵉR 5

"Now, what exactly are we going to see?"

Allison laughed as she led Carter through the GD corridors. "Extradimensional visualization."

"And what is that when it's at home, again?"

"Quantum physics shows us that there are other dimensions beyond our own," she explained, falling into lecturer mode. Carter didn't mind—he was pretty sure if he'd ever had a teacher who looked like her, he'd have shown up for every class.

"Sure. This is the third dimension, right?"

That earned him one of her "are you kidding, or really that dense?" looks. It was an expression Carter knew all too well. "No, Carter—there are three physical dimensions to any solid object. That's different. I'm talking about dimensions as in planes of existence. Everything we know—this world, the planets, the stars, all of it—that's all the same dimension. The same reality."

"Oh. Gotcha. So other dimensions mean other realities."

"Exactly."

"And whoever we're going to see has figured out a way to take us to them?"

Allison laughed at him again. At least when she did it, it wasn't mean. "No, though that could theoretically be possible someday; scientists have been working on ways to link two dimensions together. But extradimensional studies are still in their infancy. Up until now, it's all been theory and numbers. Dr. Russell is hoping to get past that."

"How so?" They took the stairs down one level, and then headed through another corridor. It was easy to get lost in GD—it was larger than most shopping malls.

"She's worked out a way to collect electromagnetic input from another dimension," Allison answered. "Then she'll filter the energy, remove any traces of our own reality, analyze the energy for any patterns, and use those patterns to organize it into a pixilated grid!" She beamed at Carter as if this was the most incredible thing she'd ever heard. Carter just stared at her. "Pictures, Carter! She's talking about finding a way to actually see another dimension!"

"Oh." He took that in. "That is cool. Snapshots of another reality, huh?"

"Exactly!" They stopped at a lab door, and Allison entered a code into the door console. The red light flicked off, to be replaced by a green one, and the door slid open. "It'll be blurry, and we'll probably have to run a variety of extrapolation programs just to make any sense of it, but this will be our first-ever glimpse into a different reality. The amount of information we could gain, both about that reality and, by extension, our own, is almost infinite!"

"Right. Cool." Carter didn't really get it, but Allison's enthusiasm was infectious anyway. She was excited, so it must be something exciting. He was okay with following her lead.

"Think of it as extradimensional sonar," a tall, striking blond woman said as she crossed the lab to greet them. "We're basically throwing energy waves into that universe, then absorbing them as they bounce back, and using that echo to build an outline or image of whatever they touched. The only difference is, we're not actually generating the energy ourselves, since it would require an immense energy output just to breach the dimensional barrier. All we're doing is tapping into the energy already there and analyzing it to see what it has rubbed up against." She held out a hand. "Nancy Russell, extradimensional visualization project. Nice to finally meet you, Sheriff."

"Uh, same here," Carter replied, shaking her hand. She had a firm grip. Also, a nice smile. And killer legs. He pretended not to notice. Why didn't all GD researchers look like her and Allison? He'd gladly become a mad scientist if it meant toiling in a lab with them all day.

"We're almost ready," Russell was telling Allison. "We're just powering up our equipment now." Behind her, three technicians were throwing switches and typing in commands on an array of monitors and computer banks. Carter watched as lights burst into being all around the room, tiny circles and squares and blinking rectangles and crackling arcs—

Crackling arcs?

"Look out!" He was moving before he'd really registered what he'd seen, and was halfway across the lab before his brain had finished processing that image—a crackling arc of electricity, bursting from a wiring juncture and spilling out along a power cord—

—which then led back to the computer banks, and toward the center of the room.

Carter was no electrician, but he knew a short when he saw one. And he knew that if it reached the monitors and the rest of the equipment, it could fry the entire system. Not to mention anyone touching it or even standing too close to it.

He couldn't let that happen.

Instead he lunged at the juncture. The wires were all bundled together there, and he was guessing one of them had come loose or somehow gotten exposed. There was no time to figure out which one. Instead he simply wrapped his hand around the entire bunch, tensed, and gave a fierce yank.

Zot!

"Yowtch!" The shock traveled up his arm and into his body, quivering its way through him in an instant, and Carter felt his hairs stand on end. His teeth rattled together, and his ears were filled with a sharp buzzing sound. The charge dis-

sipated in an instant, however, and he sagged against a nearby console, the wires still in his hand, their circuit broken.

"Carter, are you okay?" Allison was next to him a second later, and immediately started checking his pulse, temperature, and eye dilation, the medical doctor in her rising to the fore. "You shocked the hell out of me!" Her eyebrows rose as she realized her own pun.

"Wow," was Russell's comment as she joined them. "Thank you, Sheriff. I don't know how that happened. It looks like one of the wires may have been tugged loose slightly, probably when we reconnected them earlier or maybe when we repositioned one of the computer banks. If you hadn't noticed when you did, and acted that quickly—well, we all could have been experiencing an energy surge of our own, and not in a good way."

"All part of the service," Carter managed to gasp out, pounding his chest to get his lungs working again. He felt like he'd just run a marathon and then stepped into a sauna, every part of him taut and vibrating but all of his energy sapped away.

"You don't seem worse for the wear," Allison decided after finishing her cursory exam. "Good thing you broke the connection quickly, though. And that you're wearing rubber soles."

"Yeah, being grounded has come in real handy lately," Carter agreed. One of the techs had joined them, and Carter let the man pull the wires from his hand. It took some effort to get his fingers to cooperate, though. He took a few deep breaths, then forced himself upright and tried to stretch everything out a bit. It wasn't easy.

"The electricity made all your muscles contract," Dr. Russell told him. "That's why you're having trouble moving—and speaking. The effect should fade, though." She gave him a smile. Nice smile. "I think you may have saved our lives."

"That's kind of what he does," Allison agreed. And did Carter imagine it, or had she moved just a little bit closer to him when Russell smiled? Like she was marking her territory?

"Found the problem," another tech announced from the far side of the console Carter had leaned against. "Fuse burnt out on one of the safeties here. When we powered up, that circuit got fed too much juice and overloaded. The excess had nowhere to go but that coupling."

"And my arm," Carter muttered. His jaw was still clenched tight, but he could open his fists again, with effort. That was an improvement.

"Everything's reset," the tech assured them. "We're all good to continue."

"Right. Let's start the power-up sequence from the beginning," Russell announced. "Just to be on the safe side. Sheriff, Director, maybe you want to wait over there?" She indicated a row of seats along the back wall, facing both the computer banks and the massive flatscreen monitors mounted on the opposite wall.

"Of course." Allison led Carter to the chairs, and after a minute he managed to sit down stiffly. Now he knew what the Tin Woodman had felt like. "I'll still want you to stop by the infirmary afterward," Allison warned him quietly once they were seated. "Just to be on the safe side. But I think you'll be okay for now, and I'd hate for you to miss this." Her lips quirked in a smile. "Especially when you've paid such a high price for admission."

Together they sat and watched as all of the equipment, which had gone dark after he'd pulled the plug, began to power up again. This time there weren't any disturbing sparks, and after a few minutes each tech announced that his station was all clear. Russell, who stood by the center console, nodded and threw a switch. Then she typed in a short series of commands and dramatically hit *Enter*.

"We've begun the collection process," she explained to her audience of two. "It will only take a minute for our extradimensional scoops to draw in enough energy to form an image." Behind her, a line of text appeared on the screen. "We've currently collected sixty-two percent of the necessary data, and we're building rapidly," she called out after reading it. "Seventy-six. Eighty-nine. Ninety-four. One hundred percent—we have enough raw data. Next step, number crunching." She typed in the next set of commands.

"I prefer my numbers smooth," Carter whispered to Allison. "Not as annoying to everyone around me. Especially during a movie." She elbowed him in the side, but did so gently.

A few more minutes passed before they heard a chime and saw more text flow across the screen. "Number crunching is complete," Russell announced. "We've filtered the gathered energy, broken it into patterns, and parsed those using a mathematical equation that maps them onto an ordered grid. Then we've applied that grid as a visual pattern, and the result is—" She tapped a key, and the large central monitor began to glow with light, then swirls of color. "Our first look at another reality!"

Carter watched, entranced, as the swirls shifted and settled, the colors clumping and adjusting to become hues and shades, creating shapes and depth. After a few seconds, he was squinting at the image, trying to make out some sort of shape within it. Just like staring at clouds, or those optical illusion pictures, he thought. And the longer he stared, the more the scene resolved itself into something that looked like—

—downtown Eureka.

"Wow!" Carter gazed at the monitor. "That's fantastic!" It was a perfect image, as if he were standing downtown instead of sitting in a lab at GD. There was his office, and there was the little park across the street, and there was the dry cleaner's, and there was the hardware store, and there was the crosswalk whose signal often went on the fritz, and there was the statue of Archimedes, the town's patron saint—the image was so clear, it seemed as though any second now the people walking past would turn and say hi.

The room's other occupants didn't share his enthusiasm, however. Dr. Russell had sagged against the console. "No, no," she was saying softly, and though Carter couldn't see her face, she sounded on the verge of tears. Allison was out of her chair in an instant, hurrying across the lab to console the taller woman. She put her arm around Russell's shoulder, and seemed to be talking to her softly. Russell nodded a few times, and may have murmured something back, but didn't glance up. Carter couldn't think of too many executives who could get away with being so touchy-feely, but somehow Allison managed it without losing even an ounce of her authority. If anything, it made her employees respect her even more. They knew she was there for them, and that she was really concerned for their well-being.

Carter rose from his seat as well and wandered closer to the two women, though he wasn't sure what he could do to help. Hell, he wasn't even sure what the problem was.

"It should have worked!" Russell was saying over and over again. After a few seconds of that, she straightened up and patted her cheeks, which were now bright red. "It should have worked! All the calculations were correct, I'm sure of it!"

"I know," Allison agreed. "I saw your figures. Everything looked perfect." She frowned. "Maybe your collection array got misaligned somehow?"

"That's possible," the tall blond researcher admitted. "We double- and triple-checked them, of course, but if we missed something . . . if they'd been set to absorb local electromagnetic signatures instead of extradimensional ones, that could easily include the normal visual spectrum."

"Sorry," Carter interjected quietly, and both women turned to look at him. "I don't get it. You didn't want it to look like that?" He gestured at the screen.

"No, of course not." Dr. Russell had regained most of her composure now, and straightened up, raising her chin. "We're supposed to be looking at a rough approximation of an image of another dimension. It would be grainy at best, like the worst old television signal you can imagine. This—" She glanced at the screen, then turned away. "This is nothing more than a standard satellite image of our own town."

"Maybe so," Allison agreed, "but that's actually an achievement all by itself. Think about it—you managed to view downtown Eureka without a satellite, just by targeting the general area and absorbing the energy accumulated there, and then extrapolating that into an image. This could have huge military applications, for one thing—we could see anyplace in the world, no matter how isolated, just by sampling its energy fields! From anywhere!"

Dr. Russell perked up slightly. "Yes, I suppose that's true. I'd only been considering the extradimensional ramifications of my extrapolation protocols, not the localized ones. But if we—" Carter recognized the impending signs of technobabble, and decided now would be a good time to excuse himself. He was pretty sure the demonstration was officially over.

"I'd better be getting back," he told them, and Allison waved at him absently. She clearly had her hands full, and Carter knew she'd be able to get Russell up and running again a lot more easily if he wasn't around to ask dumb questions. He let himself out of the lab and, after a quick stop at the infirmary to make good on his promise to Allison, he headed back toward the front lobby. His stomach was growling, so he figured he'd stop by Café Diem for lunch, then check in with Jo and see if she'd gotten any leads on the Thunderbird case.

On his way up the stairs, a shadow fell across him, followed by the echo of approaching footsteps. Carter glanced up and saw someone heading toward him. After a second he recognized the tall, gangly figure. "Hey, Taggart!"

The lanky Australian—Eureka's resident hunter, tracker, and animal expert—had been descending the steps with his head down, eyes not entirely focused. He glanced up when Carter called out, looked around, looked at Carter, and nodded. "Oh, g'day." Then he kept on going.

Odd, Carter thought as he moved to one side to let Taggart pass. Taggart was extremely outgoing. Usually he'd stop and chat for ages, about any topic under the sun. In fact, plenty of times in the past Carter had been forced to eventually walk away, leaving the Australian still expounding on some esoteric trivia or recounting one of his bizarre adventures around the world to whomever was still around to listen—or to the empty air. Taggart liked pretty much everybody, and though he and Carter had started off a little rocky—with Taggart tranking him and tossing him in a cage like a stray dog because Carter had been walking through Eureka without proper clearance—they had long since gotten past that and formed at least a tenuous friendship. Ever since, Taggart had always seemed happy to see Carter. This time he'd barely even rated a hello.

Then again, he usually saw Taggart at Café Diem, or out on the streets, or out in the woods surrounding Eureka. This was GD, so Taggart might be in "lab rat" mode, doing his best to behave like a proper GD researcher rather than his usual freewheeling self. Or he might just be preoccupied with something.

Carter shrugged and made his way up the remaining steps to the main floor. Then he headed out to the parking lot and his Jeep. Taggart acting strange was just Taggart. Right now, Carter was more concerned with the New York–style pastrami on seedless rye he knew Vincent could whip up for him, and the old-fashioned chocolate malted that would accompany it.

Those were far more important than feeling slighted because one of Eureka's odder residents hadn't taken the time to bend his ear for a change.

CHAPTᵉR 6

"Okay, that's weird."

Carter leaned over his steering wheel to peer up through the windshield. It was just a little past noon—no wonder his stomach was demanding food so strenuously—and the sun was high, only a few wisps of pale white cloud marring the otherwise perfect blue sky.

Except for the small dark patch off to the left.

It didn't look big from here, no larger than a hardcover book, though Carter was sure part of that was because of the distance. But it was low—low enough to almost brush the roofs in that part of town—and such a dark gray it was almost black, and too filmy and flickering to be anything but a storm cloud.

A really small one.

On a clear, sunny day.

Yep, definitely weird.

But possibly exactly the break he'd been looking for.

He straightened up and returned his attention to the road, pulling his phone from his pocket with one hand while the other maintained its grip on the wheel. He dialed the number from memory. "Jo?"

"Carter."

"There's a storm brewing."

That made her pause for a second. "The sky looks clear here—hold on." Another brief pause. "Got it. Heigel and . . . Plato, I'd say."

"I'll be there in ten."

"I'll be there in five." She hung up.

Carter couldn't decide whether to growl or grin. Did she have to turn everything into a competition? And then win—every time? But of course she did. If she didn't, she wouldn't be Jo.

Well, fine. Because he'd been lying about it taking him ten minutes.

He sped up.

Braking at a stop sign along the way—no reason to actually break the very traffic laws he was supposed to uphold, just like he couldn't really justify running the siren— Carter spotted a familiar figure. Tall, skinny, a little stooped, and wearing a straw hat to protect his bald head, the man wore a loud green flowered shirt over equally loud orange cargo shorts.

No one had ever accused the Bakers of being subtle dressers.

"Hey, Dr. Baker!" Carter called through his window. He had no idea which brother it was, of course. Even Jo and Henry didn't seem able to tell them apart. Hell, sometimes he was sure the Bakers themselves couldn't tell one from the other, and that was just plain creepy. But par for the course around here.

Dr. Baker—whichever one it was—glanced up and saw him. He nodded but didn't wave or say hello back. Instead he simply crossed in front of Carter's Jeep and continued on his way.

Strange. The Bakers were quiet as a rule, but they'd always been polite. And after a recent incident where they—and half the town—had been transplanted outside Eureka, and Carter had helped solve the problem, they had been far friendlier.

Usually whenever he saw one of them they smiled and said hello.

But not this time.

First Taggart, and now one of the Bakers.

He'd definitely showered this morning. And he was too far away for Dr. Baker to have smelled his breath. Was it something he'd done recently? Or something in the water? Or just Eureka's residents acting in their usual bizarre and unpredictable fashion?

Well, whatever. He could live without the Bakers greeting him enthusiastically every time he crossed their path. Right now he had a thunderstorm to chase, and a mystery to solve.

And a deputy to race.

He hit the gas, and his Jeep's tires squealed as he sped away from the stop sign.

Carter took the corner of Heigel and Plato, hard—and then cursed under his breath. Jo's car was already pulled up in front of one of the houses there. The house that had the miniature thundercloud hovering directly over its tiled roof.

How did she always arrive ahead of him?

He pulled up behind her and hopped out, trying to ignore the smirk she directed his way. But that same smirk turned to a grimace when her companion spoke.

"Hey, Sheriff. Took you long enough."

"I didn't realize it was a race, Fargo," Carter replied, ignoring Jo's glare—the glare that clearly said "you saddled me with him, this is all your fault!" Which, in a way, it was.

But they might need a science geek for this. Henry would have been perfect, but as the town's mechanic, mayor, fire chief, and a dozen other roles, he was probably a little too busy to just roam around with them all day. And Jo was a lot of things, and ridiculously good at almost all of them, but science geek? Not so much.

Hence, Fargo.

"Looks like the place," Carter commented, glancing up at the thundercloud. Little flickers of lightning rolled through it here and there, and he could hear the thunder that accompanied them, though it was oddly muted. This was probably due to its size; the entire storm couldn't be more than twenty feet across.

But that was more than big enough to house a Thunderbird, he was guessing.

"Think the second one hatched?" he asked as the three of them approached the house. It was a modest two-story dwelling with a mixed stone and brick front and a small awning over the front door. An awning that wasn't going to shield them from the sheets of water pouring down onto the front steps. The rain was heavy enough for them to hear it from the front lawn, and Carter guessed that walking through it would be like stepping into a heavy curtain—of hard-hitting rain.

His third shower of the day. Swell.

"Possibly," Fargo answered, tailing him and Jo. "Though if it did, it reached a much greater maturity than the last one, and in record time." He smiled. "Dr. Korinko and Dr. Boggs should be pleased."

Yeah, of course, Carter thought. Because having your prize research stolen, then set off prematurely and turned into a house-sized hurricane, was exactly what they'd been hoping for. But still, he knew what Fargo meant.

"I don't see any evidence of the Thunderbird itself," Jo pointed out, squinting up at the cloud. "Though that storm is more than dense enough to hide it, especially since the Thunderbird looks like a storm itself."

"Does it create storms, or is it a storm?" Carter asked. "I wasn't really clear on that part."

"Me either," Fargo admitted. "Dr. Korinko only said that it generated thunder and lightning, wind and rain. She didn't say if it contained those within it or could somehow separate them to produce storms that would remain independent of the Thunderbird's own location." Which just proved why they needed Fargo along on this one—Carter hadn't followed through on his initial thought to realize that a Thunderbird might be able to create storms and then move on, leaving them behind like stray feathers.

"Well, either way, this is the best lead we've had all day."

Carter stopped just shy of the water curtain and took a deep breath. "So here we go." And he plunged into the storm.

His clothes were soaked to his skin in an instant. It only took him three long steps to reach the shelter of the awning, but by then his hair was plastered to his head, his socks were squelching in his shoes, and he could barely see for the droplets clinging to his eyelashes. The water was cold, too—cold enough to make him start shivering again, despite the mild temperature beyond this little weather pocket.

Jo was right behind him, and just as soaked, but she didn't seem to notice any discomfort. Fargo, on the other hand, looked like a drowned rat with glasses, and huddled in on himself as if that would somehow help him dry more quickly.

Carter tried to shake off as much water as he could before turning and ringing the doorbell.

"Dr. and Dr. DelSantos," Jo said softly as they waited. "And their two children, Marta and Tomas."

The door swung open just as she finished speaking, and a teenage boy stood there. His eyes widened as he took in the badges, belts, and guns. "Um, hi?"

"Hi—Tomas, right?" Once again Carter silently blessed his deputy's encyclopedic knowledge of Eureka's residents. "I'm Sheriff Carter. This is my deputy, Jo Lupo, and that's Douglas Fargo from Global Dynamics. Have you got a minute?"

Tomas nodded. He was a good-looking kid, average height and dark skin, buzz-cut hair and dark eyes. The hint of a tattoo peeked up from the collar of his T-shirt, and another showed on his forearm, just above the bracelet there—one of those rubber bands kids wore to show support for various causes. He looked like a surfer, or maybe a skater.

"This is about the storm, isn't it?" Tomas sagged a bit. "Sorry about that. It just got a little out of hand. It should end soon, though, honest."

"Out of hand? Care to tell me about it?" Carter was careful to keep his tone friendly. He also didn't bother to ask if they could come in. No sense dripping all over the hall carpet.

"It's my science project," Tomas explained. "I'm working on a way to shape storms. Alter their size and direction, funnel them to areas that are more in need of rain while by-passing heavily populated regions to minimize any related damage." He shrugged, and gave them an apologetic grin, one that made Carter glad his daughter was already away at college. He had a feeling most high school girls would have swooned if Tomas had grinned at them like that, and he didn't want to see Zoe smitten. Bad enough she had Lucas, but at least he wasn't this confident—or this unafraid of Carter.

"That's an excellent concept," Fargo offered, uncurling from his soaking little huddle. "Most storm-protection ideas involve deflecting the storms, or somehow negating them, but that could deprive areas of much-needed rain. If you could simply sculpt the storm to skirt the edges of any cities, it could be allowed to run its course without threatening urban centers."

"Exactly!" The boy's eyes lit up. "I've been having decent success so far, at least with the lower-impact storms. But the stronger the winds, the more the storm's own force tends to skew it out of shape, making it harder for me to reshape."

Carter interrupted before Tomas and Fargo could get into a lengthy discussion about meteorology. "Okay, that's all very cool, and good luck with your project. But that doesn't explain the little drizzle you've got going on over our heads." He glanced back at the rain just behind them and shuddered. He wasn't looking forward to heading back out through that.

"I needed a storm in order to practice my shaping techniques," Tomas replied. "And it had to be big enough that local wind conditions could affect it, so I could be sure my methods would resist them." He glanced past them. "So I built a storm. I was careful to keep it over our house only, and I asked my parents first." His smile faltered. "Am I in trouble?"

Carter sighed. "No, you're not in trouble, Tomas. But next time, let us know you're doing something like this, okay? That way we'll know when someone calls in about the world's smallest thunderstorm."

"Sure, no problem." Tomas paused for a second. "Hey, hang on." He disappeared, and then returned carrying a small computer tablet. "Let me see . . ." He frowned, thinking, then typed quickly. And waited.

Carter heard a shift in the sound behind him. The rain was still pelting the ground, and the roof, but it sounded somehow—distant. He looked back, and gaped.

The storm was still going full-force, sheets of rain dropping from the sky to crash into the ground—except the steps and the walkway that led down through the front lawn to the curb were clear.

The water had literally parted on either side of that the walkway, leaving them a narrow path through the shower.

"Thanks," Jo told Tomas, and he beamed at her. "And good luck on your project."

"Definitely," Fargo agreed. "I think it's got great commercial application."

"Thanks!" The boy looked thrilled to receive such encouragement. Not that he seemed to need it.

"Thanks, Tomas." Carter offered his hand and the teenager shook it. "And I'm sure you'll do great."

"Thanks, Sheriff. Sorry to drag you out here," Tomas called as Carter followed Fargo and Jo down the pathway.

"Not a problem," he answered over his shoulder. "I needed to cool off a little, anyway."

Back at Jo's car and Carter's Jeep, the three of them turned to look back at the house and its private storm. "Impressive," Carter admitted, shaking his head. A high school student shaping thunderclouds. What would they think of next?

"But it has nothing to do with our missing Thunderbird," Fargo pointed out. "Which makes it just another dead end."

"A dead end we wouldn't be worrying about if you hadn't destroyed any possible evidence back at the lab," Jo snapped.

"What's this?" Carter glanced between them.

"It's not my fault!" Fargo protested—which was pretty much his signature phrase, as near as Carter could tell. He certainly uttered it often enough. "When I activated the sprinklers to take care of the containment gases, they washed away any trace evidence the thief might have left behind. But it was either that or flood the entire building with those chemical compounds!"

"Did you have to throw away the door's access panel while

you were at it?" Jo demanded. She nodded to Carter. "Yeah, when he got in there to manipulate the lab's systems he tossed the panel. It's gone. We think the janitors saw it as trash and swept it up. And I talked to them—they'd already put the day's load into the incinerators, so if it was in there it's nothing but ash now."

Carter sighed. That figured. The panel might have had the thief's fingerprints on it, in which case they'd know exactly who they were looking for rather than wandering all over town chasing clouds. Well, there was nothing they could do about it now. "We were all a little busy at the time," he reminded his deputy. "And none of us knew we were going to have to chase this down later."

"Even so," Jo grumbled. "A little more care then and we'd be in better shape now." Carter knew most of her anger was actually at herself for not catching the thief in the lab, but he still felt a pang of sympathy at the hurt that flashed across Fargo's face.

"A little more speed then and you'd have caught him in the first place," Fargo muttered in response, then shrank back as Jo turned on him, fists clenched. "Hey!"

"Enough!" Carter reprimanded them both. He felt like he was dealing with two squabbling children. "Do I have to separate the two of you?"

"Yes!" Jo replied immediately.

He just shook his head.

"Keep looking," he instructed instead. "And try to get along, okay? The sooner we find this thief and retrieve the egg, the sooner Fargo can go back to GD and we can get back to whatever other problems have cropped up in the meantime."

"What're you going to do?" Jo called out as Carter headed for his Jeep.

"Me?" he answered, pulling open the door. "I'm going to get something to eat."

She was still glaring at him as he drove away.

CHAPTᵉR 7

"Hey."

Carter waited, but Dr. Russell didn't respond. She had her back to him, though, head down on her crossed arms on the desk, so perhaps she hadn't heard him. He stepped all the way into her lab and tried again.

"Dr. Russell?"

"Hm?" This time she turned slightly, and favored him with a wan smile. It was pale echo of the warm look she'd given him this morning. "Oh, hello, Sheriff."

"Hey, are you okay?" He walked across to the desk and leaned against it, not too close to invade her space but close enough to talk easily. From there he could see that she'd probably continued crying for some time after he'd left, even with Allison's attempts to suggest positive sides to the experiment's failure. What little makeup she'd been wearing had long since run and then dried, leaving faint streaks of mascara down her cheeks. She was still just as striking, however.

"I don't know," she admitted quietly. "I've been working on this project for the past two years. I thought we'd worked out all the variables, answered any possible problems, closed off any risk of course deviation. But still—" She waved her hand at the screen. It still showed the same image of downtown Eureka.

"Didn't you say something this morning about the inputs being misaligned?" he asked her softly. But she shook her head.

"It was a possibility, but we checked them again, and then again. They're exactly as they should be." She straightened up and tossed her hair back—it was a bit tousled now, though the look suited her. "Basically I just need to face the fact that I screwed up somewhere."

"I'm really sorry." He didn't know what else to say.

"Not your fault." She gave him another weak smile. "Nobody's, really. Just my own." She looked like she might start crying again.

"Do you want me to leave you alone?" Carter asked. He'd noticed that the techs weren't around—he'd been heading down to check on the GD security logs and had decided to swing past her lab, and the door had been open.

"I'm sorry, I'm afraid I'm not very good company right now," Dr. Russell answered.

"No problem." He hopped down off the desk. "If you do need anything, though, just let me know. Okay?" She nodded, but he wasn't sure she'd really registered what he'd said. That was all right.

He backed up, but paused at the top of the steps to look at the monitor again. The image really was very cool, despite it not being what she'd wanted. He could watch all of downtown from there, see everybody—there went Taggart, in fact, and two of the Bakers, and he recognized David Boyd. And he could make out the edge of his office from this vantage point, and if he looked down along the street, he could see—

Huh.

That was odd.

He blinked and looked again.

Nope.

Carter frowned and studied the picture. Was he wrong about the angle, or the distance? No, he was sure of it—he covered that same ground at least twice a day, and often more like three or four times. And yet—

It wasn't there.

He had no idea what that meant.

But he had a feeling it was something big.

He considered pointing it out to Dr. Russell, but wasn't sure she was in any shape to hear him.

Instead, he went looking for the one person he knew was always willing to listen to what he had to say.

"Carter, this had better be important," Allison said as she let him drag her toward Dr. Russell's lab. "I've got a conference call with some of our researchers in Iceland in half an hour. They're researching magma coolant systems, which we could use to prevent volcanoes from erupting even as we use their heat to power whole continents."

"I have no idea if it's important," he admitted, leading her into the lab. The door was still wide open. "That's why I need you to tell me." He stepped inside and moved off to one side, then gestured at the monitor. "What do you see?"

"Downtown Eureka, same as before." Allison kept her voice down so as not to disturb Dr. Russell. The blond researcher was still slumped over the main console.

"Yes, but look more carefully." Carter waited. Allison stared at the screen, but finally she shrugged. "Okay, it took me a while, too," he admitted. "But look. That's the crosswalk, right? With the sign that's always going out and Henry's always having to fix it? But why is there a speed limit sign next to it? We don't have one there—it's a block farther down." Allison frowned. "And what about the statue of Archimedes?" he tried again. "Look at the base. Remember we were having that problem with pigeons, after that one experimental bird got loose and started breeding? And Henry and Taggart whipped up a little sonic doohickey to keep them from using the statue as their own private birdbath? Where is it?"

Allison nodded. "I don't see it."

"Right. Now, are you ready for the big one?" Carter rubbed his hands together. "Look at the buildings. There's my office, right? And next to it is the hardware store. And next to that is the dry cleaner's. And next to that, just at the edge of the picture, is—"

"Café Diem," Allison answered at once. "I know the town's layout, Carter. But what—" She stopped midsentence, and stared. Then she walked a few paces, so she could see that edge of the screen more clearly, and stared some more.

"Oh. My. God." The words were barely a whisper.

"I know," he agreed. "But what does it mean?"

"What does it mean? Carter, it means— Dr. Russell!" The researcher bolted upright at Allison's shout, and was out of her chair in an instant. If this had been the army, she would have saluted.

"Yes, Director!"

Allison smiled and lowered her volume. "Doctor, look at the screen. Look carefully." They all turned to watch, just as Jo crossed into view. His deputy looked the same as ever, though Carter noticed she was completely dry. He wasn't sure how she'd managed that—his clothes were still damp, and his hair was still wet as well. But Jo looked none the worse for this morning's deluge as she crossed the street—and headed into a small coffee shop.

A coffee shop that Carter was absolutely sure didn't actually exist.

"Oh. Oh, my." Russell gaped at the screen, then turned to Allison. Her eyes were shining again, but this time it wasn't from tears. "It worked!" she all but shouted. "It worked!"

"It certainly did!" Allison agreed. The two of them were practically jumping up and down, and both were grinning like idiots. "And do you know what this means?"

"Um, I don't," Carter offered, raising a hand. "What's going on, exactly?"

"Dr. Russell's demonstration wasn't a failure at all," Allison explained happily. "It just worked even better than we'd ever expected. We really are looking at another dimension here!"

"But it looks just like this one," Carter argued.

"I know!" Allison gave Dr. Russell a big hug. "Dr. Russell has just proven the existence of parallel dimensions!" she announced happily.

"Parallel what? Is that like parallel parking, only bigger?"

Both women laughed, then Dr. Russell sobered up. "I need to get my technicians back in here at once," she stated. "We've got to start analyzing all of this, and recording it!"

"Absolutely! Let me know once you've got a preliminary report put together," Allison told her. She turned and guided Carter back toward the door. "We'll give you room to work."

"Thank you," Dr. Russell called after them. "And, Sheriff? Thank *you*!"

He nodded and waved as Allison led him away.

"Okay, what's the big deal?" he asked once they were back in the hall. "What's this about parallel dimensions?"

"There's an old theory in quantum physics," Allison explained, "that every time a decision could go one of two ways, it does both. It goes one way here, but then there's another reality where it goes the other way. It's called divergent realities. As a result, for every decision or choice there is, theoretically, a universe where the other choice was made and those consequences played out."

Carter processed that. "So there's a universe where I turned left instead of right when I pulled out of my driveway this morning?"

"Exactly. And in that universe, turning left might have meant you got hit by a truck, or got to the office late and missed an important call, or noticed a potential problem before it could get worse." Allison shrugged. "Each of those paths would have led to other decisions, other choices, and each would have then split off into its own reality as well."

He nodded. "And what we're seeing is a world where, somehow, one of those decisions meant Vincent never opened Café Diem."

"Right. And who knows what other little changes exist between that world and our own?" She grinned. "Like I said, it's an old theory, but it's only been a theory because there's never been a way to prove it. Until now. This is an amazing accomplishment!"

"Oh. Well, that's cool." Carter only vaguely understood what she was talking about, but that was okay. The important thing was, he'd been right to show her what he'd noticed. And now both she and Dr. Russell were thrilled. That had to be a good thing.

They got back to the lobby, and Allison checked her watch. "I've got that call in two minutes." She smiled at him. "I'll see you later."

"Okay, sure." He smiled back, as always. He'd never been able to resist her smile. "Later." And he headed out again. His socks were still damp, so he decided his first priority was to go home and get a dry uniform. Then he'd check in with Jo and see where they were about the Thunderbird egg. It had already been a busy day, and it wasn't over yet.

Zane was calculating vectors for the new project he had going with Arnold Gunter, something that built off Gunter's work on the MRS, but a bit less dramatic and thus hopefully more immediately usable. He had his computer pad in his hands but was doing most of the math in his head, as usual. That and the earphones that were blasting Scandinavian death metal were probably why he almost didn't see Allison heading toward him down the hall.

"Whoa!" He sidestepped just in time to keep from barreling into her, or her into him. "Everything okay, boss?" She looked a little dazed, which wasn't like her at all. Allison Blake was the original calm, cool, and collected.

"Hm?" She stared at him, but he wasn't sure her eyes were really focusing on him. He pulled off the headphones.

"Are you okay?" He liked Allison—of all the people he'd worked for, she was the only one who gave him enough freedom to be truly creative while still providing enough clear discipline to keep him from getting out of hand. That was impressive. He even considered her a friend, which he never would have believed in the old days. Must be JoJo's influence, mellowing him.

Right.

"I'm fine," Allison answered, but she frowned at him. "Thanks." Then she turned and continued the way she'd been heading.

Zane watched her go for a second, puzzled. She wasn't acting like herself. Should he go after her and find out what was going on? After a tick he shook his head. Friend or not, Allison was still his boss, and still the director of all of GD. She had to manage every project in this place, most of them heavily classified, and she wouldn't appreciate Zane poking his nose into somewhere he didn't belong. He'd asked if she was okay; she'd said she was. Nothing more he could do.

Pulling his earphones on again, he turned the music back up and was soon lost in vector calculations once more. Humming along to the music, he continued toward his lab, making occasional notes on the pad as he went. And keeping an eye out for any other possible collisions.

CHAPTᵉR 8

Carter leaned back in his chair and propped his feet up on his desk. "So what you're saying is—"

"—we've got no leads," Jo finished, pacing the space between his desk and hers. "None at all. Nothing from the security logs, nothing from the access panel, nothing from the lab itself. Nothing anywhere."

"Got it." He scooped the baseball off his desk and tossed it up in the air, then caught it and tossed it again. "We have no idea who stole the egg, no idea what they want with it, no idea where they are, and no idea if they're caring for it properly or if it might explode into living lightning at any second."

"Exactly." Jo reached out, lightning-fast, and snagged the baseball before it could fall back into his waiting hands. "And that might not have been the case if you hadn't saddled me with the world's greatest detective as a sidekick."

"Oh, come on. He's not that bad, is he?" Carter watched her warily, both her eyes and the hand that was gripping his baseball so tightly her knuckles had gone white. He already knew from the one time they'd played baseball—albeit Eureka's high-tech virtual version—that she had a killer fastball.

He really didn't want to be on the receiving end of it, especially not at this close range. And him without a bat.

"He's worse," his deputy insisted through gritted teeth. "He asks questions about everything I'm doing, stands so close I can hear him breathing, touches things without thinking, throws away valuable potential evidence without a second thought—he's a disaster!"

"Are you sure this isn't just because he's always had a crush on you?" Carter quickly held up his hands, then, because Jo's eyes had flared and her arm had cocked back of its own accord. "Whoa, just kidding, just kidding. No need to go all Wild Thing on me."

She sighed and tossed him the ball, which he caught after only a minor fumble. "I know. And you know I consider him a friend. It's just that he's annoying enough when we're dealing with him at GD. To have him tagging along while I'm trying to track down leads—it's even worse."

Carter got serious for a second. "So you don't think he's going to be any help to us at all? Even if we find the egg?"

Jo went totally still. One of the things he really liked about her was that she could be brutally honest, even with herself. "No, I think he could be helpful," she conceded finally, though he could see she was having a hard time letting those words spill from her mouth. "The only people who know more about the Thunderbird project are Allison, the two researchers in charge, and their lab assistant. We can't ask Allison to take time away from her own work to wander around with us just in case we wind up needing her expertise, and we can't be sure the docs or the assistant weren't in on it. Plus, Fargo knows us, and knows how we work, so in theory he's better at staying out of our way than the others would be. In theory."

"But of course it's Fargo, so he's right *in* our way half the time," Carter finished for her. He laughed, but not at her. "Sorry, Jo. I know it wasn't fair to make you drag him around. But I do think we'll need him when we find the thing, and that means keeping him close at hand."

"So *you* drive around with him for a while," Jo suggested.

This time he did laugh at her. "Me? Oh, no. He'd drive me crazy!"

He was really glad he'd gotten the ball back before he'd said that.

"Okay, let's talk about our suspects." He switched gears. "You met Korinko—you think she's capable of stealing her own project?"

Jo didn't even have to think about it. "No. She was genuinely upset when she found out what had happened. Either she's a really good actress or she had no idea. Plus, she wanted to know all about the one that did hatch, which means she wasn't there at the time."

"Could have had an accomplice," Carter pointed out. "She gives him the codes, he steals the eggs for her, she's got an ironclad alibi."

"Possible, but I don't think so," Jo argued. "She just didn't strike me as the type."

Carter nodded. He'd learned long ago to trust Jo's instincts. "What about Dr. Boggs?"

"I'm not as sure about him," Jo admitted. "He was harder to read, and he seemed a little more preoccupied. Like this wasn't his biggest concern, which struck me as weird. They've put the last few years of their lives into this project."

Carter thought about that. "You met with Dr. Korinko when she arrived, right?" His deputy nodded. "And then went in to inspect the lab?" Another nod. "Did Dr. Boggs arrive before you came back out?"

"Yeah, he was waiting in the hall with Dr. Korinko." She grimaced. "Which means he'd already heard about the break-in, and about the loss of the eggs . . . "

"So he might have been preoccupied because he was going over everything in his head so they could reconstruct their notes and all that lost data," Carter finished. This was one of the many reasons he and Jo made such a good team. They often thought along the same lines, or at least reached the same conclusions even if they started from different places.

"Right. In that case, never mind. His reaction made perfect

sense." Jo sighed. "Besides, he's really tall and really skinny. I didn't get a good look at the thief, but I'd have noticed that."

"Could have been an accomplice again," Carter reminded her. "But it sounds like we can rule both of them out, at least for now." He started to toss up the baseball again, then thought better of it. "That leaves the lab assistant."

"Andee Wilkerson," Jo supplied. "She's got the day off and has been out at the lake with her boyfriend. She's not answering her phone." For just a second, Carter thought he saw a sappy expression cross the face of his tough-as-nails deputy. Was she thinking about picnics like that with Zane? But her face was back in its usual sharp, unforgiving lines now. Maybe he'd just imagined it.

He was one of the few people in town, however, who knew that Jo Lupo did have a sappy romantic side to her. She just kept it under lock and key most of the time.

"Okay, so we'll talk to her when she gets back into town," Carter said, stating the obvious. "Though if she and her boyfriend are the thieves, spending a day incommunicado at the lake would make for a perfect cover. She could have gone up there with his phone, in fact, so both their signals would match their alibi. Then he could have met her there with the eggs. She'd know exactly how to keep them safe and stable."

"True, but why do it?" Jo shook her head. "Andee's been a lab tech for eight years, and she's been on the Thunderbird project with Boggs and Korinko since the beginning—she'd worked with Korinko on another project before this one, and they requested her specifically. Why suddenly decide to betray them? And would she really wait all those years for something to steal?"

"She could have needed a lot of money in a hurry," Carter suggested. "A dying relative, a gambling debt, plans for a big wedding, a baby on the way—there are lots of reasons." He was tossing the baseball from hand to hand while he thought. "Whoever stole the eggs knew exactly how to get into GD and get past its security. That means either a master thief or a genius who knows GD's security measures."

"The second one describes just about everyone who works there," Jo commented.

"I know. But whoever it was also knew how to get past the eggs' containment field. That's got to require a bit more specialized knowledge, right? Do any of the other labs use the same sort of field? Who repairs them when they break down? Who installs them in the first place? Do the maintenance guys check on them along with the lights and the locks, or is that a different department?"

Jo nodded. "Plus, we still need to figure out what the thief plans to do with the egg," she added. "Is he going to sell it? Who's going to buy this thing? A rival think tank? A corporation? A small country?" She frowned. "If we can figure out who he—or she—is hoping to sell to, we can work out how he's planning to get it out of Eureka, and then we may be able to catch him in the act."

"Good." Carter set the baseball back on his desk and stood up. "You take that angle. See if anybody's been asking the same questions, too—if this was an inside job, our thief might not know a good fence for the eggs, in which case he must have asked around before he decided to pull the job. I'll nose around GD, find out about the containment fields. We'll compare notes and see if any of the same names pop up." That would certainly be nice, though he wasn't counting on it being anywhere near that easy. Things in Eureka almost never were.

Jo glanced at the clock. "You're not going to find out much at this hour." It was almost six. Carter shook his head. Ever since Zoe had left for college, he'd had a harder time keeping track of the hours. It made a big difference when you no longer had a kid in high school who had to eat a decent dinner at a decent hour.

"You're right. I'll head over there first thing tomorrow morning." It wasn't like the containment fields were going anywhere, after all. And unlike most problems in Eureka, the missing Thunderbird wasn't so urgent it couldn't wait until morning. He headed for the door. "Got plans for dinner?"

Jo nodded. "Zane and I are going to pick up some food from Vincent, then head out to one of the ridges. There's a meteor shower."

"Nice." Carter felt a flash of envy. His first date with Tess had been watching a meteor shower from the hood of his Jeep. He thought of her fiery hair and her sharp tongue and her wicked smile. They'd been good together. But she'd gotten a job in Australia on that new radio-telescope array, and it had been too good to pass up. They'd tried to keep things going long-distance, and he'd even gone out to visit her, but it had proven too hard for them both. She'd been the one to break things off, and though it had hurt at the time, Carter knew she was right to do so. They had separate lives to lead. He still missed her sometimes, though.

"Well, don't let me keep you," he told Jo as she caught up with him and they headed out together. "You don't want to miss the sights."

His deputy smiled, though, and kept pace beside him. "The shower's not for another few hours," she replied. "And it never hurts to keep a guy waiting every once in a while." Something in her smile and in her eyes, though, told Carter she knew what he was thinking. Jo wasn't delaying to make Zane miss her; she was keeping him company because she'd seen that he was lonely.

Like he'd said, she had a sappy side. And every once in a while he saw glimpses of it.

But he'd never say that out loud. She was still armed, after all.

Instead he just smiled. "In that case, let's take our time." And together they strolled down the block at a nice, leisurely pace. Neither of them said anything more, and Carter realized that she was another close female friend he could have a comfortable silence with.

By the time they reached Café Diem he was in a good mood, and had already decided to catch up on the other night's baseball game once he got home, followed by some random action movie. Maybe two. S.A.R.A.H. had a whole array of them archived, and he could order up a few beers and some donuts or chips and kick back and watch them as loud as he wanted, as long as he wanted.

There were definite advantages to being a bachelor again. And to having a sentient house, or a "Self-Actuated Residential Automated Habitat." He might as well make the most of them.

CHAPTᴇR 9

"How's it going? Have you found Howard the Duck yet?"

Allison and Dr. Russell both turned to look at him. They sported identical "what the hell are you talking about now?" expressions. Carter squirmed. He enjoyed having two attractive women eyeing him, but not like that!

"Howard the Duck," he tried again. "Old comic book, made into a movie with Lea Thompson. Ducks in another dimension are like people here." Their expressions didn't change. "Wow, tough room."

That got Allison to smile, at least. "Sorry, Carter. Things are a bit hectic right now. In a good way, though."

"A great way," Dr. Russell agreed. Gone were any traces of the depression he'd seen the day before. Now she was radiant and enthusiastic, almost vibrating with energy. Amazing what a difference a little thing like a major scientific breakthrough could make!

"Cool, so it's all going well, then?" He edged his way into the lab proper, but stayed up near the observation chairs in back. Russell's techs were swarming around the consoles like worker bees and he didn't want to get in their way. Or get stung.

"It is," Allison agreed. She rose and moved a little closer, leaving the researcher back by the main console. "Dr. Russell's been cataloging the differences and similarities between our own Eureka and this parallel version. You already noticed several discrepancies, and she's found a few more, but there are far more similarities. Which means that, in the grand scheme of things, we're looking at a dimension very close to our own."

Carter remembered her explanation of divergent realities the other day. "Because it's like a tree, with each choice leading to two or more branches, and the farther you venture from your own branch, the more different it'll be in every way?"

She beamed at him. "Exactly! We've seen plenty of people we recognize, and plenty of places as well, so this other Eureka has to be on the same major branch we are, and probably only a few choices removed from our own."

Carter nodded, glancing up at the screen. "Have you found Café Diem yet? Maybe it's just in a different location."

Back by the console, Russell frowned. "That's been the only real hitch so far," she admitted. "We haven't been able to shift our observational focus yet." She must have seen his expression, because she quickly clarified. "We can't change where we're looking. Not yet, at least. I've got my assistants realigning the arrays slightly. I think I've worked out a rough three-dimensional analogue, so I should be able to adjust the arrays' position and sample visual inputs from another part of that other Eureka without wandering too far astray." She smiled again. "After breaching the dimensional barrier, shifting our lens by a mile or so shouldn't be much of a problem."

Carter had learned from long experience that the words "not a problem" often led to trouble in Eureka, but he tried to keep that from his face. Dr. Russell had worked long and hard on this project, and now she was enjoying the glow of success. He didn't want to be the one to dampen that.

"Well, keep me posted," he said instead, turning back toward the door. "I'd love to see other views of the place, once you've got them up and running. Maybe I'll see myself with a handlebar mustache—I thought about growing one once." Once. For maybe five minutes total.

Allison laughed. "If we see that, we'll definitely give you a call," she promised. "Now go away—you're distracting us." She said the last part with a smile, so he took it as the gentle ribbing it was meant to be. Then he left them there, looking over printouts and screens and discussing things he didn't understand in the least, and headed down to the maintenance department to ask about those containment fields.

"Let me know once you've shifted the focus," Allison reminded Dr. Russell again as she made her way toward the door herself, a little while later. "I want to be there for that."

"Of course," Russell promised. "It shouldn't be more than a few hours, now."

"Great." Allison waved and walked out. She still couldn't believe how well the project had done. They'd hoped for some vague information about other dimensions, and about the structure of reality in general. But this! To actually prove the divergent-realities theory, and be able to see into another world so clearly? It was astounding! They hadn't told anyone else yet—Allison wanted to make sure Russell had her findings well documented first—but when they did, the news would turn the theoretical physics world upside down. This could be as big as proving the Earth was round, or that it revolved around the sun!

She was still pondering some of the implications—political as well as scientific—when she spotted a familiar rotund figure up ahead. Familiar, but oddly out of place.

"Vincent?"

The man turned and glanced back at her, his curly brown hair flying about his head as he did. Yes, it was Vincent. But what was he doing here at GD?

"Can I help you?" he asked. He sounded harried, which was also strange. Vincent was one of the most laid-back people she knew, despite having to run Café Diem and fulfilling Eureka's food needs almost single-handedly.

"I was going to ask you the same question," Allison told him. "What are you doing here? And in that?" She gestured at the white lab coat he had on. She hadn't even known Vincent owned a lab coat.

"Ha ha, very funny," he snapped. "Was there anything else you wanted to joke about? Perhaps you wanted to know why I was wearing shoes as well?"

Allison bristled slightly despite herself. She'd never heard him take that tone before, and certainly not with her. She liked Vincent, but nobody got away with talking to her like that at GD. "Now, listen—" she started, but he cut her off.

"No, you listen." He glowered at her. "I'm very busy, and I don't have time for idle chitchat or strange little games. If you need something, you can stop by my lab. Otherwise, I'll thank you to leave me alone." And he turned and hurried off down the corridor.

"Now just a minute!" Allison took off after him, but for such a short and portly man Vincent proved to have surprisingly long strides. He rounded a corner before she could reach it, and when she did he was gone. She stopped and looked around. Where had he gotten to? She could see down the corridor, and it was empty. There were a few doors along it, but she hadn't heard any of them open. And at least a few of them had restricted access, so he wouldn't have been able to use those anyway.

What was going on here?

She stood there for a minute, looking and listening, half expecting Vincent to pop back up and apologize. He didn't. Finally she shook her head and turned to head back the way she had come. She could ask him about it at Café Diem later—and he'd better have a good explanation! In the meantime, she had work to do.

She just hoped this wasn't a sign that the day was about to become truly surreal. They had plenty of days like that around here, and she almost never got anything done when they occurred.

CHAPTᵉR 10

"Divergent realities." Jo nodded. "That's pretty cool."

Carter eyed her warily from his perch on the edge of her desk. Why was he not surprised that his deputy knew exactly what he meant without him having to explain it? Was everyone in this town smarter than he was? Or just better informed? "Yeah, it was weird seeing you up on that screen." He remembered the image from yesterday. "You were completely dry—unlike me—but otherwise you looked the same."

Now she was frowning up at him from her desk chair. "Wait, I looked the same? How much the same? Do you just mean my hair and my height and no visible tattoos, or do you mean"—she gestured at her body—"this?"

It took Carter a second to realize she was referring to her uniform. Fortunately, he figured that out before he said anything. That could have been embarrassing. "Oh, yeah, you were still my deputy."

"Great," she muttered. "That figures. Even in another dimension I don't make sheriff!"

"I'm sure you did somewhere," Carter assured her. "Every

choice creates a new reality, right? So there've got to be a bunch where you got to be sheriff."

She brightened. "Yeah, I guess so." Then she frowned again. "Too bad it isn't one of those we're looking into."

"Maybe Dr. Russell will be able to switch to a different reality," he offered, thinking about it. "You know, like changing the channel." He imagined being able to "channel surf" different realities—seeing himself in different clothes and hairstyles and maybe even jobs—and he shuddered. Maybe seeing one other world was enough.

The office phone rang, and Jo snatched up the receiver immediately. "Sheriff's office, Deputy Lupo speaking." She put extra emphasis on the word "deputy." "Uh-huh. Okay, we'll be right there. Thanks."

"What's going on?" Carter asked, getting to his feet.

"That was Mrs. Murphy, who lives over on Kasold," Jo explained, standing as well. "She just got a remote alert that something's breached her house's privacy fence."

"Ah, okay." Carter hitched up his belt. "I'll check it out. Why don't you collect Fargo and start making those inquiries about fences and whatnot for the Thunderbird? We're running out of time on tracking it down before it hatches." He'd already struck out with the containment fields; the maintenance guys at GD had told him that all the labs used the same basic field for their experiments and just modified it as necessary, so anyone in the building would know how the field worked and how to shut it off or at least cut through it. That included maintenance and security but not the janitorial staff, so at least they knew the janitor hadn't done it. But they still had a building full of suspects, plus anyone outside who had access to similar equipment. Which put the ball squarely in Jo's court for now.

She grimaced but nodded. "Fine, I'll go get him." She paused. "You know, I may ask Taggart what he knows about all this."

"Good idea." Taggart was the resident expert on wild animals and strange creatures, as well as their local hunter. He might know something about the Thunderbird that would make it easier to catch. He also might have some ideas on who would want such an unusual animal, and ways they could get it out of Eureka without setting off any alarms.

And Jo was definitely the one to ask him about it. Taggart had harbored a major crush on her for years—like many of the men in Eureka—but she had actually dated him for a while. That had ended shortly before she started going out with Zane, but she and Taggart were still close, and he'd be far more likely to tell her what he knew, especially if it was something he wasn't supposed to talk about.

"Let me know how it goes," Carter said as they both headed out the door. Jo nodded and turned to her car, while he stepped over to his Jeep. As usual, Jo peeled out first. Carter just laughed and shook his head, then he pulled out and took off in the direction of Kasold Drive. Time to see about a privacy fence.

It didn't take much deduction to figure out which house belonged to Mrs. Murphy. The street was lined with handsome ranches and Tudors, all with nice big lawns and long driveways. Eureka had plenty of space, so all its residents could have big homes and large yards.

But only one of those yards was throwing off sparks.

He pulled up across the street and got out. A handful of kids were lingering nearby, eyeing the crackling stretch of grass, and Carter ambled over to them. "What's going on?" he asked.

One of the boys—they looked to be around junior high age—shrank back, but the other three stood their ground. None of them said anything for a second, however. And none of them met his eyes.

Carter was both a cop and a dad. He knew guilt when he saw it.

"Okay, somebody had better start talking," he warned, "or I'm going to get irritable. And you really don't want that to happen." He let the threat hang in the air between them. Then one of the boys gulped and glanced up at him.

"It's our fault," the boy explained. "We didn't mean it, honest."

Carter nodded and kept his face and posture unthreatening. "Okay, start at the beginning. What's your name, anyway?"

"Ray," the boy answered. "Ray Aventura." He was short and skinny, with thin, slicked back dark hair and a narrow face. Twenty years ago he'd have worn Coke-bottle glasses with tape around the middle and a pocket protector. At least here in Eureka he didn't have to worry about being picked on for stuff like that. Here, nerds were king.

"All right, Ray, what happened?"

One of the other boys tugged at Ray's sleeve, like he was trying to stop him from saying anything, but Ray shrugged him off. "Mrs. Murphy, she's got this privacy fence," he explained. "It zaps you if you get too close to her property." Carter nodded—plenty of Eureka residents had something like that. "But she's got hers set really wide. It actually covers half the sidewalk. And she's got a piece on the lawn by the street, too. If you walk exactly down the middle of the sidewalk, you can usually avoid getting zapped. Much." He grimaced, as did the other boys. Carter didn't blame them. The privacy fences were nonlethal, but that didn't mean they didn't hurt.

"Have you talked to her about resetting it?" he asked.

All the boys nodded. "Lots of times," one of them said, speaking up for the first time. "But she won't. She says it's her property and she has a right to protect it."

Carter frowned. That was true as far as her own lawn went, but the sidewalk was town property and anyone could walk on it. "So you decided to teach her a lesson," he guessed. He could see from their expressions that he'd pegged it.

"It's not that hard," Ray told him with just a touch of pride. "The fence is just a low-grade energy field. If you can isolate its harmonic frequency, you can manipulate it, even shut it down."

"Only things didn't go as planned."

The boys all shook their heads. "She must have a secondary generator, which has a slightly different frequency," Ray guessed. "It creates an oscillation field instead of a single harmonic. When we tried to tap into the frequency and shut it down, it overloaded instead." He glanced at the lawn, which was still coughing up sparks. "And that happened."

Carter nodded. "Okay. Any idea where she keeps the generator?"

"Sure." Ray pointed at the side of the house. "It's that little box right there, next to the door. We tried to shut it off ourselves, but we couldn't get close." Carter noticed the boy had a scorch mark on his arm and another on one cheek.

"Better that you didn't," he told them. "That would have been trespassing, and Mrs. Murphy could actually press charges." He gave them his best reassuring grin. "But she asked me to help, and I'm the sheriff—I'm allowed to walk on people's lawns." One of the boys actually chuckled. "Wait here, okay?" They all nodded.

He left the boys there, trusting them to stay put, and made his way across the street to Mrs. Murphy's driveway. He could feel his hair standing on end as he set foot over the curb, and gritted his teeth. This was going to sting like hell.

Zap!

"Ow! Damn it!" The spark had arced to his left hand, and he shook it off as hurried up the driveway. Did she have her privacy fence set above normal levels? It certainly felt that way, and that would explain the second generator. He'd have to speak with her about that. But first things first.

Zot!

"Ow!"

Crackle!

"Ouch!"

Sizzle!

"Hey, come on!"

He finally reached the side of the house and saw the small black box—and realized he had no idea how to turn it off. And he didn't have time to ask. Each shock had been more painful than the last one, and it had been all he could manage to stay on his feet the last time. Another like that and he'd pass out, which wouldn't do anybody any good—least of all him.

Still, it was a fuse box, essentially. There should be a breaker switch, right?

He reached for the box and made contact with its smooth metal surface—just as another crackle sounded beside him. Great. But then he realized that might be exactly what he needed. He waited, holding his breath, and felt the energy build up all around him. Then—

Pop!

The discharge leaped to his arm—and coursed down it, into the box. Which flashed and flared and smoked. And the soft hum he'd been feeling in his bones and his teeth suddenly disappeared.

Yes!

Wobbling slightly, Carter rose to his feet. Then he made his way back over to where the boys waited. Slowly.

Good thing nobody has a dog on this block, he thought to himself. He could just picture having to comfort some distraught neighbor after Fluffy the poodle turned into instant rotisserie. Not pretty.

Though it did make him hungry.

"I'll speak to Mrs. Murphy when she gets home," he assured the boys. "I'll make sure she pulls her field back in so the sidewalk is completely clear."

"Thanks!" Ray was definitely the group's spokesman. "Um, are we in any trouble?"

Carter pretended to consider that for a second, just to make them sweat. "I didn't actually see you do anything to the privacy fence," he finally said slowly. "And you pointed out the box so I could shut it off before it could endanger anybody else. So I don't see any reason to bring you downtown." The boys all sighed and visibly relaxed. "Just do me a favor. Next time, call me first, okay?"

"We will," Ray assured him. "Thanks!"

Carter nodded and climbed back into his Jeep. His hands were still shaking slightly as he turned the key in the ignition. What was it about this week and getting shocked? He was starting to wonder if he should carry a lightning rod around with him.

Ray and his friends were still standing around after the sheriff drove away. Mike was arguing that they should follow through with their original plan, now that the privacy fence had been shut down properly.

"We need to make sure she knows not to do this again," he argued. Derek nodded.

"No way," Ray countered. "Sheriff Carter said he'd take care of it. And he knows who we are now. If we do anything, he'll know to come after us."

"He knows you," Derek pointed out. "Not the rest of us. Not by name, anyway."

"Oh, so you'd leave me to take the heat alone?" Ray demanded. The others all looked away. "We're a team, right?" They nodded slowly, one by one. "So it's all or nothing. Besides, how hard do you think it'd be for him to find out your names, too?"

They were still discussing it when the sheriff's Jeep pulled up at the curb once again. Ray and the others froze. Had he somehow known what they were about to do? Man, he was good!

They watched as the Jeep switched off and its driver-side door opened. Then a man climbed out and looked at them. "Everything okay here?" he asked.

Dumbfounded, Ray just nodded.

"I heard there was a problem with a malfunctioning privacy fence," the sheriff continued, glancing around. "Seems quiet, though."

"It got shut off," Ray told him after he found his voice. "It's all good."

"Oh. Really?" The sheriff seemed surprised. "Well, okay then. You boys have a nice day." He slid back into the Jeep, started it up again, and roared away.

Ray glanced over at his friends, but they looked just as confused as he was. What was going on here? He knew who the guy was—he'd seen him a few times before, at Eureka town functions and when they'd had a class field trip to GD.

But what was Douglas Fargo doing wearing the sheriff's uniform and driving his Jeep?

"Dude, this is all too weird," Shay whispered. "I vote we just go get slushies and hit the arcade instead."

The rest of them looked to Ray, and he nodded. Whatever was going on, they were better off well out of it. "Let's roll," he said. And he and his friends hightailed it down the street, leaving Mrs. Murphy's lawn unharmed except for the blackened spots where her own privacy fence had burned out patches of grass.

If need be, they could always come back and write "Free the sidewalks!" with plant-killer later.

CHAPTᵉR 11

"Taggart!"

The lanky Australian glanced up as Jo approached. He was, as she'd expected, out in the woods around Eureka. Since he was wearing his usual pocketed vest and carrying his rifle, she assumed he was either hunting or animal watching, which really amounted to the same thing. She'd only seen him fire the rifle a handful of times, and then only when absolutely necessary. For someone who had all the appearance of a big-game hunter, Taggart was a ridiculously soft touch when it came to animals.

And not just animals, she reminded herself as she saw his eyes light up. They hadn't gone out for long, but it had been . . . fun. In the end, Taggart hadn't been the man she was looking for. But she did still like him, if not in that way.

The problem was, she knew he still liked her in exactly that way. And he made no bones about showing it. He and Zane had apparently formed a grudging respect for one another, and Taggart had told her once that he was happy for her as long as she was happy—but he'd also said that he'd be there for her if she ever changed her mind.

"Jo! G'day! What brings you out here?" Taggart stood and loped toward them, gliding through the grass in a way Jo knew many of her old Ranger buddies would have envied. He slowed slightly as he saw the little researcher puffing along behind her, though. "Fargo. Didn't expect you out here, mate."

"Me, either," Fargo agreed, leaning against a tree trunk and gasping for breath. "Jo, would it kill you to slow down a little?"

"Probably," she answered without looking back. She was trying to not be as hard on him as she had yesterday, but that didn't mean she was going to cut him any slack, either. That just wasn't the way she was built. Besides, a little exercise was good for him.

"I take it this isn't a social call," Taggart commented as he reached them. He smiled. "Still, always good to see you, Jo."

"Good to see you, too," she admitted. "But no, not a social call. Sorry. We need to know if you know anything about the Thunderbird project."

"Thunderbird, eh?" He scratched his bristly chin. "That's Korinko and Boggs's deal, eh? I don't know much about it, no. The basics, sure—they're tryin' to create a living thunderstorm—but not much more. They've been pretty tight-lipped." He grinned. "Why, they run into a brick wall? Need ol' Taggart to bail them out?"

"Not exactly." Jo glanced around out of habit, though of course they were alone out here. "Somebody stole the eggs they'd created. And trashed their lab."

"Oh, that's bad," the tall hunter commented. "That's bad. So you're lookin' for tracking, not ornithology?"

"A little of both, really." Jo sighed. "We don't have any leads right now, but we figure whoever stole the eggs wants to sell them. We need to know who might be interested in buying them, and how they can smuggle them out of Eureka." She didn't mention that one of the eggs had already hatched. No sense in sharing information if it wasn't necessary. It wasn't that she didn't trust Taggart. But he did like to talk to people.

He scratched at his chin again. "Yeah, I see what you mean. 'Fraid I'm not much help there, though. Never had reason ta smuggle anything out of town before, y'know? Don't traffic in black-market beasties much, either. Though I'd think it's less likely you're lookin' fer a collector and more likely it's a rival research group, or someone who can use the Thunderbird itself."

"So you don't know what the Thunderbird's living requirements might be?" Fargo cut in for the first time. "What it would eat, for example? Or what kind of environment it would live in?"

"Nope, sorry," Taggart answered. "Like I said, Korinko and Boggs've kept details to themselves all this time. Never even got a good look at the eggs. Wish I had. Bet they're beauties."

"You said eggs." Fargo jogged forward to confront Taggart, an attempt that would have worked better if the hunter hadn't towered over him by almost a foot. "How'd you know there were eggs?"

"Jo just mentioned 'em," Taggart replied easily. He didn't seem at all intimidated, but then he'd known Fargo for years. "Wish I could 'elp more," he added. "If I 'ear of anything, I'll give a holler."

"Thanks, Taggart," Jo told him. "I appreciate it." She turned to go. Then stopped. "Come on, Fargo," she snapped over her shoulder.

"All right, all right," he grumbled, hurrying to catch up with her. "I've got my eye on you," he called back to Taggart, who just smiled and waved.

"You've got your eye on him?" Jo commented as they trekked back to her car. "Please."

"What? His answers seemed fishy to me." She didn't reply, and they walked the rest of the way in silence. Fargo was busy imagining a confrontation with Taggart again, this time without Jo to hold him back. Unfortunately, all of those daydream scenarios ended with the lanky hunter turning him into a pretzel.

"What now?" he finally asked as they were strapping themselves into her car.

"I have no idea," Jo answered, putting the car in gear and stomping on the gas. They fishtailed for a second on the dirt road, then she took control and they shot away, back toward town.

Great, Fargo thought. *Another dead end. No wonder everybody laughs at me all the time.*

And to make matters worse, now he was dying for a pretzel.

"It's going great," Zane assured Allison, showing her the data on his computer pad. "We've got the initial nodes isolated, and all we have to do now is sync them up in sequence."

"And prevent the feedback from distorting your signal, or frying the receiver," she countered, indicating a spot in the calculations. "Have you fixed that yet?"

He grinned at her. "Yeah, all right," he admitted. "I should've known you'd catch that."

"That is my job," Allison reminded him.

"I know, it's just that I could usually fool my previous bosses." Which was true. Allison was no dummy. "No, we haven't fixed it yet. But we will." He was telling the truth, too. He was sure he and Gunter could crack that little problem.

It was just a matter of time.

"Okay, good." Allison glanced at her watch. "Put that all in the progress report, and tell Arnold we—" Her phone rang, interrupting her, and she glanced at it briefly, then looked again and answered it. "Dr. Russell? What is it?" She listened, then smiled. "Absolutely! I'll be right there!"

"Is that the extradimensional visualization project?" Zane asked as she hung up. "I'd love to see it."

"How do you even know about that?" Allison asked as she turned to go. Then she laughed and gestured for him to catch up.

"I have my ways," he told her, grinning as he bounded after her.

They reached the lab a few minutes later and found Dr.

Russell waiting for them. "I've got the arrays realigned," she explained, shaking hands with Zane and waving toward the main screen. "We've collected sufficient input to form our visual matrix, and we're ready to translate it to the monitor."

"Excellent." Allison rubbed her hands together. "Let's see what you've got."

Russell hit the switch on the main console, and the monitor overhead turned black, then to fuzz. The fuzz gained streaks and blobs of color, and then began to clear as those bits began to merge and shift and shape themselves into coherent images. In less than a minute, they were looking at a perfectly clear image—

—of the extradimensional visualization lab.

And at Dr. Russell and her crew, staring back at them.

Or, at least, staring at her large overhead monitor, which was showing an image—of them watching her from here!

"Oh. My. God." Allison whispered. "That's amazing!"

"I thought it best to use a location I knew intimately," Russell explained quietly, never taking her eyes off the screen. "So I thought, what better place than my own lab?" She shook her head. "It makes sense that if that world's Eureka has a me, and she's working on this same project, she'd come to the same conclusion."

"Yeah, but what are the odds that she'd collect input from our reality while we collected it from hers?" Allison wondered out loud. They had to be staggering. Beside her, Zane waved and they all watched as his image in the monitor they were seeing through their screen waved as well.

It was enough to give her a headache.

"Any chance we can talk to her?" Zane asked.

"I haven't worked out how to isolate soundwaves yet," Russell said apologetically. "Visible light is a broader, stronger spectrum, so it's easier to absorb and process. I have some ideas, though." She looked at her other self and smiled. "And if we both work on it, we should be able to solve it that much faster."

"We absolutely need to find a way to communicate," Allison agreed.

"On it," Zane replied. He ran out of the room and returned a few minutes later, pushing a whiteboard in front of him. "Here you go."

On the screen, the other Dr. Russell nodded. She said something to one of her techs, and he departed in a hurry. A few minutes later he was back with a whiteboard of his own.

"Hello," Dr. Russell wrote on hers.

"Hello, yourself," the other Russell replied. They both laughed.

"I'll leave you two to get acquainted," Allison commented wryly. "Let me know if anything new develops."

Russell nodded and returned to writing.

"I should get back to my own work," Zane admitted. He followed Allison out. "Still—wow. A genuine divergent reality. And we're communicating with the people there! It's amazing!"

"It really is," Allison agreed. She headed back to her office. The question was, what did it all mean? And why did she have a bad feeling that it could become more than the confirmation of an age-old theory and a fun little peek at another version of themselves?

CHAPTᵉR 12

"So you're no closer to figuring out who did it, or to finding the missing Thunderbird egg?" Allison frowned. "Not the news I was hoping for."

"Me either," Carter agreed, leaning on her desk. "We've got our eyes open, but so far nothing. The minute the thief moves we'll go after him—"

"But that might be too late to stop him from selling or escaping with the egg," she finished. "There has to be something we can do!"

"Open to suggestions." Carter watched her for a second, but she shook her head. "Yeah, me neither."

"What about atmospheric disturbances?" Allison offered.

"Already on that one," he told her. "Fargo patched into the local weather surveillance. We'll know the instant there's the sort of activity associated with thunderstorms. But that means we're still just reacting and not acting, and by the time we notice anything it could be too late."

"You'll think of something," Allison assured him. "You always do."

"Yeah, well, thanks." He grinned and ducked his head.

"Hope you're right. So, how's the mirror-universe thing going?"

As he'd hoped, mention of that project perked Allison up immediately. "Great! The two Russells figured out how to sample and process sound, so they're actually able to talk to each other now using the monitors and speaker sets. It's basically video-conferencing, but across realities."

"I'd hate to see their phone bills," Carter muttered, and chuckled at the look he got in response. "Well, that's cool." He straightened up. "I'd better get back to it. Let me know if you hear anything."

"Of course. See you later." She half waved and turned back to her computer, but paused to watch him leave from the safety of her desk. Her relationship with Carter was a strange one, no doubt about that. She knew he was interested in her, and she was interested in him, too. But somehow it never seemed to work out.

But perhaps it would, someday.

In the meantime, she had reports to look over, and budgetary requests to approve or deny. Bureaucracy stopped for no man—or woman.

With a sigh, she got back to work.

Taggart was trotting down one of the corridors in GD on his way back to his lab—he'd taken a little detour after lunch to check in with Abe Pappersea and see how his extrasensory huskies were doing. Cute little pups, and the way they could find anything, even in pitch-black and buried in three feet of mud, was astounding. He was still remembering the way the one had nuzzled his hand when he rounded a corner and almost slammed right into a tall, broad-shouldered man in a handsome tailor-made suit. They both recoiled just in time.

"Slow down, Taggart," the other man warned. "This isn't high school, and you won't get detention if you're late to class."

"Uh, right, thanks," Taggart managed to blurt out. He was too busy staring at the other man to say anything more coherent. Dark wavy hair, dark beard and mustache, long nose, thin lips, sharp pale blue eyes. Good-looking, confident, and very much in control. Exactly as he remembered.

The man stared back at him. "Something wrong, Taggart?"

"Nah, of course not," he stammered. "Just lost in thought, is all. Cheers!" And Taggart took off down the corridor. The other man didn't follow. But that didn't slow Taggart one bit. He knew who he had to tell about this encounter, and he really wasn't looking forward to it. Better to get it over with quickly.

Carter was just leaving Allison's office when Taggart burst toward him from one of the side corridors. The lanky Australian was in a full sprint, long arms and longer legs flying everywhere.

"Whoa, where's the fire?" Carter asked as Taggart almost ran him down.

"G'day, Sheriff." Taggart slowed to a halt. "Glad t' find you here. You'll want ta hear this."

Curious, Carter followed Taggart into Allison's office.

"Sorry t' interrupt," Taggart started as he approached Allison. He had his hunter's cap in his hands and barely glanced up—it was like watching the world's tallest schoolboy go to the principal's office to be punished. "But you need ta hear this."

"What, exactly?" Allison asked.

"I was just down in corridor B-twenty-three, and I saw somebody down there." He gulped. "Someone I shouldn'ta, on account a' he's dead."

Allison stared at him. So did Carter. Finally, she asked, "Dead? You're saying you saw a ghost or a spirit?"

But Taggart waved that aside. "He looked very much alive ta me. An' the way he reacted, he wasn't at all surprised to see me. No disorientation like you read about with spirits, no 'Wait, where am I?' He actually reprimanded me for not lookin' where I was goin'!"

"Okay, slow down," Carter urged, holding up both hands.

"You said you recognized him. Who was it?" There were plenty of restless spirits he could imagine haunting the halls of GD.

Taggart glanced up, looked at Allison, then looked back down again. "I don't want ta say," he muttered.

"Taggart." Allison's tone wasn't sharp, but there was warning edge to it. She was a patient woman, but he was testing her.

"Stark," the tall Australian burst out, the one syllable like a gunshot. It had as much effect as one, too, as both Carter and Allison reeled back, stunned. "I saw Nathan Stark."

"That's—" Allison finally found her voice, but couldn't continue.

"Impossible," Carter finished for her. "It's impossible. Stark died. I was there. I saw it. There was nothing anyone could do to stop it." But glancing over at Allison, he saw the one thing he hadn't ever wanted to see in those pretty eyes in connection to Stark.

Hope.

She had loved Stark. They had been married for years. Even after they'd separated, she'd still had feelings for him—feelings she had warred with when he'd returned, especially since she and Carter were starting to have feelings as well. Stark's change in attitude and demeanor, the softening around those arrogant edges, and his up-front declaration that he still loved her and hoped to win her back, had worn away at her reluctance. She had rediscovered her love for him, and had accepted when he asked her to marry him again. And then, on their wedding day, he had died saving the universe. That had been more than a year ago, and Allison had come to terms with his death. Or so Carter had thought. But given the fact that, as with many Eureka deaths, Stark's demise had been unusual, had been steeped in esoteric superscience, and had left no body—Carter knew a part of her had hoped that Stark had somehow survived.

He'd thought she was past that. But now, with Taggart's claim, that hope was alive again.

And a part of Carter—the part of himself he didn't much

like—wanted to smash it quickly, before it had a chance to spread.

"I'll check it out," he assured her, working to keep that internal struggle from showing on his face or sounding in his voice. "You stay here. I'll let you know what I find."

It didn't surprise him in the least when she stood and stepped around the desk to join him. "No, I'm coming with you. If Nathan really is alive, or a spirit, I need to see for myself." Her voice shook slightly, but her steps were steady, and Carter knew there was no way he could talk her out of it. Nor would it have been fair to try.

"B-twenty-three, you said?" he asked Taggart instead.

The lanky hunter nodded. "I'll just head back ta my lab, if ya don't mind," he called after them as Carter and Allison headed out. "One encounter a day with the hereafter is plenty for me!"

Allison led the way down to the corridor Taggart had named, and Carter trotted along beside her. He wanted to say something about not getting her hopes up, about hallucinations and chemicals and tricks of the light, but couldn't bring himself to be that mean. If it had been someone he loved—like Allison herself—and he thought he had even a chance of seeing her again, let alone finding her once more, how would he react if someone tried to prevent that? He'd be furious. And he might never forgive them. And whatever else happened between him and Allison, she was one of his closest friends. "I'll always be here for you," he'd told her the day of her wedding, right before informing her of Stark's death. "You know that." And he'd meant it. He couldn't bear the thought of her turning away from him. So he kept quiet and hoped there was some other explanation besides her ex-husband returning from the dead.

The corridor was completely empty when they reached it. No signs of anyone, and no ghostly goo like in the movies, either. Carter tapped on one of the lab doors along that stretch, but got no answer. The second one he tried slid open after a second, however.

"Yes?" The man who answered the door looked vaguely

familiar—short, heavyset, with a reddish-brown fringe beard and a matching fringe of hair. "Oh, good morning, Director!"

"Professor Glowgoski," she responded. "Sorry to disturb your work. Did you see anything . . . unusual a few minutes ago, by any chance?"

Professor Glowgoski chuckled, an impish expression crossing his broad face. "You mean like Taggart running as if all the legions of hell were behind him?" He sobered when he saw their expressions. "Sorry. Yes, I did think that was strange."

"Did you see anything that might have spooked him?" Carter asked.

The burly professor shook his head. "No, and I even glanced back the way he'd come, just in case it was some escaped experiment I should worry about. There was nothing there. Just Taggart, looking like a scarecrow on a rampage." He chuckled again, but quickly stifled it.

"Thank you, Professor. There's nothing to worry about. You can go back to work," Allison assured him. He frowned and watched them for a second, then shrugged, nodded good-bye, and turned away. His lab door slid shut behind him.

"So we have Taggart running away, but from nothing," Carter mused. "He says he saw Stark, and he's not one to make things up, though Taggart has been known to indulge in . . . mind-altering substances."

"If you're trying to politely say that he gets stoned and high as a kite and who knows what else, I'm well aware of that," Allison told him, just a little sharply. "But he's never let any of that interfere with his work. Taggart saves his amusements for his off hours. I think he was sober when he saw . . . whatever it is he saw."

"Which means we're looking for a ghost, or something like it," Carter pointed out. "Because if Stark had been here in the flesh, Professor Glowgoski would have seen him, too."

"I know." She sighed. "And yes, I know he's dead. You can't blame me for hoping otherwise."

"I do know that," he assured her quietly. "And you know I'd have saved him if I could."

She perked up. "Say that again."

"I'd have saved him if I could?"

"Yes!" Allison was suddenly energized, her eyes alight. "What if you could have, Carter? What if, somewhere else, you did?"

It only took him a second. "The other Eureka!"

They both raced down the corridor and to the one beyond, heading for Russell's lab.

Both Russells glanced up, startled, as Allison and Carter burst through the door. It was eerie seeing the two versions of the tall blond researcher. There were minor differences—the one in the monitor wore her hair in a tight braid, while their own Russell had hers cut in a cute but professional bob—but they were clearly the same woman, and their facial expressions were identical. It was like looking into an odd version of a funhouse mirror.

"Sorry to barge in like this," Allison explained, panting for breath as she walked over to the console, "but I have a quick question for the other Dr. Russell, if you don't mind."

"Of course," both Russells replied. They flashed the exact same smile at each other. Carter found it disconcerting and a little eerie the way the other Russell's voice was actually coming from speakers to either side of the monitor. It was almost like an echo, but not quite.

"Nathan Stark," Allison began, ignoring the way her own Russell gaped at her.

"What about him?" The other Russell looked puzzled but not overly concerned.

"Is he . . . alive?"

Now she looked surprised. "Of course he's alive! I saw Director Stark just this morning, to update him on my—our—progress." The two Russells shared another smile, this one triumphant.

Allison, meanwhile, sagged back against the desk. Carter hurried over to her in case she fainted. Not that Allison was the type to do that, but you never know. This was a major shock.

"He still runs GD?" she asked after she'd recovered enough to speak again. "So he never left?" Her mind was racing, trying to figure out where their realities had diverged in his case. And hers.

"Of course he left," the other Russell answered. "For years. He was working in the outside world, for the Department of Defense. Then he came back and took over as director. And he's been here ever since." She was looking at Allison strangely. "You should know that."

Allison gulped. Behind her, Carter tensed. She clearly couldn't bring herself to ask, so he did it for her. "Why should she know that?"

The question was uttered so softly, the second Russell frowned at first. Then she nodded. "You should know," she explained slowly, "because you're the one who married him."

That did it—Carter caught Allison as she stumbled, and helped her to one of the chairs set up in front of the computer. She just stared, tears in her eyes, and clutched his hands when he offered them.

He couldn't even imagine what she was going through. She had loved Stark, and given him up, then found him again, and then lost him.

But apparently in that other Eureka, he had never died. They had found a different way to solve the problem. Nathan Stark had survived, and she had remarried him.

There was another question, and Allison forced herself to ask it. "Jenna?" she whispered, and the second Russell indicated that she hadn't heard the question clearly. "What about Jenna?"

"Your little girl?" The other Russell beamed at her. "She's beautiful! I saw her just a few weeks ago, at the company picnic. She's absolutely adorable, and she clearly has the director wrapped around her little finger."

Allison nodded once. Then she rose and walked out of the room without another word and without looking back. Carter let her go. He could see the effort she was exerting, trying not to cry in front of him or the two Russells. He had to respect that. He wanted to run after her, to comfort her, but knew she'd let him know if she wanted his support. Right now, she needed privacy to process what she'd just heard.

"Is she okay?" the second Russell asked the first, who glanced at Carter helplessly.

"She'll be fine," he replied slowly. He was almost sure of it. Allison was one of the strongest people he knew. "She's just had a major shock." He took a deep breath. "Our Nathan Stark died almost a year ago. He gave his life to save us all. Allison is the director now. And Stark never met his daughter."

He turned and walked out, not quite sure where he was going. But he had a feeling they had just let something loose, something that could stagger them all. Something, in its own way, even bigger than the discovery of another reality.

They'd just unleashed the endless possibility of what might have been.

He hoped the town was strong enough to handle it.

CHAPT€R 13

"Okay, explain to me again what it is you're doing."

Zane sighed. "I'm beefing up the security systems."

Carter rolled his eyes. He was standing in classic cop position, legs slightly apart, hands at his sides, ready for action, scanning the area for any potential trouble. "That much I got. How, exactly?"

"It's complicated."

"Well, uncomplicate it." Carter leaned in so that he was blocking the light as Zane bent over the security console. "I need to know what to watch out for when trying to catch whoever's trying to break in."

"Fine. I'm rewriting the security protocol algorithms on the fly," Zane explained. "Before, it was a simple set of yes/no questions: 'Is he carrying a gun?' 'Does she have radioactive material on her person?' 'Is his head on fire?' Things like that." He frowned. "Obviously, that wasn't enough." Allison had brought him up to speed on the Thunderbird situation, and asked him to lend a hand.

Carter was nodding. "As long as you knew what questions

it would ask, and what clues it would look for, you could work around it."

"Exactly." Zane glanced up at him, and got a grin in return. He sometimes had to stop and remind himself that Carter was by no means stupid. He was actually a damn good cop— he'd caught Zane, after all, and that was something most of the law enforcement in the company had failed at, more than once. Just because Carter wasn't a genius was no reason to underestimate him.

"So, what, you're setting it up with something like S.A.R.A.H., so it can ask its own questions and change them depending on the situation?"

"Good god, no." Zane shuddered. "Can you imagine tying S.A.R.A.H. to GD's security system?" Now Carter shuddered with him. They were both remembering the times Carter's experimental artificial-intelligence house had gone haywire and threatened both the people inside and anyone nearby. "We don't need a real AI here, and I wouldn't want to risk it. But I'm programming a wider range of questions and set-ting them to cascade. That way it's not just yes/no. Even if you manage to trick the system about one thing, it could still notice something else that would trigger a whole new set of questions."

Carter considered that. "Is this going to be one of those things that comes back to bite us on the butt?" he asked after a minute. "Are we going to be getting calls about regular GD researchers who got detained, or cuffed, or zapped, or sprayed in goo, because they had watches or pens or a penny stuck in the sole of their shoe?"

"I hope not." Zane shrugged. "No guarantees, though."

"Great." Carter rubbed at his face with one hand. "Just the kind of reassurance I was hoping for."

"It should work," Zane assured him. "You've got to meet several criteria before you get flagged by the system, or trip a major one like carrying a gun. And I've set it to moderate its response based on the perceived threat level, so it can do everything from magnetizing your ID to the wall to hitting you with enough electricity to stun you unconscious before you can blink." He grinned. "I'd try to avoid that one, if I were you."

"Is it still set to recognize Jo and me as authorized to carry weapons on-premises?" It was an important question to ask.

"Absolutely. The two of you are the only ones who can carry guns in GD without Allison's direct approval." Zane double-checked, though, just to be sure. The last thing he wanted was for his new security upgrades to try taking out JoJo. She'd never let him hear the end of it.

"What about setting it to pick up traces of the Thunderbird itself?" Carter asked.

"I'd love to, but I don't have much to go on." Zane scratched his chin and yawned. Man, when was the last time he'd had coffee? It had to have been hours. "The Thunderbird lab was fried, so I don't have any clear readings there. And whoever did this killed the security cameras in the lab and along the hall first, so all we have are readings from before all this happened, when the eggs were still nice and quiet in their containment fields." He stood up and stretched. "I do have it programmed to watch for any major electromagnetic anomalies, and that would include a hatched Thunderbird. But short of the thing flying through the security gates, there isn't much I can tell you."

Carter nodded. "Okay, thanks." It wasn't Zane's fault he couldn't do more. It wasn't anybody's fault, really—not even Fargo's, or at least not entirely—but he was still frustrated. So far he'd found absolutely nothing to help them track down the missing egg or its thief. And the longer they ran around chasing their own tails, the more likely it was that the thief would manage to sneak the egg out of town. Or lose control of it, in which case they'd have a crazed sentient storm on the loose. They needed to figure this out. But how?

Jo and Fargo were having the exact same problem.
"This is getting us nowhere," Jo rasped, slamming her palm down on the hood of her car. They'd just spoken to Sheila

Menninger, a Eureka resident who supposedly had access to black-market sources for equipment, chemicals, and other supplies. But Sheila had claimed she didn't know anything about the egg, and wouldn't know what to do with it if it did come to her. "I buy stuff people can't get approved to purchase through official channels," she'd explained when they'd confronted her. "But it's all legal, and I don't sell things from here. I could go to prison for that!" Which was true—all of Eureka, and especially anything related to GD, was under military security, and the penalties for violating that were severe. "Besides, I don't deal in animals," Sheila had continued. "Too messy. I'll keep my ear out, but really I doubt anybody would try bringing something like that to me."

"Then who would they bring it to?" Jo had demanded in her best tough-cop voice. It had made the other woman shrink back from her, despite having a good six or seven inches and thirty pounds on Jo, and her voice had quavered a bit when she'd answered. Not that it helped.

"I don't know. I swear! Like I said, I don't deal with animals. Nobody's ever asked me to get them anything alive, and nobody's ever asked me to sell anything for them, either."

"All right, all right." Jo had stepped back, and watched, secretly pleased, as Sheila had sighed in relief. It was all about the attitude. That, and the fact that she could have broken the larger woman into pieces in seconds without working up a sweat, and they both knew it. "Just let us know if you do hear anything."

"Absolutely." Jo was pretty sure she meant it, too.

But that didn't help them much right now.

"Another dead end," Fargo complained as he climbed back into Jo's car. "So much for 'crack detective work.'" He even made little air quotes with his fingers.

"Yeah, because you're doing so much better on your end," Jo snapped at him, slamming her door and twisting the key in the ignition until the car's engine roared to life. "You're supposed to be our science adviser, so advise already! Give me something I can use!"

"I'd love to!" His voice came out in a whine, and in his

head he cursed himself for it. He sounded like a petulant child. "I don't have much to go on, here."

"Well, neither do I," she retorted. "But there has to be something! There's a thief out there, and every minute we waste following dead ends lets him get farther away." She slammed the car into gear and hit the gas so hard the acceleration flung Fargo back in his seat.

It wasn't fair. He really was trying; he'd been wracking his brain ever since the theft, trying to come up with some way to detect the egg or track the thief or both. But so far nothing had burst into his head.

He admitted privately that he'd been hoping—even fantasizing a bit—that they'd crack the case together, thanks to some clever insight on his part. And then Jo would see that he was really the man for her, not that arrogant bad-boy pretty-boy Zane. She'd fall for Fargo, for his charm and sophistication and intellect, and then—

Oof!

"I said, do you have any idea who else might bring in—or take out—restricted tech?" Jo demanded. Fargo rubbed his shoulder where she'd punched him.

"No," he replied, trying to keep his voice from going shrill again. "The only person I know who ever did anything like that was Victor Arlan."

Jo slammed on the brakes, sending Fargo flying into the dash despite his seat belt. At least the airbags didn't activate.

"Arlan," she muttered. "Of course!" She grinned and slapped Fargo on the back. "See, you can be useful when you put your mind to it!" Then they were racing down the street again.

Fargo wasn't sure which hurt worse—his shoulder, his chest, or his back. Still, Jo had complimented him, so at least his pride was intact. Right now it might be the only part of him without a bruise.

CHAPTᵉR 14

"I just saw Dr. Carlson!" Steve Whiticus insisted. "He walked right by me, then stopped to ask why I was wearing these!" Steve indicated the strange glasses that completely covered his eyes. "What exactly is going on here?"

"Don't worry," Allison assured him. "Everything is under control. You should go back home before you strain yourself." Whiticus was a meteorology expert and one of the few GD researchers to work from home. He'd suffered an eye injury a few years back, and it had damaged his retinas to the point where even weak light hurt like a migraine. He had special filters built into his glasses to help shield his eyes, but even with those she could see him wincing.

"But it was Dr. Carlson," Whiticus insisted. "I'm sure of it! We used to be neighbors!" Carl Carlson had been another GD researcher, a mild-mannered, friendly, slightly awkward little man who worked on cellular regeneration and mostly kept to himself. That is, until an experiment with the strange object known only as the Artifact had somehow rendered him invulnerable to harm. He had disappeared right before their eyes after warning them that they weren't ready to understand how the Artifact worked or what it could do. There was no way he was back, she thought. But she doubted Whiticus would lie about a thing like this.

"I know." Allison kept her tone calm and soothing. "There have been a lot of strange sightings lately. Don't worry about it. I promise you, everything is fine."

Whiticus finally left, shaking his head, and Allison sighed and dropped back into her office chair.

It was getting worse.

More and more people were calling her or stopping by to say they'd seen an old friend and colleague who had moved away, or quit, or been fired (and, in most of those cases, imprisoned)—or who had died.

Clearly they were seeing people from the other Eureka. That was why there were subtle differences—Carl Carlson hadn't known about Steve Whiticus's special glasses because in that world Whiticus must not have been injured.

But where were these strange sightings coming from? She'd seen people on Dr. Russell's monitor, of course, but that was in the extradimensional visualization lab. Now she had employees saying they'd sighted people from that other reality out in the halls.

People like Nathan.

She pushed that thought away again. She didn't have time to deal with it, or the emotions it caused, right now. Running GD came first. It had to.

Making a decision, Allison typed in a command on her computer. Then she leaned in toward the monitor—and the microphone built in above it.

"Can I have your attention, please?" she asked. She knew every monitor in the building was carrying her face and words right now. She could see the ones in the main lobby out of the corner of her eye, and employees crossing the lobby obediently stopped and turned to see what she had to say.

And what was she going to say? She'd debated. She could have concocted some kind of cover story, claimed it was a hallucinogenic gas leak, or released images stored in the building itself, or some other silliness. But she didn't want to have to lie. These were her people. And besides, she had no idea if these sightings would continue to increase. She didn't want to make up some phony explanation now and get caught out later when the situation changed.

So she settled on the truth.

"As some of you may know, Dr. Nancy Russell has been conducting an experiment into extradimensional visualization." She smiled, reliving the excitement of the initial discovery. "She has succeeded beyond our wildest expectations. Dr. Russell and her team have been able to assemble clear images of another reality—a reality surprisingly like our own. The theory of divergent realities has now been proven, and what we are seeing is another Eureka—a Eureka very much like ours, but with some differences as well." She could almost hear the surprise and interest rippling through the building. "Many of you have seen people around the building today, people you know but who do not seem to know you, people who look or act differently from what you expect. Even people who are no longer with us." She forced herself to push on. "These are images from that other Eureka. You are seeing alternate versions of the people we know, versions whose lives have diverged a little or in some cases a lot from those same people here."

She took a breath. "We don't know exactly how the visual spectrum is bleeding over from Dr. Russell's lab, but clearly it is. And it seems to be spreading throughout the building. But I assure you that it is not dangerous. You are merely seeing into another world. And they are seeing into ours. So please do not be alarmed. Do inform me or Dr. Russell whenever you see something of this nature, however, so we can keep a record of these sightings."

Something else occurred to her. "As far as I know, no one has actually been able to touch one of these alternate versions," she pointed out. "They seem to be like ghosts here, or holograms—they have no mass, and no solidity. Even so, it is probably best if you do not try to touch them, just in case. We don't know what would happen if matter from our two realities ever came in contact."

She smiled again, to offset the fear that last statement might have caused. "For now, just think of this as a chance to see what some of your friends and co-workers would have been like if their lives had gone a little differently. Thank you."

Allison switched off the announcement system and rose, stretching first and then smoothing the front of her suit. Hopefully that would help calm people's nerves and settle any fears.

But she still needed to find out why this was happening, and if there really was any danger.

Which meant another trip to see Dr. Russell.

She hoped she wouldn't run into any of the other side's residents on the way.

Her trip down to Dr. Russell's lab was uneventful, thankfully, but Allison stopped dead when she stepped into the lab itself. Standing there in the monitor, speaking with the two Russells, was a man she knew only too well. A man she thought she'd never see again.

Nathan.

"Hello, Nathan," she managed, crossing the room and stopping to stand beside her Dr. Russell. He was sitting beside his, leaning back, legs crossed and up on the console. She felt her breath catch in her throat. Same old Nathan.

"Hey, Allison." His voice was exactly as she remembered it, husky and smooth at the same time, deep and rich and vibrating with the same warmth that danced in his eyes. God, how she'd missed that voice, and that look!

"I was just telling them about the announcement you made," her Russell told her, glancing up at her. "They could hear some of it, but not all."

"I made a similar announcement," Nathan added with that slight smirk that had always made part of her want to laugh and the other part want to hit him. "Great minds think alike. But that's not really a surprise."

"So your people have been seeing mine?" Allison forced herself to concentrate on the problem at hand.

"It's been a bit more than that, actually," he conceded. "They've been finding themselves in a GD that looks almost, but not exactly, like our own. And running into people who look a lot like people we know, but with some subtle differences." She didn't miss the way his eyes flicked over her, as if searching for any differences, and tried to fight back a blush. He could still get to her, apparently.

But then, in his world, he'd had plenty of practice.

"So the pull has been toward our side," she noted, and Nathan and both Russells nodded. "Your people are coming here, but ours aren't going there."

"Seems that way," he agreed. "It doesn't seem to be dangerous, though if it continues to increase it could be. The real question is, why is this happening?" He glanced at his Russell, and at the equipment behind them. "I was thrilled when Russell told me she'd cracked the dimensional barrier, and ecstatic when she said she'd proven divergent realities by sighting another Eureka. But the way this experiment has gone beyond its original parameters—not to mention the bounds of this lab—is becoming disturbing."

"I agree." Allison clenched her hands, which desperately wanted to run their fingers through his hair. He wasn't even here! But seeing him there, alive and well, and talking to him, listening to him, watching him—it was killing her. "We need to figure out what's causing this and why, so we can extrapolate and see if it's going to continue, or taper off, or somehow get stronger."

"We'll get right on it," the two Russells insisted, speaking at the same time, and then grinning at each other. They began talking softly, sharing ideas at a rapid-fire pace, entering concepts and theories and lines of code into their respective computer consoles.

Which left Allison and Nathan eyeing each other quietly.

"You look good," he said, breaking the silence first. "Healthy. Happy. I'm glad."

"They told you?" She couldn't bring herself to say anything more about it, but he nodded.

"I don't know the project in question," he admitted. "It's

not anything we have running here, so that's clearly one point of divergence. But if we did, and that was the only way—" He shrugged.

"I know." He'd do exactly the same thing. Nathan had been like that. He'd often mocked Carter for acting like a hero, leaping into danger without a second thought, but he'd done the same thing himself when he thought there weren't any other options. He just believed in exploring other possibilities first.

"You look good, too," Allison told him. And he did. Comfortable, relaxed, in control—the way he always had. Just like her own Nathan had looked, right up until the end.

He gave her one of his half smiles, along with his usual shrug. "I manage." He waved his hand idly, and she saw the flash of the wedding ring on it. Then she had to look away, because she couldn't see anything else through the sudden tears.

"I'm sorry." He leaned in closer, letting his hands drop out of view below the console, and lowered his voice. "I know this has got to be hard for you."

"Does your—does the other me know?" Allison asked when she'd regained her composure. She'd started to say "wife" but couldn't manage to get the word out, even though the woman he'd married was her in a very real sense. But it wasn't this her, and she couldn't bear the thought of him being married to anyone else, even though he wasn't really her Nathan, either.

He nodded, but looked uncomfortable, which didn't happen often. Or at least it hadn't with her Nathan, and she assumed it was the same over there. "She wants to see you," he said finally, "but I'm not sure that's a good idea. There are some things—sometimes it's better not knowing how your life could have gone differently."

Allison frowned. Why would he worry about the other Allison getting upset by meeting her? She was the one who'd had it all work out! She had Nathan, *and* she had Jenna!

"Is there—" She stopped, then started again. "Is there something wrong?"

He frowned, clearly choosing his words carefully. "I don't think we should get into it," he replied eventually. "Let's just say my Allison has suffered as well, and leave it at that. I really don't think you want to know any more."

Allison felt her heart seize up.

Kevin.

He was talking about Kevin.

She wasn't sure how she knew, but she was absolutely certain.

After all, the other Allison had Nathan. And she had Jenna—the other Russell had said she'd seen their daughter not long ago, and she was beautiful.

Which left Kevin. Losing her son was the only other thing that could have made her suffer in the same way.

Or maybe Carter. But if that were the case she didn't think Nathan would have hesitated to tell her. He and Carter had never gotten along, and Nathan had always delighted in giving Carter grief, even indirectly.

No, it had to be her son. What had happened? Was he—was he alive?

She wanted to ask, but couldn't.

Nathan was right. Sometimes it was better not to know. Even though her own son was alive and well, the thought that another version of him had died probably would have overwhelmed her.

In much the same way that learning her husband had died in another reality would have been devastating.

"I think you're right," Allison managed to say, forcing each word out slowly and carefully. "Some things we shouldn't know. And I'm not sure she and I should meet yet. Maybe at some point."

"Of course." He nodded, and looked relieved. Then he hoisted himself to his feet. "Assuming we can figure out why my people are popping over to your reality for these little sightseeing tours, and make sure everyone is safe and secure on both ends."

"Absolutely." Allison glanced over at her Russell, who was still conferring with her alternate self. "We should let them work at the problem for a bit. We can reconvene once they've got something tell us."

"Sounds like a plan." He smiled at her, and gave a short bow. "I'll see you around." Then he turned and walked away, toward the lab's door and the edge of the monitor's view.

Allison just stood there for a minute, unmoving. Finally, when she felt she could trust herself again, she exited as well.

She made it halfway back to her office before she collapsed against a wall, crying great gulping tears.

Fortunately, no one from either world was there to see it.

CHAPTER 15

"She'll be okay, Jack," Henry assured him, patting him on the back. "She'll be fine."

"I know. I know she will." Carter took a deep breath, then bit savagely into his cheeseburger. "I just . . . she took it pretty hard, you know?"

"I do indeed." For an instant, less than an instant, Henry's eyes were haunted, and Carter cursed himself. When would he learn to think before he spoke? Henry had been in love with Kim Anderson for years, all the way back to his days as a GD researcher. She had been interested in him as well, but had somehow wound up with their mutual friend Jason instead. Years later, she and Jason returned to Eureka. When Kim and Henry discovered Jason had been using a device to erase memories and steal their ideas, she divorced him. She and Henry finally admitted their feelings for each other, and they were happy.

Until sabotage on the Artifact project created an energy burst that destroyed the Artifact lab's observation chamber.

And killed Kim, who had been the lead researcher on the project.

Henry had been devastated. It had taken him a while to pull himself back together. But he'd managed it.

Until a ship he and Kim had designed years before, a ship that GD had sent out to map the universe, had returned. And when some sort of virus corrupted the ship's onboard computer, it cloned one of its creators and dumped all of its stored information into her cells.

But that meant Henry found himself face-to-face with an exact clone of his dead love. Kim lived again.

Only, it wasn't her. Not really.

But that didn't make it any easier when they discovered that Kim 2.0 was dying, and that the only way to obtain the ship's information before her cells degraded and all that priceless data was lost, was to dissolve her. To kill her.

And Henry had to watch his love die all over again.

So yeah, he knew what Allison was going through better than anyone.

Carter swallowed. "I'm sorry, Henry. I'm an idiot."

His best friend shook his head and managed a smile. "You're not an idiot, Jack. But thank you." He sighed. "So trust me when I say, she'll be okay. It may take a little time, but she'll come through this."

"Okay."

They finished their food in silence. They often met for lunch or dinner here at Café Diem, and Carter had wanted to catch Henry up on everything that had been going on, both with the Thunderbird theft and with the other Eureka. Because in addition to being Eureka's duly elected mayor, Henry Deacon was also one of its best and brightest. And he was Jack's best friend. He was the person Jack always turned to first for advice.

Unfortunately, so far Henry hadn't been any more help than anyone else.

"I'll let you know if I hear of anything regarding the Thunderbird," Henry assured him as they both rose from the lunch counter and waved good-bye to Vincent. "Keep me posted about Russell's progress."

"You got it."

They turned to go, and almost bumped into one of the Bakers. Today's shirt was evidently gray, with stylized blue-rose patterns plastered across it. The Bakers always had the most entertaining shirt choices.

This Dr. Baker didn't even spare Carter a second glance, so whatever had gotten the brothers mad at him the other day must still hold true today. Baker did see Henry, however—and reeled backward, as if he'd seen a ghost. Or a rabid dog.

"You can't be here!" Dr. Baker accused, pointing at Henry. His hand shook. "You aren't supposed to be here!"

"What are you talking about, Dr. Baker?" Henry asked, his voice as calm and soothing as always. Henry was great with people, which was part of why he'd been elected mayor. Another reason was that he almost always had a solution to whatever the current problem was. "Of course I can be here."

"No!" Dr. Baker stared at him, and began backing away. "You can't! You're gone! They said you were never coming back! They promised!" Then he turned and ran from the restaurant.

Carter glanced at Henry. "Any idea what that was all about?"

"No." Henry frowned. "But whatever it was, I don't like it."

"Welcome to my world." That got a laugh out of Henry, and he was smiling again as they walked to the door—

—which opened just as they were reaching for it.

And Dr. Baker stepped through.

The first thing Carter noticed was the shirt. It wasn't gray with blue roses. It was midnight blue, with tiny stars.

The second thing was that this Dr. Baker nodded at them and said, "Good afternoon, Henry. Hello, Sheriff Carter." No fear. No snubbing, either.

But he did look distracted.

"What's with the quick change?" Carter asked, gesturing at the starry shirt. "Didn't think the other one went with your socks?"

He got a blank look in return. "I don't know what you mean, Sheriff."

"Were you just in here, or was that one of your brothers?" Henry tried. "Just a minute ago?"

"It wasn't me," this Dr. Baker declared. Then he frowned. "But . . . I don't think it was one of my brothers. I'm not sure."

"You're not sure?" That was really weird. For Eureka, anyway. The Bakers seemed to always know where their brothers were, and what they were doing, and even what they were thinking. Half the time, Carter wondered if it was just one Baker and he did all the rest with mirrors.

Dr. Baker was still frowning, and his eyes were slightly unfocused. He whispered something, and Carter had to lean in close to catch it: "There are too many of us."

He glanced at Henry, who nodded. He'd heard it as well.

"Go ahead and have lunch, Dr. Baker," Carter encouraged, guiding the balding scientist over to a stool. "We can talk more later." Baker nodded vaguely, but when Vincent stepped over, the routine of ordering food seemed to calm him, and he was able to place his order without any hesitation. Carter left him there and returned to the door.

"We need to tell Allison about this," he suggested.

Henry nodded. "Absolutely. And Dr. Russell. It's clear that things are getting out of control." He pulled open the door. "After you."

"What are you telling me?" Allison asked. They were in her office, and had just finished relating the encounter with the two different Bakers.

"We think"—Carter glanced at Henry, who nodded for him to continue—"we think that the two Bakers were from the two different Eurekas. The first one was from the other Eureka. That's why he wasn't as friendly toward me, and why he seemed so surprised to see Henry. Obviously something's happened to Henry over there, and he's not in town anymore."

"The second Dr. Baker was one of ours," Henry picked up. "He knew us both right away, and didn't seem surprised to see us. He was confused, though, because he said there were too many of them. Too many Bakers. Both his brothers from our reality, and his brothers from the other reality."

"Which is also why they had different shirts," Carter

added. "You know they all dress alike every day. The Bakers in the other Eureka must be wearing gray shirts with blue roses today."

Allison thought about what they'd said, drumming her fingers on the desk. "If what you're saying is true—and I'm sure it is—we've got a serious problem. Initially the bleed-over seemed confined to right around Dr. Russell's lab. Then it started spreading through GD. Now you're telling me these other Eurekans are popping up in town as well."

"And it didn't just start happening, either," Carter blurted out, realizing something. "Yesterday, on my way over to see Tomas DelSantos and his storm-shaping project, I crossed paths with one of the Bakers. I said hi, and he barely acknowledged me. That's not like them. At least, not these days. But it's the same reaction I got from the first one in Café Diem today. The Baker I saw yesterday wasn't one of ours!"

Allison shook her head. "That's not possible, Carter. We've only just noticed these . . . visitations. And they definitely started in Russell's lab, which makes sense because that's where the equipment is. The DelSantoses are half an hour from here. And you're saying you saw someone from the other Eureka over there yesterday?"

"I know what I saw," he insisted. Now that he thought about it, the idea made perfect sense.

Allison stood up and stepped around her desk. "We need to speak with Dr. Russell right now," she declared. "I think we need some serious answers."

"Uh-oh." Carter kept his voice down as they stepped into the lab, but both Allison and Henry heard him and stopped.

"What's wrong, Jack?" Henry had learned all too well over the years that Carter's instincts were usually right. And that listening to those instincts often saved lives.

"Look." Carter gestured toward the main console, where Dr. Russell leaned in close over her microphone. On the large screen, her other self was crouched in as well, and they were whispering hurriedly to each other. "That's not two scientists casually exchanging ideas, or even getting giddy about sharing research. That's two people trying to fix a problem, preferably before the boss finds out." He flashed a quick grin. "Bet they both jump when I call their name." Then he raised his voice. "Dr. Russell!"

It didn't take a genius to notice the way both women started and looked up, then flushed and looked away when they heard his shout.

"What's going on, Dr. Russell?" Allison asked, covering the distance between them in quick, strong strides. "People from the other side are starting to appear all over town. What haven't you been telling me?"

"I've—we've been trying to figure that out," Russell admitted, rubbing at her forehead and the crease that had been there since the other day. "The readings don't make any sense, though. They have to be wrong."

"What readings?" Henry asked, stepping up beside Allison. Carter hung back. Sometimes having a badge made people too nervous to think straight, and right now he figured they needed Dr. Russell clearheaded. "What did you find?"

"Our realities," the other Dr. Russell answered, her words echoing slightly from the speakers set up in front of the monitor. "They're side by side. Perfectly parallel, and completely separate. Totally inviolate."

Henry nodded. "Of course. The parallel universes have been theorized as discs in a platter, suspended at a precise and unwavering distance apart."

"Exactly." Dr. Russell looked like she might be sick. "Until now."

"What do you mean?" All humor and sympathy and friendship were gone from Allison's voice. There was nothing now but steely authority and resounding impatience.

"It has to be our experiments," the other Russell offered. "Somehow, by tapping into the energy in the other universe, we've transferred some of that energy between our worlds. And with both of us doing that from our respective sides, we've set up a two-way transfer, an exchange. A link."

"You've connected the two realities," Henry said softly, studying the readouts flashing by on the monitors. "You've bridged the gap between our universes."

"Yes." Russell bit her lip. "But that's not all. Bridging the gap would be dangerous enough—think what could happen if energy from one world wound up in the other without there being a corresponding transfer going the other way? We could offset the energy level of both realities!"

"And energy must remain constant," Allison agreed. "Neither created nor destroyed. Change that level, and who knows what it could do to our universe?"

"Exactly." Russell's fingers were tapping nervously on the console's edge, Carter noticed. There was more, and worse, to come. "But it's not just that we've established a link between the worlds. If our readings so far are correct—and we've gone over them a half dozen times already, to be sure—the link is actually pulling our realities closer together."

Henry made a noise that was somewhere between a gasp and a cry. "You've thrown off the balance, and shifted their positions as a result!" he said in little more than a whisper. "Like adding a grain of rice to a perfectly balanced plate and causing it to tip! And they're tipping toward each other!" His eyes went wide. "But if we don't stop that and right them somehow—"

"Our two realities will overlap," the other Russell confirmed.

Carter stepped forward a little bit and half raised his hand. "And this would be bad?" he asked. The fact that no one rolled his eyes told Carter how serious this was.

"Very," Allison agreed. "No two things can exist in the same space simultaneously—not two atoms, not two people, and definitely not two universes." Carter flashed back to the recent incident with the Matter Relocation System, or MRS, again, as it switched buildings and people with other buildings and people elsewhere. "If our two realities were to fill the same space—" She closed her eyes.

"They would destroy one another," Henry finished for her. "Total, instant annihilation of both."

Carter nodded. "Right, definitely bad." He tilted his head and studied the three people—and one image—in front of him. "So how do we stop it?"

"We don't know!" both Russells wailed. "We need to figure out why this is happening, first," Dr. Russell continued, while her double nodded vigorously. "We can shut down the energy input arrays, of course, but that probably won't be enough to halt their drift. They're already out of position, and still shifting closer and closer, which is why we're having people appear from their world. We have to figure out what caused that change and then reverse it, so we can push our two realities back into place before it's too late."

Carter started to ask something else, then stopped as the door behind him opened. He turned and glanced back, just as a strikingly beautiful woman stepped in. Average height, well built, dusky skin, long hair, pretty features, lovely eyes. Well dressed, very elegant, but still comfortable and approachable. He looked over his shoulder, then toward the door again.

"Yeah, this was what we needed right now," he muttered.

CHAPTᵉR 16

"I need to talk to him," Jo insisted for the fifth time. "Now."

"You're welcome to come down here and speak with him during normal visiting hours, Deputy Lupo," the warden replied. They watched on the video screen at the sheriff's office as he smiled—it was the kind of smile that said, "I hold all the cards, and I'm going to enjoy lording that over you." "Otherwise, I simply can't help you."

"Of course you can," Jo argued. "Get Victor Arlan, bring him to your office, and put him on the phone."

"That would violate all of our standard protocols," the warden replied calmly. "We can't go making exceptions for a prisoner just because someone calls and says it's important." He flashed that same phony smile again. "Not even if it's a valued member of the law-enforcement community."

"It is important," Jo snapped, "and it's classified." Her smile was now a lot sharper, and even though they were hundreds of miles apart the warden gulped. "Do you have top secret clearance?" She widened her smile. "Well, I do. Now get me Victor Arlan."

"There are rules and regulations to be followed—" the warden sputtered, but Jo tuned out his words because Fargo, sitting off to one side, had just written something on her notepad. It was a single word:

Mansfield.

This time Jo dropped the smile, slumped slightly, and sighed. "Okay, fine," she said. "I can see you aren't willing to help us out. That's a shame. I'll just have to let General Mansfield know that we weren't able to get the information he'd requested."

"G-general Mansfield?" The video quality was excellent, Jo thought; she could see the tiny beads of sweat popping up on the warden's brow. "I didn't know, you didn't say!" Of course he knew who Mansfield was—and what he did to people who disobeyed him. The prison was where Eureka sent its convicted criminals, and though nominally part of the normal judicial system, it still answered to the military.

"I didn't realize I needed to," Jo replied. She paused for effect. "Oh, right—you don't have the clearance to know our command structure." Her smile sprang back into place, not unlike a steel trap. "Now, then. Victor Arlan?"

The warden nodded and scrambled out of his chair. "I'll get him myself!" he called back as he fled the office.

Jo glanced over at Fargo, who gave her a big grin and a thumbs-up. She nodded in return. "Not bad, Fargo," she admitted.

A few minutes later, a new face appeared on the screen. This man was older, more solidly built, and his face was heavily lined. The fringe of hair around his head was grayer than it had been the last time Jo and Fargo had seen him, and he looked tired, but then, federal prison could do that to you. He still looked like a kindly old grandfather, and he smiled sadly when he saw them.

"Deputy Lupo, nice to see you again. Fargo. Are you still holding a grudge?"

"Why would I do that?" Fargo snapped. "Just because you tried to frame me for all the stealing you'd done, and then almost got me killed? No, not almost—my heart stopped, so you did get me killed!" Which was technically true. Victor had been in charge of the Vault, where GD stored all its old and unwanted experiments. But they were still cutting-edge, and so over the years he had quietly sold many of them on the black market to build himself a tidy retirement fund. He'd worried that someone would figure out what he'd done, though, so right before he retired he framed Fargo for the thefts by planting one of the Vault devices on him. Unfortunately, Fargo had activated the device, and had been trapped in an ever-expanding force field—one that threatened to destroy Eureka itself. The field was linked to his heartbeat, which meant the only way to shut it down was to stop his heart. Jo had done the honors, and they had revived Fargo a few seconds later. Not surprisingly, he was still a bit sore about the subject.

"I told you I was sorry," Victor reminded him gently. "I really didn't expect you to turn it on." But of course Fargo had, as anyone who knew him well could have guessed.

"That's not why we're calling," Jo cut in. "Victor, we actually need your help."

He leaned back in the warden's chair. "Really? Because I don't have a lot of access to anything where I am now." He held up his arms, and the chains connecting them clanked against the desk.

"All we need is information," Jo told him. "You were selling things from the Vault on the black market. We need to know who you sold them to, and how to get in touch with them."

Victor frowned. "Why would I tell you that?" he asked, and he sounded sincere. "If those people find out I told you anything, they could come after me, even here."

"I can talk to Mansfield, tell him you cooperated on an investigation, and try to get your sentence reduced," Jo offered.

"Really?" Victor leaned forward eagerly. "You could do that? I haven't seen my grandkids since I was sent here!" The sad smile returned. "Not that I blame Marcie for that. I wouldn't want them to see this place, either."

"No promises, but I'll do what I can," Jo told him. "And we won't tell anyone how we got the information, either."

Victor glanced around him. "Okay. I only dealt with two

people: John Beardsley and Rose Kenning." He leaned in closer and lowered his voice still more. "You contact them through this site." He scribbled something on a piece of paper and held it up to the screen. Jo thought he was being a little paranoid, but copied the URL down anyway. When she nodded that she was done, Victor folded the paper up and stuffed it in his mouth, then swallowed it. She tried not to roll her eyes at him.

"Okay, thanks." She nodded. "I'll let Mansfield know you were helpful. Take care, Victor." She'd always liked him, and might have felt bad that he'd been sentenced to hard time in a military prison just for selling off what GD considered to be junk. It wasn't like he'd hurt anyone. Still, he'd known the penalties when he'd started. And the law was the law.

"You, too, Jo," Victor replied. He looked at Fargo. "And you, Fargo. I really am sorry." Then he heaved himself to his feet and stepped out of the camera's view. A minute later, the warden was back in sight.

"Thank you for all your assistance, warden," Jo told him politely, keeping her voice civil. "I'll be sure to let General Mansfield know how helpful you were." She hung up before he could do more than look worried about exactly what she meant.

"I'm guessing we need to contact those fences, right?" Fargo asked. He already had his laptop open and was typing furiously.

"Yes, but we need to be smart about it," Jo warned quickly. Was he actually writing them to introduce himself and ask about the Thunderbird? That could be disastrous. "We can't let them know who they're dealing with!"

Fargo harrumphed. "Like I didn't know that? Please!" He turned his monitor so that Jo could see the screen. "There! A brand-new fake identity, totally untraceable! We can leave them a message, give this e-mail as a contact number, and wait. When they do get in touch with us, they'll probably want to do a video chat, but I've set up filters so they won't be able to recognize our faces or our voices."

Jo studied what he'd done, but finally had to straighten

up and nod. "Nice work, Fargo," she admitted. "I hope this isn't something you do often." She cracked a smile to let him know she was only teasing. Mostly.

"Only when I want to stir up trouble in chat rooms and on fan sites," he assured her. He broke into a huge grin. "Man, I've gotten some huge flame wars going!"

"That's great." Jo stretched and checked her watch. "Okay, let's go ahead and leave a message for them. Then we can grab some lunch. I'm starving!"

"Me, too." Fargo called up the site Victor had given them. "This detective stuff is hard work."

Allison stared.

So did Allison.

Carter stared at them both.

At first glance, they were identical. But then he started to notice differences. His Allison—his world's Allison, he corrected himself quickly—was dressed a little more sharply. Her hair was loose and styled, her jewelry understated but elegant. The other Allison was dressed a little more casually, a little more plainly, her hair pulled back in a ponytail, unadorned except for a wedding ring and a small locket around her neck.

It was like looking at the soccer-mom version of Allison, Carter decided.

Which probably wasn't far from the truth.

"Hi," the other Allison said first.

"Hello," his Allison replied.

"I—Nathan told me, but I didn't—I never expected . . ." She trailed off, gesturing at the lab, at the two Dr. Russells, and at her other self.

"I know. It's a lot to take in." Allison moved a step or two closer, as did her twin, but both of them stopped several paces apart. Carter wasn't sure what would happen if they did touch, but he wasn't anxious to find out. It looked like they weren't, either.

"I—" the other Allison started again. But she couldn't bring herself to finish.

"How's Jenna?" his Allison asked. That seemed like a nice safe question. She already knew the other Jenna was fine.

"Fine, she's fine." The other Allison smiled, her eyes sparkling. "Well, she's a handful, of course. And keeping us up at all hours. But she's great. She's trying to stack blocks already!"

"Mine, too." His Allison laughed. "And she's kicking her legs like she's going to bypass the whole crawling thing and go straight to running marathons!"

"Or wind sprints!" They both laughed, the peals identical. Then the other Allison sobered. "I'm sorry," she said. "I heard about . . . your Nathan. I don't know if I could have handled that."

"You would have. I did," Allison pointed out gently. "But thank you." She didn't mention how she'd cried after seeing him again, but she thought her other self might have guessed it anyway. After all, it was what she would have done in the same situation.

"How's—" her other self began to ask. Her eyes filled with tears, and she had to look away. "How's Kevin?"

Allison blinked away tears herself. "He's good," she answered after a second, though her voice was thick. "Well, he's the same. Though he's got a new tutor and he's doing well. She manages to break through his wall from time to time, and he seems a little more aware of the world around him in general." She shuddered, wrestling with herself. Did she dare ask? Could she live with what she might find out? Could she live with not knowing. "What—?"

The other Allison shook her head. Her shoulders were heaving, and they could hear gulping sounds as she battled to get her sobs under control. Allison wanted to go to her, to comfort her, but she didn't dare. They had no idea what would happen if two people from the different realities touched, much less the same person from either side. Instead she clenched her hands into fists and held them against her legs, hating to see herself so torn up.

"The Artifact . . ." the other her managed to gasp out finally. "It was . . . the Artifact. It . . . consumed him. Linked to his mind, and . . ." She stopped, unable to go on.

Allison nodded and wiped at her own tears. She'd nearly lost her Kevin to the Artifact as well. At first his link to the strange object had seemed a godsend, because it had pulled him out of his autism. But then she'd discovered that the link was burning him up inside. It was killing him. Henry had saved Kevin, using the old SRT in the GD director's secure bunker to deconstruct her son and then reassemble him without the Artifact's influence. And Carter and Nathan had risked life and limb to reach the bunker in time to warn Henry of an oversight that could have killed Kevin immediately. She owed the three of them her son's life, Allison knew.

Apparently in the other reality they hadn't been as lucky.

"Can I— Can I see him?" the other Allison asked softly. She finally turned back toward them, her face streaked with tears, her eyes bright. "I'd really like to see him." One hand went to the locket around her neck, and Allison knew at once whose pictures were contained within.

Her heart went out to her other self, but still she shook her head. "I don't think that would be a good idea," she said as gently as she could. "I think it would only make this harder for you."

That earned her a sharp glare. "I can handle it!" the other Allison insisted. "And I want to see him! I'm his mother!"

Allison felt a flash of anger herself, and gave in to it—it was easier than letting the grief swallow her up. "No, you're not. I'm his mother."

"So am I! We're the same person!"

"We're two versions of the same person," Allison corrected. "And Kevin is part of my reality, not yours." *You got Nathan!* she wanted to scream, but didn't.

As always, Carter sensed her mood. He stepped between the two of them. "Everybody's a bit worked up," he offered quietly, his tone nice and reasonable. "Why don't we all just relax, and maybe talk about other things. Like the weather. Or baseball."

Allison laughed—leave it to Carter to find a way to bring sports into this—but her other self just glared at him. "Who the hell are you?" she demanded.

Carter gaped at her, mouth wide open, eyes huge. But Allison was pretty sure his expression only mirrored her own.

CHAPTᵉR 17

"You . . . don't know me?" Carter asked slowly. He felt like he'd just entered his own private nightmare.

"Should I?" The other Allison eyed him up and down. "I recognize the uniform, of course, but you? I'm not used to seeing you wear it."

"This is Jack Carter," his Allison offered. Was it his imagination, or did she say that with a touch of protective pride, like someone saying "This is our state capitol" or "This is our little boy"? "He's the sheriff. He has been for several years now."

Her double shook her head, her ponytail whipping around behind her. "Sorry, we've never met." She started to offer her hand out of reflex, then stopped and let it fall instead.

"So . . . what? I don't exist over there?" Jack asked. "Who's the sheriff, then?"

He couldn't quite read the expressions that flickered across her face. Amusement, some respect, a little concern, and maybe . . . bewilderment? Which all matched his own reaction nicely when she answered, "That'd be Fargo."

"Fargo?" Allison was clearly just as surprised as he was. "Douglas Fargo? Douglas Fargo is Eureka's sheriff?"

"Sure. He got tired of being treated like an underling, campaigned for the job, and won it," the other Allison explained. "He's done a solid job of it, too." Her mouth quirked in a private smile Carter knew all too well. "Though I'm sure having Jo to back him up doesn't hurt."

"I can't believe it." Carter dropped into a chair next to Dr. Russell. "No wonder the people who've popped up here haven't recognized me! I've never met them!"

Then he realized that Dr. Russell—both Drs. Russell— were staring at him. "What?"

"That's it!" their Russell told him. She and her counterpart beamed at each other. "That's the discontinuity! We've been trying to figure out where our realities diverged, and you've been the answer all along! They split off when you came to Eureka!"

"That makes sense," Allison agreed, pacing as she thought about it. "You took over from Bill Cobb when he lost his leg. But if you weren't here, we'd have held open elections for sheriff. That must be when Fargo took over, over there. Warren left at the same time, and Nathan came back. In their world he . . . never left. Which means I never became director. And . . ."

"If I wasn't here to help Stark crack the bunker," Carter continued, seeing where she was going, "and Fargo wasn't around to help Zane handle the code breaking because he was busy being sheriff . . ."

"Then Henry never found out about the mistake in his plan," Allison finished. She glanced at her other self, who was watching them go back and forth. The fact that she was clutching at her locket suggested she knew what they were talking about but couldn't follow all the details. But Allison and Carter did. If Henry hadn't corrected his calculations in time, the trip through the SRT would have killed Kevin. And Henry would have been put away for murder as well as for causing a fake emergency. Which was why the other Dr. Baker had said Henry wasn't supposed to come back. In their world, he'd been sent to prison for good.

"What about Vincent?" Carter asked, remembering what

Allison had told him about her encounter with the curly-haired chef. "How did my not being here make Café Diem disappear and Vincent wind up working for GD?"

"I don't know," Allison admitted. "It could have been any of the times the restaurant was almost destroyed and you saved it. Or any of the threats that you stopped before they could get out of hand. We'd have to trace all of those outcomes to see which it was. But somewhere along the line, your absence caused that change."

Carter rubbed at his face. "Okay, so now what? Does knowing that help anything?"

"Absolutely," both Russells answered. "Now that we know the point of divergence," the other reality's Russell continued, "we have a better sense of how our two realities connect. Which means hopefully we can figure out what's drawing them closer together." They both grimaced. "Before it's too late."

A sound near the door made them all turn. Allison—the other Allison—was saying something. But they couldn't tell what it was, because her words were fading. Along with the rest of her. Carter watched as her outline blurred and she seemed to wash out, like an old image being erased. He could see through her now, to the door beyond. What was happening to her?

On a hunch, he turned and glanced at the lab's main monitor. Sure enough, a hazy image was forming behind that Dr. Russell, over near the door. Squinting, he could just make out a long ponytail. It was the other Allison; she was returning to her own world!

"Fascinating," the two Russells breathed, cutting their gazes between monitors and room. Carter had to admit it was impressive, in a creepy sort of way, to watch her vanish from here and reappear there. In a way, the process showed more than anything else so far just how close their two worlds had become.

And apparently that was far too close for comfort.

In less than a minute their Allison was entirely back in her own world. She glanced down at her hands, brushed them against her face as if reassuring herself that she was all there, then stared at the monitor. Her eyes zeroed in on Allison, and for a second they just locked gazes. Then she turned and fled from the room.

"What was that all about?" Carter asked Allison quietly.

She shook her head. "I'm not entirely sure. Part of it is seeing herself in another life, of course. And part of it is knowing that I still have Kevin. But the rest—there's more to it than that, I think."

"She lost Kevin, but you lost Stark," Carter pointed out. "I'm not sure which of you got it worse."

"She did," Allison answered without hesitation. "You were married, Carter. And you have Zoe. Think about it."

He did, and saw at once that she was right. He could live without Abby; he'd certainly managed all right, especially once he'd moved here. But losing Zoe? That would kill him.

"What was she trying to say when she got pulled back across?" he asked, changing the subject. "It seemed important to her, judging by the way she was gesturing."

Allison shrugged. "I have no idea. It could have been anything. It might just have been shock and fear from hearing about our realities colliding." Allison smiled. "She was never GD's director, so she hasn't had to deal with as many near-catastrophes as I have."

"Yeah, well, let's see what we can do to avert this one, okay?" Carter asked her and the Russells. The twinned blond researchers nodded. "I'm going to go check in with Jo, see what's going on with the Thunderbird egg."

Allison nodded. "All right. Keep me posted. And I'll let you know if we figure out anything over here."

Carter waved vaguely with one hand as he headed to the door. Then he was gone, and Allison turned back to her Dr. Russell and the twin in the monitor.

"And we are going to figure things out, aren't we?"

Both of them nodded quickly, and neither of them met her eyes.

"Got it!" Fargo smacked his hand on the desk in tri-umph, and immediately yelped and shook it. "Ow!"

Jo snorted at him, then sobered. "What've we got?" She leaned over him to peer at the screen.

"We've been invited to conference privately with each of them," Fargo answered, calling up the messages. "They've given us video chat log-ins. I'm guessing they're single-use only, which is how they keep from getting traced. Each time they contact someone, it's with a new log-in, and probably through a different set of servers. Clever."

"Yeah, well, let's hope we don't have to trace them, then," she reminded him sharply. "Set it up, and let's find out what they know."

Fargo enabled the scramblers he'd set in place, and then opened a window to the first video chat and entered the log-in. The screen cleared almost immediately, to show a shadowy figure against a hazy background. "He's using similar scramblers," Fargo whispered. Obviously these fences knew what they were doing.

"I got your message," "John Beardsley" said at once, leaning back against a chair or couch they couldn't see. "What can I do for y'all?" Despite the filters, Jo could determine a few things: "John Beardsley" was definitely a man, for one thing; a tall, long-limbed fellow at that. Not skinny but not fat, just medium build. Square head, slightly long jaw, lots of hair on top that stood up in every direction. Relaxed, laidback, and very in control.

"We're looking for something we hear you might have," Jo replied, talking into the tiny mike built into the top of Fargo's laptop. "A Thunderbird egg."

John Beardsley tilted his head to one side. "A what, now?"

"It's an egg," Jo repeated. "Bioengineered. Stolen from GD a day or two ago . . ." But Beardsley was already shaking his head.

"Sorry, little lady, but you've got the wrong cowpoke," he drawled. "I don't handle livestock—too messy. And I haven't heard anything about any Thunderbird."

Jo studied the shadowed figure for a second. "Well, thanks anyway," she said finally. And she closed the window.

"That's it?" Fargo demanded, turning in his chair so he

could see her properly. "You ask him about the Thunderbird, he says he's never heard of it, and we're done? Just like that?"

"Just like that," Jo agreed. "He was telling the truth, Fargo."

"How do you know?"

She peered down her nose at him, one eyebrow cocked. "I'm a cop, Fargo. That's what I do. I'm certain he was telling the truth. So, on to the next one."

Fargo grumbled for a few more seconds before calling up a new video chat window. "Okay, Rose Kenning."

This time the image was clear, as was the person facing them—but it wasn't a real person. At least, Jo had never seen a real person with tiger-striped rose-and-lilac skin, glittering silver hair, and huge crimson eyes that matched her tiny, bow-shaped lips. Rose, indeed! She sat on an enormous faceted throne in what looked like an elegant restaurant. A handsome tea service was laid out in front of her, complete with scones and crumpets and jam.

"Hi!" "Rose" burbled enthusiastically. "You were looking for me? What can I do for you?"

"We're looking to buy something that just came out of GD," Jo explained. "A Thunderbird egg."

Rose shook her head, which sent sparks flying from her eyes and her hair. "GD? Never heard of it. Sorry!"

Jo pursed her lips. "You're lying," she said carefully. "You've dealt with GD merchandise before."

"Who are you?" Rose's large eyes narrowed to impossibly thin slits. "Are you the law? If so, this is entrapment!"

"We're just interested parties," Jo insisted. "We heard you could get GD goods; that's why we contacted you."

"Sorry, I don't think I can help you." Rose reached for something past the screen, which Jo was sure was the disconnect button.

"Wait!" Fargo lunged forward as if he could stop her physically. "Look, we'll make it worth your while!"

The narrow gaze flattened out, looking just like a cat pretending indifference. "Oh, really? How, exactly?"

Fargo glanced around, then up at Jo, then away, then back at the screen. "Cloning algorithm," he said quickly, as if hoping Jo somehow wouldn't hear him. "Lets you duplicate files in a fraction of the normal time, no data loss, no file degradation even over multiple copies."

"Show me," the animated painted lady demanded.

Fargo hit a few keys, and his laptop chimed as it transmitted the information. On their screen, they watched as Rose pulled a monitor into view and scanned it.

Then she smiled, her whole face crinkling. "Lovely! Thanks ever so much! Now, what were we talking about?"

"GD. Thunderbird," Jo reminded her through gritted teeth.

"Oh, yes. You'd heard I could . . . acquire GD material." She all but purred as she tossed her long, shimmering hair back over her shoulder. "Well, I can, sometimes." She blinked insanely long lashes that hadn't been there a second ago. "But I don't know this Thunderbird. What sort of project is it?"

"Bioengineering," Jo answered. "Biological and bioelectric."

"Ooh, clever!" Rose's eyes had gone huge. "That does sound intriguing!" She pouted. "But I'm afraid I haven't seen it. And nobody else has mentioned it to me."

"Could they have taken it to somebody else?" Fargo asked.

For just an instant, Rose bristled, all of her hair standing on end. Then she huffed. "I can't imagine who! Everybody knows I'm the best when it comes to dealing with biologics!"

"Will you tell us if you do hear anything?" Jo asked. "We'd be very interested in making an offer on it."

"I will, I will," Rose assured them. "And thanks ever so much for the lovely gift!" She winked, then the window winked out as well.

As soon as the image was gone and she was sure the connection had been cut, Jo swatted Fargo on the arm. Hard.

"Ow, hey!" he complained at once, shrinking away from her and raising both hands to fend off any more blows. "What was that for?"

"Bargaining with her? Giving her GD software?" Jo hissed. "That's a felony, Fargo. I could arrest you for that!" She was pissed. You don't sink to a criminal's level, even when you're trying to catch another criminal. And despite all his quirks and faults, Fargo was a decent guy. He should know better.

But Fargo just smirked at her. "It wasn't GD software," he corrected, rubbing his arm.

"Oh, really? Then whose was it?"

"It was mine," he told her, looking her straight in the eye. "I wrote it myself, in my spare time. So it belongs to me, and I can trade it away if I want to."

"Oh." Jo frowned. "Well, sorry, then." She punched him in the arm to show there were no hard feelings, but he only winced again.

"Ow! Too bad it didn't get us anything," he said, hopping out of the chair before she could decide to hit him for anything else. He moved to the desk across the room instead, to maintain a safe distance.

"Don't be so sure," she corrected. "We know whoever has the egg hasn't tried to sell it yet, so that's something. It's still here in Eureka, which means we have a little more time to find it. And, if your new girlfriend sticks to her word, she'll let us know if it ever does go up for sale."

"Right." Fargo shook his head. "But what do we do in the meantime?"

The sound of the door opening interrupted them. Both of them looked over in time to see Carter enter. He stopped when he saw them.

"Great, I was going to come looking for you," he said. Then he looked at Fargo. "Comfy?"

Which is when Fargo realized he was sitting at Carter's desk.

"Might as well make yourself at home," Carter muttered, perching on the corner of Jo's desk instead. "The other you certainly has."

Fargo and Jo exchanged glances. What the hell was Carter going on about?

Then he told them.

"I'm sheriff?" Fargo asked. "Me? Really?" He grinned.

"He's sheriff? Really?" Jo groaned and sank into her

chair. "So not only am I still a deputy over there, I have to work for . . . him?"

"Hey!" Fargo lifted his chin. "That's Sheriff Fargo you're talking to!"

"Not over here, it isn't," Carter reminded him. "Over here, you're sitting in my chair."

Jo chuckled as Fargo grumbled to himself, but he did get up and sulk back across the office.

CHAPTᵉR 18

"Hey, Vincent," Carter said as he pushed through the door to Café Diem. "Can I get a— Oof, sorry!" That last was for the guy he bumped into, who was heading out just as he stepped in. "I didn't see you—"

Then he stopped and stared.

Average height. Average to slim build. Long face. Mostly bald. Glasses. A lot like a younger, slightly heavier version of Dr. Baker. With less interesting shirts.

And Carter knew him.

"Walter? Walter Perkins?"

"Yes?" Walter stopped and frowned. "Do I know you?"

Carter mentally smacked himself. "No, of course not. Sorry. Have a good day."

Walter nodded and walked away, though he glanced back over his shoulder once, clearly confused.

Carter sighed. Walter Perkins had been the cause of the very first incident he'd dealt with in Eureka—the same incident that had cost Sheriff Cobb a leg and led to his stepping down as Eureka's sheriff, and Carter's taking his place. Walter was a scientist at GD, a quantum physicist researching tachyons and wormhole theory. He'd built a tachyon accelerator in his basement, away from GD's prying eyes, but had lost control of it. At first they had thought he'd died helping them shut down the accelerator, but later they'd learned that he'd simply been shunted into an energy form that had flickered in and out of material existence. Allison and Zane and others had helped Walter regain proper cohesion, and then promptly put him in lockdown for violating GD security protocols.

It had been one helluva way to get to know the town, and the new job.

And now here he was, Walter Perkins, wandering the streets free as a bird.

But of course, this wasn't their Walter Perkins, who was presumably still in solitary detainment. Carter made a mental note to check on that. This was the other reality's Walter Perkins. Apparently his experiment had never occurred, or had been dealt with in some other way, not requiring Carter's help and not killing Walter or turning him into an electronic ghost, either.

Unreal.

For a second he considered going after this Walter Perkins and letting him know what had happened to his alternate self, warning him in case he was playing with a similar experiment. Then Carter shrugged. Would a guy like Walter really listen to some crazy-sounding "you could destroy the world" sort of warning from a guy he didn't even know?

Probably not. Why would he? Carter wouldn't, if their situations were reversed. Even if he told Walter about the divergent realities, the guy still didn't have any reason to accept his word about what had happened to Walter himself. For all he knew, Carter was an escaped nutjob, telling crazy stories to anyone who'd listen.

Carter shook his head as he resumed his path to the restaurant's counter. He was going to have to get used to this, seeing people he knew but who didn't know him and who were just a little different from their usual selves. He couldn't keep jumping, or stopping to stare, every time he saw one of them. Still, he'd have to let Allison know that at least one more alternate version had popped up in Eureka. And not just visually, either.

They'd bumped into each other. Literally.

And Walter had been carrying a to-go bag.

"I don't know what we're doing back here," Jo complained, pacing down the corridor. Fargo quickened his own pace to keep up with her. "I already checked the lab and didn't find anything useful. And Carter looked over the security logs—nothing there either. This is a waste of time." She glanced around. "The Thunderbird lab isn't even on this level!"

"No, it isn't," Fargo agreed, "but you know as well as I do that things around here have a habit of being connected in ways you'd never expect. And it's not like we have any other leads to pursue, right? So why not prowl the halls here for a little while, in case something pops up?"

She glanced at him, one eyebrow raised. "Prowl the halls? You've been reading gumshoe novels again, haven't you?"

Fargo looked away so she wouldn't see him blush. So what if he enjoyed the old pulp detective stories and the noir tales that came after them? And so what if he occasionally imagined himself as starring in them, wearing a battered fedora and suspenders and an old, cheap suit, smoking a cigarette and carrying a forty-five in one hand and a bottle of whiskey in the other? He had a vivid imagination.

Of course, the images of Jo as his femme fatale, wearing a slinky dress and a little velvet hat with a filmy veil that drifted over her face but only drew attention to her eyes behind its shadowy curtain, her full lips visible just below the veil's fluttering edge—well, that didn't hurt any, either.

But probably best not to tell her about that part.

"It isn't making any sense!" a voice insisted from a nearby doorway. "There had to be a trigger of some sort! Most likely electrical or electromagnetic in nature. But what?"

Fargo grinned at Jo. "See? Told you this would be useful!"

He led the way to the door and knocked on the frame, since the door was already open. It was a large lab, with arrays of computers and consoles, one enormous video flat-screen mounted on the far wall, and several smaller ones positioned at other locations around the room. A handful of lab techs scurried about, checking various panels and wires and circuits and readouts, while a tall blond woman stood by the main console, conferring through the screen with—

Herself.

Aha! Fargo had heard about the extradimensional visual-ization project, of course—he made it a point to keep up on all the latest experiments at GD, so that he could help Al-lison stay informed and on top of everything. And of course Carter had talked about Dr. Russell's recent breakthrough. He'd hoped to stop by and take a look at some point, after this whole Thunderbird egg thing was over. But what he'd just overheard made him wonder if somehow the two weren't actually connected.

"Dr. Russell?" he called out as he stepped down into the lab and approached her. He could feel Jo behind and slightly to one side of him. Must be a military thing.

"Yes? Oh, hello, Fargo." Dr. Russell turned and gave him a brief smile. "Hello, Deputy Lupo. What can I do for you?" Fargo had a bit of a crush on Russell as well—she was tall, blond, gorgeous, and a genius; what was not to like?—and in his head she suddenly became another femme fatale, a lady in trouble, garbed in a tight but demurely long skirt and a plain white blouse that was buttoned to her collarbone but strained against her impressive chest, clutching a pocketbook to her side and gazing at him with her big eyes, pleading for his help in solving this problem that was threatening her very life. He gulped and tried to push the image away. He had a girlfriend now, and Julia was awesome. But that didn't mean he didn't occasionally have these little . . . scenarios anyway.

"Sorry, I couldn't help overhearing," Fargo answered, forcing himself to concentrate on the real world. "You were saying something about an electrical trigger?"

"Yes, well." Russell leaned against the console and brushed a stray wisp of hair from her forehead. "Something reset my input arrays and caused my equipment to somehow do more than just absorb and process electromagnetic input. We wound up linking our two worlds instead, and that shouldn't have happened." Behind her, her other self nodded. "There wasn't any tampering—nobody but myself and my assistants touched any of the equipment, and everything here is self-contained, so there's no way anyone could have gained access from outside this room. Which means it probably wasn't deliberate—no sabotage, no pranks, nobody trying to hack in and steal the software. We figure it must have been some sort of electromagnetic activity instead. Something interfered and screwed with the settings somehow." She sighed. "But until we know what it was, we won't be able to backtrack and filter out that alteration to see exactly what happened and why. And how to fix it."

"Could it have been the Thunderbird?" Jo asked, stepping forward. She'd obviously thought the same thing Fargo had. "It's a bioelectric entity, and one got loose upstairs yesterday morning. It shorted out all of the systems in its own lab—maybe the effect somehow registered down here as well, and that's what made your systems go haywire?"

"It's possible," the other Dr. Russell agreed from the monitor, and Fargo glanced over at her. That was uncanny. She looked exactly the same, only she had long hair in a braid instead of the sort of pageboy cut this Dr. Russell did. He tried, unsuccessfully, to banish the sudden image of both Russells as damsels in distress, twin blond bombshells begging for his attention. Now was definitely not the time for such flights of fancy!

"The lab's heavily shielded, of course," the other Russell continued, "but if this Thunderbird produced sufficient energy, it could have leaked through. Especially if it was on some wavelength that slipped past our safeguards." She nodded at him. "Good thinking, Sheriff."

Fargo tried to ignore the glare Jo sent his way at that, or the sudden flush of both pleasure and jealousy he felt for himself. Not fair at all!

"Do you have readings on this Thunderbird?" their own Russell asked. "We could analyze them, run them through our logs, and see if the system registered the presence of those particular energy signatures."

"Uh . . . no, we don't," he had to admit, scuffing one shoe on the floor. "There were two eggs, and the first one hatched. It sort of blew out the security systems when it did, and fried the lab's equipment, so we don't have any clear traces of it." He could feel the heat of Jo's gaze on his neck, and deliberately avoided looking her way. Yes, he might have had something to do with that. But he'd been trying to help!

"Ah, that's too bad." Russell sighed. "Without the readings, we can't do anything more than speculate. We're checking all of our data for anomalous readings anyway, of course, but even if we find any, we won't know for certain they came from your Thunderbird."

"It's not *my* Thunderbird!" Fargo snapped, suddenly exhausted from all this pointless searching, and irritated that everyone seemed to hold him responsible for this mess in the first place. "I didn't create the thing! I didn't steal it! And I definitely don't have it!" He could feel Jo watching him, and both Drs. Russell as well. Watching, and judging. And blaming. That was it! He just couldn't take all the silent accusations anymore. He turned and stormed for the door, heading off in a random direction down the corridor. He didn't even care where he went right now, as long as it wasn't here.

"Uh, sorry about that," Jo told the two Russells. "This whole Thunderbird thing has been pretty stressful, and I think the pressure's just getting to him. But I'll let you know if we figure out some way to check the Thunderbird's energy signature." She turned and hurried after Fargo. She actually felt sorry for the wiry little researcher. She knew he was trying his best, and she was frustrated with their lack of progress as well. And yes, they did tend to pick on him a bit, and blame him when things went wrong, and roll their eyes at him, and ignore him.

But that was no reason to be upset, was it?

CHAPTᵉR 19

"We can't just have these people wandering around town," Carter said again. And again, Allison shook her head.

"What do you want me to do, Carter?" she asked. "Have you arrest them?"

He considered it, ignoring the way she rolled her eyes at him. "No, that wouldn't work," he decided finally. "We don't really have that kind of space. Besides, it's not like they've done anything wrong. And they are Eureka citizens."

"Yes, some of them twice over," Henry joked. They were in Allison's office at GD, and Carter had just told them about his run-in with Walter Perkins. "You're right, though—we need to do something about them. It's not safe to have them on the loose. We have no idea what could happen when they interact with people here, and it could be dangerous."

"Like 'touch your other self and go boom' dangerous?"

Henry laughed. "You've been watching too many bad science fiction movies," he teased. Then he turned serious again. "But there could be some electromagnetic discharge," he conceded. "We're occupying the same spatial coordinates as the other Eureka, but in a different dimension. Like having two sounds in the same receiver but at a different frequency. If they touch, they could cancel each other out, or build upon each other, or both warp from the contact. We can't be sure."

"Well, touching anything in general doesn't seem to be a problem," Carter pointed out. "Café Diem didn't explode when Walter got his lunch to go. And we didn't blow up when we ran into each other, though that was only for a second."

"That's a good sign," Allison agreed.

They all thought about it for a minute.

"What about keeping them here?" Carter said finally. "You've got the space for it. You could put them in a conference room or something, bring in some coffee and donuts, set up a movie. That way we'd know exactly where they were."

She thought about it. "Well, I guess they've already got security clearances, so there's no problem with letting them in GD. And you're right, that way they'd be comfortable but out of harm's way until they return to their own reality. And it'd be better than trying to cram them all into your little jail cell." She grinned at him.

"Great." Carter headed for the door. "I'll do a sweep of town, look for anybody acting out of the ordinary—which should be fun, since nobody here acts normal anyway. If I find anybody from the other Eureka I'll escort them back here."

"I can help with that," Henry offered, also turning to go. "And I'll let Vincent know to send any strays here as well."

Carter nodded his thanks. "You set up the conference room," he told Allison, "and let me know which one it is so I can bring our guests there directly."

"I'll take care of it right now," she assured him, turning back to her computer as he left. She needed a room that was big enough to fit a decent number of people, comfortable enough to hold them for a while, and preferably close to the main lobby but not near any sensitive areas. She called up GD's floor plan and then started checking the various possibilities for the one that would best suit their needs.

* * *

"Oh, what's he doing here?" Fargo whined as Jo half led, half dragged him back into Dr. Russell's lab.

"Just lending a hand," Zane replied, glancing up from the keyboard he was hunched over. He gave his patented lopsided bad-boy grin. "Hey, JoJo."

"Hey, yourself," she replied, her voice going a little bit more husky-raspy at the sight of him. She could feel the way Fargo stiffened in response, and scolded herself mentally. It wasn't his fault he still had a thing for her, and she knew that seeing her with Zane was killing him. And while she did enjoy tormenting Fargo sometimes—and while he certainly deserved it a lot of the time—she also felt a little bad for him. Nobody should have to see the object of their affections—or at least someone who had been for a long time—doting on someone else.

And dote she did. Try as she might, she couldn't keep the smile from her face when she looked at Zane, who was tall, well built, and way too good-looking with those dancing eyes and short black hair and boyish face. They'd butted heads when he'd first arrived in Eureka, a barely reformed criminal who'd traded prison time for work here. But over time she'd come to see the good man lurking behind the rebel mask, and he'd begun to tame his wild ways and show the decent, caring, hardworking person he really was. Sparks had continued to fly between them, but now it was in a good way, and Jo could no longer imagine a life without him.

A part of her wondered if her other self was involved with that world's Zane. She wasn't sure she wanted to find out.

"Zane is helping me check the energy readings," Russell explained. "I told him about your Thunderbird theory."

"Makes sense," he agreed, nodding to Fargo. The two of them had gotten along a lot better since the time they'd been forced to work together to help Carter and Nathan Stark break into GD's secure executive bunker, though Zane still made cracks at Fargo's expense sometimes. But who didn't, really? "I don't know a lot about that project, but if it was generating the kind of energy output you'd expect from a compacted thunderstorm, it could definitely play havoc with the circuits in here."

"If it could pierce the shielding," Fargo pointed out, echoing Russell's earlier thought. "If only we had a reading to compare it to."

"Ah, but we might." Zane grinned.

"The lab's systems all got fried when the Thunderbird hatched," Fargo argued. "And the thief had shut down the cameras and monitoring systems before that, and blanked them all the way to the front entrance. We've got nothing." He said the last belligerently, daring Zane to prove him wrong.

"Nothing from that lab," Zane agreed, surprising Fargo and Jo both. He was still grinning, though. "But what about the labs next door?"

Jo saw Fargo's eyes widen. "Of course! They wouldn't help us figure out the thief's identity, but if all we're looking for is the Thunderbird's energy signature, it would have bled through those walls easily because the bio labs aren't energy-hardened like this place. We can take a reading from Dr. Wilder's lab, or Dr. Hemming's, just before the hatching, and then just after, subtract the first from the second—"

"And know exactly what wavelengths we've got for your little winged stormbeastie," Zane agreed. His fingers danced across the keyboard, manipulating information with deceptive ease, and Fargo stepped up beside him, their animosity forgotten as they tackled the problem together. Jo crossed her arms and watched them, trying not to laugh.

"There!" Fargo jabbed a finger at the screen they had commandeered for this. "That energy spike has to be when it hatched!" The readings were displayed on the screen, with a clear spike at seven twenty-five in the morning.

"Yeah, energy levels're off the charts." Zane nodded and typed in something else. "And here's that lab's energy levels right before that." A second reading graph appeared on the screen. Then he did something, and the second one floated upward to overlay the first. It winked out after a second, taking most of the first graph with it.

"And there we have it," Fargo announced. "The energy

signature of one infant Thunderbird!" He turned and held his hand up to Zane, who high-fived him. Then they both glanced at each other, and at their hands, before dropping the offending limbs, backing away, and pretending the other didn't exist. Jo swallowed another laugh. Boys.

"We can check this against your logs," Zane told Dr. Russell, but she was already shaking her head.

"Seven twenty-five?" she asked. "Don't bother. I didn't even have equipment powered up at that point. I got in around seven fifteen, but I spent half an hour going over my notes and checking my calculations. My crew didn't get here until seven thirty, and we had a short meeting before we started flipping switches." She sighed. "It definitely wasn't the Thunderbird."

"How's it going in here?" The question made all of them look up, even the other Dr. Russell on the monitor, as Allison entered the lab. "Any progress?"

"Well, we've worked out what it isn't," Zane answered, displaying his usual lack of concern for authority. He treated Allison like he would any co-worker or friend, except that he generally did at least vaguely what she told him to do. And he sometimes called her "boss" or "chief." "It wasn't the Thunderbird."

Allison frowned, then nodded. "I hadn't even considered that possibility," she admitted, "but it would have made sense. It's almost a shame that wasn't the answer." Her gaze took in Jo and Fargo's presence. "I assume that's why you two are here?"

Jo nodded. "Fargo thought we should check around GD again, see if anything turned up," she explained. "And we overheard Dr. Russell talking about some kind of electrical trigger. Fargo thought it could have been the Thunderbird." She wanted to make sure Fargo got the credit for the idea. He deserved it. "Since it wasn't, I guess we'd better get back to our investigation. Come on, Fargo."

"Right." He nodded to the others, then as an afterthought held out his hand to Zane. They shook, both looking a little awkward. "Nice working with you." It was clear he'd had to force the words out.

"Same here." Zane glanced up at Jo, and his eyes twinkled. "Later, JoJo. Dinner tonight, maybe?"

Again, that smile appeared all on its own, and she even felt herself blush a little. "Dinner sounds great," she agreed. "I'll call you." She turned and marched out before she could embarrass herself further. But not fast enough to miss the *harrumph* Fargo uttered in her and Zane's general direction. Well, whatever. She was being nice to him, but that didn't mean he got to interfere with her own happiness.

Now if they could just find this stupid Thunderbird egg, and whoever took it, she'd really be happy.

"Okay, so it wasn't the Thunderbird," Allison repeated after Jo and Fargo had left. "What was it?"

"We're checking," Dr. Russell assured her.

"I think I've got something, too," Zane offered. He leaned back so they could both see the monitor behind him. "These are the energy readings for this lab, from yesterday morning." He indicated where they ramped up. "Eight oh-three, right about when you said you began switching things on."

Allison let her eyes skip along the visual record of the lab's energy input and output. "What's that?" She indicated a spike. It was from eight fifty-two.

Russell frowned. "I don't know. We were supposed to start the demonstration for you at nine, so that was still a few minutes early." Then she brightened. "Oh, right. That was when we had that energy surge, remember? One of the fuses burnt out, overloading the safeties. Sheriff Carter noticed, and leaped to the rescue." Allison noticed that Russell's smile widened and her pupils contracted slightly as she remembered the incident. She was interested in Carter! Allison had a strong urge to say something, to object somehow, but forced herself to swallow it. What right did she have to interfere? If Dr. Russell liked Carter, and he liked her—well, good for them.

Which didn't jibe with the way the thought of them together made her suddenly nauseous.

She shook that off and concentrated on the here and now. They were talking about Carter and the energy surge. Then she gasped.

Carter!

"How big of a surge was it?" she asked, her eyes going to the screen again. "Could that have caused the problem?"

Zane was running diagnostics. "Wow, that had to have been one hell of a jolt!" he muttered. "Remind me to ask Carter the next time I need somebody to hold a lightbulb for me!" He lost himself in calculations for a minute or two, typing furiously. Finally, he nodded. "Yeah, I think that was it." The screen shifted to show the readings from Russell's energy inputs. "Check it out—that zap supercharged your arrays, giving them a serious suction grip. They didn't just analyze the energy from the other Eureka; they drew it toward us."

"And created the link between our two realities," Russell whispered.

Allison shook her head. And, of course, Carter was right there at the middle of it all.

Then another thought occurred to her. "When was the first instance we had of anyone from the other side appearing here?" she asked Russell. She was wracking her own memory, and the two of them came up with the same answer at roughly the same time.

"Taggart!" Carter had mentioned seeing Taggart in the stairs on the way out after the demonstration had seemingly failed, and had said that the lanky Australian hadn't stopped to chat. Later he'd realized that was because the other Taggart didn't actually know him at all.

Okay, but who was the next one?

There was Vincent; Allison had seen him in the hall herself.

On her way out of this lab.

Shortly after Carter had gone.

Taggart had run into Nathan—when Carter was here in the building, talking to her in her office.

Sheriff Fargo—she still laughed picturing that one—had been in town. Only those boys had seen him.

But Carter had just left.

And when *she*—the other Allison—had appeared in this lab, Carter had been standing beside her.

"It's Carter," she whispered, then repeated it more loudly when both Russells and Zane glanced at her. "It's Carter. He's the key. The transferences all happened when he was around, or when he'd just been there." She shook her head. "Somehow, it all revolves around him."

Why wasn't she surprised?

CHAPTᵉR 20

"All right, I'm here," Carter huffed as he burst through the door. "What's the big emergency?"

Allison, Zane, and Russell all turned to study him. Something about the look in their eyes made him feel like a lab experiment. He had a sudden urge to make sure they weren't holding stickpins and little paper tags behind their back. For a second, they just studied him. The back of his neck itched. His heart hammered in his chest, and only part of that was because he'd raced through the corridors to get here after receiving Allison's urgent message. Then, finally, she spoke.

"You are."

"Huh?" He looked behind him, but nope, no sign of people sneaking in to shout "Surprise!" or "April Fools'!" or "You're on *Candid Camera*!" Which made sense, since it wasn't anywhere near his birthday, or April first, and as far as he knew they'd canceled *Candid Camera* years back. Plus, Allison didn't look even remotely like she was joking.

Which just made him want to say "Huh?" again.

But he was the sheriff here, duly elected, and he couldn't let himself look like an idiot. He had to be a calm, cool, competent professional at all times. So he straightened up, took a deep breath, hitched up his belt, opened his mouth—

—and stuttered "Wh-what're you doing? Hey now, slow down!" as Allison, Zane, and Russell all moved toward him with that strange gleam in their eyes that you only ever saw in bad science-fiction movies, the kind with crazed scientists about to enact some horrible scheme on the unsuspecting public.

There, or every day here in Eureka.

"Oh, quit being such a baby," Allison scolded as she grabbed him by one wrist and led him down into the lab proper. Russell latched on to the other, and Carter might have enjoyed being dragged along by the two of them if Zane hadn't chosen that same moment to plaster something small, round, and cold to his left temple. "Hey!"

"It's a sensor, Sheriff," Zane assured him, though the laughter behind his words was clear. "We're just going to take a few readings. Sheesh, you're jumpy. Switch to decaf, why don't you."

"What exactly is going on here?" Carter asked Allison as she and Russell guided him to a spot right in front of the main console and then lifted his arms so Allison could tug his shirt loose and Zane could apply more shockingly cold sensors to his chest, stomach, and back. He really hoped they didn't want to place any lower than that, because while he'd had fantasies about Allison removing his clothing, this definitely did not match any of them.

"It's the anomaly," Allison explained, waving some sort of device around him and causing a hum and a beep to emerge from each sensor she neared. "What knocked Dr. Russell's input arrays out of whack, and caused the two universes to begin drawing closer. It's you."

"Me? Oh, that's just great." Carter sighed, and slumped slightly. "First I don't even exist in the other Eureka, and now I'm the scapegoat in this one? How is this my fault?"

"I didn't say it was your fault, Carter," Allison corrected him, her tone a little gentler now than it had been when he'd entered. "You didn't do anything wrong."

"Quite the opposite, actually," Russell pointed out, giving him a warm smile. And this time he was sure Allison's moving closer and reaching across his chest to adjust one of the sensors on his neck wasn't just her prepping him for whatever they were about to do. "You saved my life, remember? That was incredible."

"Happy to be of service," Carter replied, smiling back, and getting a sharp tug on the sensor from Allison in response. "Hey, careful there!"

"Sorry." She didn't sound it in the least. "But, yes, you were your usual heroic self, throwing yourself into danger without a second thought. Unfortunately, the shock you received did something to you, and the energy surge itself is what altered the programs and the inputs to create the situation we're now in." She explained how he had been present, or nearby, or recently there, with every appearance of someone from the other side, and Carter shook his head.

"I'm nobody in the other world," he said with a little laugh, "and here I'm apparently the center of everything. Swell."

"All synced up and ready to go," Allison told Zane, ignoring Carter's little self-pity party. Zane nodded and typed into his ever-present notepad, activating some sort of program. Carter felt as much as heard the sensors increase their hum and vibrate ever so slightly against his skin.

"Commencing scan," Zane reported, eyeing his screen. "We should be getting preliminary readings any second. Whoa!" Allison and Russell both stepped over beside him, and Carter craned his neck. No one had actually said he couldn't move, but he was assuming that was the case. "Check this out!"

"What's going on?" Carter demanded. "Am I about to explode or something?"

"Definitely *or something*," Allison reassured him. "You're giving off massive electromagnetic readings, but the frequencies are strange. Very strange." She frowned. "I'd venture to say 'otherworldly.'"

"You've been magnetized," Zane elaborated. "Somehow, that charge must have zapped you, made you into a living input array. Your body was set to absorb energy from the parallel reality Russell had targeted—the same one we're looking at, and slowly colliding with, now. That's why people from the other side keep breaking through around you, or where you've just been. You're drawing them to you."

"I'm a magnet for the other world?" Carter tried to process that. "So why haven't I been sucked through to that side, then?"

"That's a good question," Russell admitted, brushing her hair back from her forehead as she thought about it. "Probably because the process began on this side, not that one, so you were already grounded here. And because you're from this reality, even if you're carrying energy from that one. This world had a stronger pull on you, so you stayed here, but with the link we'd created from the demonstration, you were able to draw others across—only as phantoms at first, but eventually with more and more solidity. And less and less dependence upon your presence, as the links grew stronger and the worlds drifted closer."

"I'll bet the fact that you weren't there in the other Eureka added to the effect," Zane suggested. "Nature abhors a vacuum, right? And Carter was a living, breathing vacuum as far as the other reality was concerned. He wasn't there, but he was here, so he was throwing off the balance. And he was pulling in energy from that side, but he couldn't draw his other self over because his other self wasn't there. So he started sucking in his surroundings instead."

"You make me sound like some cartoon villain with a giant crazy straw," Carter muttered. "Slurping up the countryside and then, I don't know, spitting it out into a little bottle I can stick on my shelf."

Russell stared at him for a second, then started laughing. Allison and Zane just chuckled and shook their heads. "You've got quite the flair for the dramatic, Sheriff!" Russell told him, her warm tone making it clear that was a compliment.

"Oh, yes, he's a real ham," Allison agreed dryly. "You have no idea." Her tone was a lot less warm.

"Okay, so I'm some sort of reality magnet." His arms were aching, so he slowly lowered them a little, then waited for a second to see if anyone yelled at him to get them back up again. Nobody said anything, and he let them drop to his sides with an audible groan that drew more chuckles from the peanut gallery. So nice having such an attentive audience. "And it's not my fault, but I'm at the heart of this whole 'worlds colliding' issue. What does that mean?"

"It means we've isolated the triggering event," Zane answered, "and now we've got complete readings on you and the energy you're absorbing, so we have something to work with." He tapped on his notepad, then hurried over to the main console and started entering figures there. "I should be able to whip up a reconstruction of the accident, and that'll give us the data to calculate exactly how far off the arrays were from their original parameters."

"From there," Russell jumped in, joining him at the computer, "we can work out what variation of my program was created by the energy surge, and hopefully work out an equation that will correct the deviation and reverse the damage."

Carter stared at them blankly. He hated it when people dropped into geek-talk, which at Eureka was about 80 percent of the time. Well, okay, 90. "You want to try that one more time, for the guy with all the electrodes?" he asked.

As was often the case, Allison helped him out. "It's like following somebody else's directions, taking a wrong turn somewhere, and getting lost," she explained. "We know what Russell's formulae were, and what result they were supposed to produce—a window into another reality. We know what we got instead—a link to that other world, a bridge that's quickly becoming a door. Now, with the readings we just took from you, we have a pretty good idea of exactly where we are."

"So you can use that to backtrack, figure out where we took the wrong turn, and then course-correct," Carter finished, catching on. "A jolt or two in the right direction, and the two worlds move apart once more, and everybody's safe."

"Exactly." He felt like he'd just given the right answer on a pop quiz.

"Nice." Carter looked over to where Zane and Dr. Russell—and the other Russell, who'd been quiet during the exchange but was clearly studying the same information on the computers in her version of the lab—were hard at work. Then he looked at Allison, who was watching them like a hawk. "I'll just get out of the way and let you guys do your work," he offered, edging toward the door. He was still worried they might decide they needed more out of him—like vivisection.

"That's fine," Allison agreed, still watching her people crunch numbers and fiddle with equations. "I'll give you a call if we need you."

"Great. Thanks." He started to go, then stopped. "Just, don't make it sound so much like the end of the world next time, okay? Unless it really is, of course."

She glanced his way and smiled. "Fair enough. I am sorry about that. We wanted to get to work as soon as possible, because the longer we wait, the closer our two worlds get and the more we're in danger of them colliding."

"I understand. But you could have told me that. I'd still have come running." Her smile was wider and warmer this time, saying that at least some part of her knew why he answered so quickly when she called, and Carter felt himself blushing a little. "Anyway, I'll see you later." He still needed to make that call to Mrs. Murphy about her privacy fence.

"Right." He was almost out the door when she stopped him. "Carter?"

"Yeah?" he turned back, heart pounding again.

But her grin now was devilish. "You might want to take off the electrodes before you go."

CHAPTᴇR 21

"Okay, explain to me again exactly what you're doing, and why." Jo crossed her arms over her chest and gave Fargo her best "I'm losing patience here" look.

For once, he was too busy to notice her attention, or to get flustered by it. But that was because, like all true geeks, Fargo's first love was science, and she had the power to distract him from anyone else. Even Jo.

"I'm calibrating this voltmeter," he explained, not looking up from the device he had half disassembled on his workbench. They'd come here after leaving Dr. Russell's lab, at Fargo's insistence. He hadn't really explained why, except to say that he had an idea and now he had what he needed to test it out.

Fortunately, Jo was no dummy. "You're using the readings Zane gave you," she guessed, and fortunately Fargo was too busy to see her little smirk or hear it in her voice. "You've got the Thunderbird's energy signature now, and you're adjusting the voltmeter to track that one frequency specifically."

"Exactly!" Fargo grinned. He loved smart, sexy girls, and Jo was both. And she'd sounded a little bit impressed, too, which was even better. If he could use the voltmeter to locate the Thunderbird, she'd be blown away. And then maybe she'd forget about bad-boy Zane and realize who the true genius was around here!

"Done!" Fargo detached the wires that ran between the voltmeter and his laptop, and then quickly but expertly put the device back together. His people skills might need a little work sometimes, and his experiments did have a bad habit of blowing up in his face, but he was good at the mechanical side of things, and reconfiguring a voltmeter was child's play—now that he had the frequencies to tune it to. He conveniently ignored the fact that Zane had been the one to provide them. He didn't want to give his archenemy any more credit than necessary.

"Back to the scene of the crime?" Jo asked as Fargo hefted the rebuilt voltmeter. It was shaped much like a TV remote, except that the top end was wider and had a small screen inset across the front.

"Yeah, we'll try to pick up the trail there," Fargo agreed. "Then we'll follow it and see where it goes." He allowed himself a small smirk. "Piece of cake."

"I think it's our best bet," Zane was saying as Allison wandered back into Dr. Russell's lab. Much as she would have liked to stay and participate in their discussion the whole time, she did still have other duties to attend to. Especially now that they'd set up the front conference room as their "detainee center," or, as they were calling it, their "visitors' lounge." Every parallel Eurekan who appeared was invited to the "visitors' lounge" to have something to eat and something to drink and to relax while waiting to slip back across the narrowing gap between the two worlds.

Fortunately, most of them had been quite reasonable so far—they were all Eureka residents in their own world, and the majority were GD employees, so they knew about experiments gone wrong and about the importance of obeying safety protocols. It helped that Nathan had issued orders to comply once Allison had gotten him the information about their plan. Even so, some of the otherworldly residents had been a bit stubborn about recognizing her authority. Especially Mayor Herrera.

"It's crazy," Russell argued, shaking her head. Her twin nodded agreement in the monitor. "That's not even real science, it's crazy super-science. You're basing it on gut instinct and half-formed theory and old movies instead of hard data."

"No, I'm using the data," Zane insisted, tapping his notepad's screen. "I'm just . . . applying it more creatively than usual. But it still makes more sense than anything else we've got going."

"What's the problem?" Allison asked, stopping in front of them. She noticed absently that Dr. Russell's techs were nowhere to be seen. Russell had probably sent them home for now. This was the theoretical work, and they wouldn't be needed until she decided to implement a plan that required additional eyes on the boards. If it came to that.

"I've got an idea," Zane announced, giving her the little grin he always bore when he had just hatched some half-baked scheme. Which usually wound up working—when it didn't make matters a hundred times worse.

She sighed. "Let's hear it."

"It's simple." He rubbed his hands together. "We're in this mess because Carter's been magnetized, right? He's pulling the other Eureka toward him, one bit of energy at a time." Allison nodded. "So we just reverse the charge. Boom!" Zane thrust his hands apart. "We push the other universe away, because now Carter's repelling it instead of attracting it. The link between our two worlds gets weaker and weaker as it stretches further and further. And he's pouring the other side's energy back into it, shedding it and pushing it away from here. When they're far enough apart, the bond snaps"—he made a quick tearing motion—"and our two worlds settle back into their proper places, nice and separate like they always were before. We can still observe it, thanks to the properly aligned input arrays, but we're now a safe distance apart again, and we stay that way." He folded his arms over his chest and leaned back, clearly pleased with himself.

"It's ridiculous," Dr. Russell argued. "You want to use Sheriff Carter like a magnet, switching the charge he's built up, trusting that to lever everything back into place. What if the reversed charge is too strong, and it sends both worlds flying into the parallel realities beyond us on either side? What if all it does is warp their world and ours, pushing us farther apart here at the epicenter but closer together along the edges? What if—?"

"I know you'd like to run all of the calculations a few dozen times, just to be sure we've considered every possibility and accounted for every potential problem," Allison interrupted. "And I completely agree." She shook her head to stop the look of surprise and victory that was starting to form on Russell's face. "But we don't have time for that. We need to come up with what we think will work best, and try it as soon as we can." She leaned in and put a hand on the tall blond researcher's shoulder. "Never mind the exact math. You're the expert on parallel realities. Do you think this could work?"

Russell frowned. "Well, yes," she admitted slowly. "It could. But—"

"Then we'll go with it," Allison insisted, letting just enough steel flow into her voice to make sure Russell understood that this wasn't a suggestion. "Between you and Zane, I know you'll figure out the calculations involved. Call Carter as soon as you've hammered them out, and let me know as well." She glanced over at a side monitor, which was showing the energy fluctuations they were experiencing all around them, and the fluctuations from the other world as well. The two were beginning to sync up. "We don't have a lot of time left."

"Anything?" Jo asked for the fifth time, tapping her foot. She hated waiting.

Fargo sighed. "No, still nothing," he answered, studying the voltmeter's screen. "Which doesn't make any sense."

They were standing in the Thunderbird lab, and had been for the past few minutes. But despite being right where the first Thunderbird had hatched, Fargo still wasn't picking up any trace of the Thunderbird's energy signature. Which couldn't be accurate; it had been right there.

He tapped in a code, and waited as the voltmeter ran a self-diagnostic. Could he have put it back together wrong? He was sure he hadn't; he'd been building voltmeters since second grade. Perhaps he had entered the energy signature wrong? But he'd copied it directly from the reading Zane had given him. Had Zane screwed it up somehow? Or, worse, had he deliberately messed with the data?

Fargo's grip tightened on the voltmeter, and his jaw clenched. That had to be it. That smug bastard! He knew Fargo and Jo were working together on this case, and he'd wanted to make Fargo look bad. So he'd sabotaged him! Zane had given him faulty data, or introduced a worm virus, or done something so he wouldn't be able to track the Thunderbird and would look like a fool in front of Jo. Fargo's eyes narrowed. Ooh, he was going to teach Zane a lesson.

The voltmeter beeped, and Fargo checked the screen. The self-diagnostic was fine; the device itself was working perfectly. It had to be the data he'd used to program it. The data Zane had given him.

"You're a dead man, Donovan," Fargo muttered as he backtracked to the hallway and plugged the voltmeter into a security panel between the Thunderbird lab and the next lab over. "A dead man."

"What's that?" Jo asked, stepping closer. She hadn't quite heard him.

"Nothing." Fargo called up the security logs—as Allison's executive assistant he had access—and pulled up the recording of the hallway right when the Thunderbird had hatched. Then he scanned those recordings with the voltmeter.

The little device began to chime immediately.

What the hell?

"You found something?" Jo asked eagerly, leaning in to see the small screen.

"Yeah, but it doesn't make sense," Fargo answered. He angled the device so she could see it better. "I pulled up the footage from the break-in, and used the voltmeter to scan for the Thunderbird's energy reading. And it found it."

"Well, sure." Jo rolled her eyes. "That's where we got the readings, remember?"

"I know, but then why isn't it picking up anything now?" Fargo pointed out. "This means the voltmeter's working fine. And it means that really is the Thunderbird's energy signature." He ignored Jo's questioning look, which clearly asked why he would have doubted that. "But I'm not finding any trace of it back in the lab where it happened."

"Maybe the containment field being broken did something to change the energy readings?" she suggested. Despite the fact that he was already taken, Fargo marveled at Jo all over again. The face of an angel, the power of a warrior, and the mind of a scientist. She was perfect!

Unfortunately, in this case she was wrong. "That's a good guess," he agreed, to make her feel better, "but the voltmeter's sensitive enough to filter out that kind of interference. It should be able to pick up traces of the Thunderbird despite whatever else is in the air."

"Okay then, why isn't it?" The look she shot him indicated that she considered all of this to be just another example of his wasting her time.

"I don't know," he replied, maybe a little sharply. He was doing his best. It's not like anybody, even Zane, could have built the voltmeter any better. Except that Zane probably would have jazzed it up somehow, given it a bigger screen or just a holographic display, upped the filters so they could screen out stronger energy signals, built in a— Fargo stopped in mid thought. Was that the answer?

"What're you doing?" Jo asked as he tapped a new command into the security console.

"I'm using the security systems to filter out any interference," Fargo explained. "They're a lot bigger and a lot stronger than the screens I've got in the voltmeter itself." He studied the results. "Damn!"

"What?" Jo looked like she was ready to wrestle the

thing out of his hand—a contest she'd win embarrassingly easily—so Fargo held it out for her to see instead.

"Look at the readings," he explained. "The security system ran them and reimaged them. See all the data it's receiving?" He indicated the wavy lines all over the screen. "That's normal background radiation, the kind you see everywhere, every day. Except that it's twice as much as it should be, and half of it is running counter to the regular signal noise."

Jo's eyes narrowed. "The other reality." Sharp as always.

"Exactly." Fargo sighed and lowered the voltmeter. "It's too much. With the added background chatter, there's no way to isolate the Thunderbird's energy signature. The voltmeter just isn't strong enough to filter it out of such a high energy level." He glanced up at Jo, then quickly looked away. "I'm sorry."

"It's not your fault," she assured him. "Well, not this time, anyway." She thought about it. "Is there any way to get something like the voltmeter but stronger? Something that could cut through all the chatter?"

"Sure," Fargo admitted, then continued as she perked up, "if you've got a spare van to haul it around. To filter all that, we'd need something at least the size of a small couch. With power supplies to match."

"Great." Jo turned away and paced the corridor while Fargo disconnected his voltmeter from the security panel and sealed the panel shut again. "Another dead end, then." She looked at him for confirmation, and he nodded miserably. "So we still don't have the first clue who took it, or where they are keeping it, or how to get it back." She paced a bit more, then turned and kicked the wall. Hard. "Wonderful." She delivered another powerful kick, actually putting a small dent in the wall. That, at least, seemed to cheer her up slightly.

Fargo considered pointing out that the walls here at GD were a flexible polymer with a low-level AI and a fleet of nanobots, and that the damage would be gone within the hour. He decided against it. Now wasn't the time.

* * *

Zane was immersed in the work. He liked collaborat-ing with the Drs. Russell, he decided. They had a quick mind, and an impressive grasp of intuitive math, even if they didn't like to use it without triple-checking their calculations first. True, both Russells were surprisingly hidebound for some-one working on such cutting-edge research as extradimen-sional visualization, and he'd had to overcome their innate resistance to looking "outside the box," but once they'd gotten past that, the Russells been a great sounding board and counterpoint. Plus, their knowledge of parallel dimen-sions far exceeded his own, so more than once they'd caught something he would have missed but that could have made a disaster out of anything they'd tried.

It was also fascinating to watch and listen to them work, be-cause more than half the time the two Russells had the same idea at the exact same time, and even said it simultaneously. But a few times one of them thought of something and the other caught on halfway through the explanation. The product of ever-so-slightly different upbringings, he figured. Wacky stuff.

Plus, the Russells were *very* easy on the eyes.

A real physics challenge, high stakes, two attractive partners—Zane was having fun.

At one point, he glanced up to see Allison watching them. He started to say something to her about how a watched pot never boils, then realized that: (1) she was dressed more "down-home soccer mom" and less "no-nonsense top exec" than he'd ever seen her at work; and (2) she was in the moni-tor, rather than merely reflected against it. He glanced back over his shoulder to be sure. Yep, no Allison. This was her doppelgänger, her other self. The non–GD director self. Or at least the married-to-the-GD-director self. Which meant he didn't answer to her.

Russell, the other Russell, noticed Allison's presence in the lab doorway as well. But she didn't stop what she was doing, which at that point was running simulations of their latest configuration. She just nodded vaguely in that direction. Because, of course, Allison wasn't her boss in that world. She was just an interested bystander.

So Zane nodded as well, gave the other Allison a quick half smile hello, and went back to work.

When he looked up again, she was gone. And within seconds he'd forgotten all about her, losing himself once again in the intricate dance that was balancing equations across two different worlds.

CHAPTᵉR 22

"**Remind me again**—*ouch!*—**why you have to**—*hey!*—zap me with—*darn it!*—electricity for this whole—*ah!*—thing to work?" Carter shuddered, his body still quivering from that last zap. He could feel each successive shock add to the vibrations that were racing through him, setting his teeth to chattering even though he wasn't in the least bit cold.

He was standing in Russell's lab again, arms out, and Allison had affixed those blasted sensors a second time. Why couldn't Eureka's super-science figure out a way to make electrodes and medical implements and dental tools work without being ice-cold? he wondered. Or was it deliberate? Did making the patient uncomfortable somehow aid the medical process?

"We're going to give you a burst of electricity," Allison explained for the third time, patiently, while making sure the electrodes were all synced and functioning. "It'll essentially reverse the charge that's already running through your system, attuning you to our world again rather than theirs."

"You'll still be magnetized," Russell picked up, earning a momentary glare from Allison that she either totally missed or completely ignored. "But now you'll be repelling the other world's energies instead of drawing them in. You'll actually be pushing that world away from us, until it's close enough to its normal relative position for inertia to take hold and settle it back into its usual location."

"Give me a fulcrum and a lever and I can move the world," Carter muttered. Allison raised an eyebrow. "What? I did study geometry in school, you know."

"It's 'Give me a *lever* long enough and a *fulcrum* on which to place it, and I shall *move the world*,'" she corrected gently. "Archimedes. But I'm impressed." Her smile was light and teasing, and helped offset the low-level anxiety Carter had gotten when they'd explained their scheme to him the first time around.

"I just didn't expect to be the lever," he added, shivering slightly at the thought.

"If it helps any, you're actually the fulcrum," Zane offered from where he perched on the console, tapping commands into his notepad. "The charge is the lever. We're just using you as the base."

"Oh yeah, that's worlds better," Carter retorted. "Thanks so much." Zane just grinned at him.

The little electrical bursts had started again, and Carter wriggled and writhed, gritting his teeth to keep them from clattering. "Is that completely necessary?" he managed to grind out finally, his voice as shaky as his limbs.

"Nope," Zane admitted, his grin getting wider. "I just think it's funny." He quickly threw his hands up in surrender when both Carter and Allison glared at him. "Kidding, I'm kidding! Yes, it's necessary. We're calibrating the electrodes, fine-tuning the process. We're also introducing the new charge to your body slowly, so it won't be as painful when we hit you with the full surge."

"Oh, this is *less* painful," Carter told Allison. "I'm so relieved." She patted him on the arm.

"Are we ready?" Dr. Russell asked. In the monitor, the other Russell nodded. Nathan Stark was behind her, watching from the observation chairs. His Allison was with him.

She wasn't watching Carter, though, he realized. She was staring at Allison instead. And her hand was clasping the locket around her neck again. Carter wasn't thrilled about that, or about her being here, but it wasn't like he was in any position to object. At least Sheriff Fargo wasn't there. Carter had yet to see him, and didn't really want to. That would just be too darned weird.

"You'll be fine," Allison whispered, then gave him a quick peck on the cheek. "Good luck." She backed away and took a seat herself, unconsciously mirroring the other Allison in location and posture.

"Okay." Carter took a deep breath. "Let's do this." At least he'd called Mrs. Murphy already, so if something went wrong here he would leave one less thing for Jo to clean up after him. The thought didn't exactly make him feel better.

Zane nodded and typed something on his notepad, then hit a switch on the main console.

Instantly the lights in the lab dimmed. The equipment all around the room hummed, and little sparks and arcs crackled here and there—but nothing as big as the one that had started all this trouble in the first place, fortunately. Carter could feel the energy building in the air, making the whole space sizzle. The air itself tasted sharp, metallic, and it made his lungs ache. It was like being at the center of a brewing storm.

And he was the lightning rod.

ZAP!!!

Carter stiffened, his whole body seizing up as the massive current lanced into him. Every electrode poured more energy into his skin, and through that to his nerves and blood and bones, and he could feel himself twitching but had no way to control it. He could barely think straight, and he couldn't hear for the rushing and crackling in his ears, or see for the lightning arcing across every inch of his flesh and blinding him. He could barely breathe, the air so charged it was burning his nose and throat, and he started to gasp. He wasn't sure how much more of this he could take!

Then it ended.

He collapsed on the floor, still writhing, like a fish out of water. His lungs slowly expanded again, and he took a deep, rattling breath, tasting sweet air that didn't hurt other than filling him to bursting. Slowly his muscles stopped twitching, and he just lay there, head against the cool rubber, and enjoyed the fact that he was still alive.

"Are you okay? Carter? Carter!" The voice was right beside him, and it sounded a little frantic. It took another second before Carter realized he'd been hearing it for a few seconds before he'd really registered it. And a little longer before he recognized it as Allison's. When he did, he finally managed to pry his eyelids apart and peer up. Yes, it was her. She was leaning over him. He smiled, the expression turning dopey when he discovered he was unable to fully control his face muscles yet.

"Hey, Allison," he slurred. "How's my hair?" It felt charred.

She studied him for a second, then glanced at the top of his head. "Standing on end," she reported, "but otherwise fine." That was good. He didn't want to have charred hair. It would smell awful. "Are you okay, Carter?"

Some of the effects were wearing off, and he found his thoughts falling into place a little more easily. "I think so." He tried to sit up, but couldn't do more than arch his back and flop about. "Maybe." Allison helped him. "Did it work?"

"We don't know yet," she answered, feeling his forehead and then checking his pulse. "The current fried the electrodes. We'll have to remove them and apply new ones before we can check to see if you're still carrying a charge, and where it originated." He could see the professional and personal concerns warring on her face. "But first we need to make sure you're okay, and that the shock didn't do any serious damage. Come on." She looped one of his arms over her shoulder and started to lever him off the floor.

Zane stepped over and helped Carter stand, then wound up supporting him when his legs wobbled and threatened to collapse. "Don't take too long, boss," Zane warned Allison as she took support of Carter's weight and guided him toward the door. "The charge should stay in his system for at least a few hours, but we want to calibrate it before it has a chance to dissipate. It'll increase the effectiveness of the process."

"We'll be back down as soon as I've checked him over," she promised. "But if it did cause any damage, we'll need to deal with that first." She gave Carter an apologetic look. "Compromising his structural integrity could jeopardize the process as well."

"Right." Zane nodded. "Okay, we'll fine-tune things on this end. If it worked, you're now a repellent force instead of an attractive one," he told Carter cheerfully, slapping him on the back and almost knocking both Carter and Allison to the floor. "But we've got to coordinate releasing bursts of energy from the other side to force that world back into position without tearing it apart." He turned back to the console and the monitor, where the two Russells waited.

"I'm repellent?" Carter asked Allison softly as she led him away. "Really?"

"Don't worry, Carter," she assured him just as quietly. "I still think you're attractive." Her smile was soft and sweet, and he wanted to respond, but the best he could manage was to make his lips twitch.

Somehow, he didn't think that qualified as attractive.

"All good," Allison reported twenty minutes later as she and Carter returned to Russell's lab. Zane and Russell were still there, and the other Russell was still in her lab in the monitor. Techs moved around them, activating relays and calibrating instruments as ordered. Nathan and his Allison were gone, however. Probably tired of sitting around waiting—or, if Nathan was the same as he'd been here, unwilling to sit still when there was work to be done elsewhere.

"Carter's fine," she continued. "No significant damage."

"My hairstylist might disagree," Carter muttered, reaching up to gingerly pat his charred, singed hair. He still felt a little jittery from the massive electrical jolt he'd received, and his mouth tasted oddly tinny, but otherwise he felt fine.

"Great!" Zane slapped Carter on the back, and it was only

after the bad-boy whiz kid removed his hand that Carter realized he'd used the friendly gesture as a cover to plant an electrode on the back of his neck. "Let's get you wired up again,
and we'll see if electrifying you did any good or was just
plain fun." Carter knew this was necessary, and he accepted
that. He just wished Zane wasn't enjoying it quite so much.

He stood patiently while they affixed fresh electrodes. Allison activated them each in turn, then synced them together,
and then they ran a diagnostic on him. Pretty amazing stuff,
really. This system was much more accurate than a standard
MRI or X-ray, and much safer, and you didn't have to lie
down and get shoved inside a room-sized tube to get results.
He'd certainly take standing still for a few minutes over one
of those any day!

"Looks like we're all set," Russell announced a few minutes later, checking her screen. "The diagnostic is complete.
Sheriff, your body's electrical charge is attuned to our own
reality once more." She smiled at him. "Welcome back."

"Thanks." He pretended to ignore but secretly enjoyed the
glare Allison was giving both of them. He'd happily flirt with
Dr. Russell regardless, but if it made Allison jealous? Even
better! "So, what now?"

"Now we turn to our good doctor's equally lovely counterpart," Zane answered, gesturing at the monitor. The other
Russell blushed a little but smiled and waved. "She's reconfigured her own energy arrays to broadcast instead of receive.
So now she's going to start pumping out short, controlled
bursts of energy. The energy'll get sucked into our arrays
and it'll emerge here, where before your charge would have
drawn it closer, binding the two worlds together."

"But now that my charge is reversed," Carter picked up,
"that energy'll hit me and rebound, and when it bounces back
it'll push the other reality farther away."

"Exactly." Zane gave him a funny look. "Okay, where's
the real Carter, the one who never would've understood all
that?"

Carter grimaced. "Give me some credit! I don't have the
first clue how you get all this stuff to work"—he waved a

hand to include the entire lab, and GD in general—"but the plan itself, that I get."

Zane nodded. "Cool."

"Do you need me to stand somewhere in particular?" Carter asked next. "Or is it enough if I'm still here in the lab?"

"Actually, you can go to your office, or go home, or wherever else you like," Russell offered. "As long as you stay within Eureka's city limits." Carter gaped at her, and she laughed. "The arrays are spread all over town," she pointed out. "Anywhere in Eureka you go, that energy will find you. And be pushed back from you." She put on her best "tough movie or TV cop" voice. "Don't even think about skippin' town!"

"Wouldn't dream of it." Carter rubbed the back of his neck and removed the electrode there while he was at it. He tossed the sticky circle at Zane, who batted the electrode away with his laptop. "But since I'm not stuck here, I want to check in with Jo about the Thunderbird, see if there's anything new. And I should talk to anybody we've got in the conference room, reassure them, that sort of thing."

Allison nodded. "I've got a stack of budget reports and status reports to go over, too. Let me know once you start seeing results," she instructed Russell and Zane.

"Aye aye, captain!" Zane saluted.

Russell was still laughing as Allison led Carter back to the door and down the hall. "I think he's a bad influence on Dr. Russell," Carter said softly as they retraced their steps to the main lobby.

Allison laughed. "Probably, but it's a necessary evil. Zane's one of the only people here capable of deciphering Russell's notes and really understanding both her theorems and her algorithms. She's very, very good at what she does, but she isn't very quick about it." Allison shook her head. "With Zane in the mix, they're solving the problem considerably faster than either of them could have done alone. Faster, more creatively, and with a built-in editor to make sure nothing went wrong in the math. One false step and we could pull that entire other reality down on our heads all at once."

"That won't happen," Carter assured her with more confidence than he felt. But he had to believe that. How many times had they saved Eureka—and the world around it—from utter destruction? Almost too many to count.

He understood her concerns, though—and her apparent stir-craziness. He was used to being in the middle of the solution. Now he was just a lightning rod, and since they'd already had him draw down the lightning, they didn't need him anymore.

He'd been sidelined.

Still, that was worth it—it was all worth it—if the experiment successfully restored the gap between their worlds and saved them all.

"I don't get it."

Zane frowned and ran the numbers again. It didn't make any sense! "We should be seeing some reversal by now," he muttered. "Or at least a slowing of the juxtaposition. But so far, nothing." He tapped the screen, as if that would make the numbers change. "If anything, we're speeding up!"

Russell, who was reading the display over his shoulder, nodded. "You're right. The rate of approach should have dropped, only a little but enough for the system to register the change." She shook her head and sank heavily into one of the chairs. "Why isn't it working?"

Looking up at the main monitor, Russell addressed her double directly. "The energy pulses were fired according to plan, right?"

"Absolutely," her twin responded. "The intervals we calculated, and we used the amount of energy we all agreed would be optimal." She checked her own systems, and mirrored readouts onto theirs. "The energy should have hit your input arrays right on target."

"They did," Zane confirmed. "We've got a serious spike in the arrays' input levels at precisely those intervals. So that's right. But why isn't it pushing us farther apart?"

"Maybe Carter didn't hold the charge?" Russell suggested.

"In which case drawing in more energy would only make matters worse."

"Maybe, but that'd be awfully fast for the charge to fade." Zane shook his head. "There's no way he shed it that quickly. Not with the amount of energy we dumped on him, or the strength of those readings right after." He thought about it. "But maybe proximity really is important. This lab seems to be the axis point—it's where everything comes together, where Carter first started drawing the other world's energy toward us. Maybe he really does have to be here so the array's energy gets dumped on him directly."

"That much energy flowing toward one person—if we're wrong somehow, and he doesn't repel it, it could kill him," Russell warned. She didn't look at all happy about that possibility, and not for the first time Zane got the impression she'd taken a shine to their stalwart sheriff. Ha! Not that he could say much, though, considering how he felt about Carter's deputy.

"It could," he conceded. "But we can be careful. We can shield him, just in case. Having him here for the next burst, to see exactly what happens and if his being on-site actually does make a difference—I think that's worth it." He knew Carter would agree. No risk was too big for the man if it meant helping others.

The Russells considered for a moment. Finally, they both nodded. "Tell him to come back," Russell agreed. "Right away. If that is the solution, the sooner the better. Because every minute we wait pulls our two worlds closer together, and makes it that much harder to push them apart again."

Zane nodded and pulled out his phone. "Yo, Carter?" He turned away so he wouldn't have to watch the readouts while he talked. "Listen, I hate to tell you this, but . . ."

Jo was sitting in the GD cafeteria, finishing her coffee, when she spotted Allison. The GD director looked a little concerned about something, but seemed to brighten when she spotted Jo. She quickly made her way toward her.

"Hey," Allison said as she approached. She loomed over Jo, casting a long shadow that threatened to envelop her. "Have a minute?"

"Sure." It was probably about the Thunderbird project. That was fine. Jo had been hitting brick wall after brick wall, despite her and Fargo's clever ideas. She needed to know if there was a point at which they just accepted the project as lost and washed their hands of it.

Conversely, if GD was willing to lend more time and resources—like bribe money—to locating the Thunderbird, that might make the search proceed much, much faster.

Allison sank down onto the chair across from her. "I'm worried," she admitted softly. "About Kevin."

"What about him?" Jo tried not to roll her eyes. For all her bluster—and her occasional bite—Allison could be such a mom.

"I don't know if you know this, but"—Allison paused, closed her eyes, took a deep breath, and finally continued—"in the . . . other world, Kevin is . . . He didn't survive. More than a year ago, now."

"I had heard. I'm sorry." Carter had told Jo about it, and about all the changes in the people they knew. Which only made her own apparent sameness that much more annoying. *Deputy* Lupo!

Allison nodded. "Thank you. But what I'm worried about is, what if he finds out? Hears it from somebody on the street and just doesn't know how to handle it? You know how he is."

She did indeed. More than once over the years Jo had been forced to help with the process of restraining Allison's son during one of his tantrums. That was the problem with someone who was severely autistic—their reactions were unusual, and often out of sync with the events that caused them. Sometimes Kevin seemed almost like a normal teenage boy. Other times, he was totally cut off from the rest of the world. Still other times he shadowed one person for an entire day, just to see what they did. Or rewrote complex math on the sidewalk, the wall, wherever was handy. Or flew into a towering rage over something insignificant. It was something Allison lived with every day, and Jo wasn't sure how she managed to handle it. Jo wasn't sure *she* would be able to, in Allison's place.

And she wasn't sure how Kevin would react to learning there had been another him, and the other him had died. It was a strange enough thing for anyone to discover, and Kevin's reactions were less predictable than most.

"I'm sure he'll be fine," Jo tried to reassure her, though they both knew there was no guarantee of that. "First of all, we're not letting information about the other side out into the general population, so it's unlikely he'll hear that from anyone else. And those of us who do know are pretty good about keeping quiet about things."

"Sure, but what if he sees someone from the other side," Allison insisted, "or, worse yet, they see him? Someone who knows he's dead, and reacts the way anybody would upon seeing someone suddenly alive again?"

"Most of the appearances have been centered here at GD," Jo pointed out. "And Kevin's school is on the other side of town, over on Edgemont. Hopefully none of the sightings will get that far." Kevin didn't attend Tesla High, even though he was the right age. Due to his autism, Allison had enrolled him at a small specialized school that catered to Eureka's more unorthodox students, those with special needs.

Allison nodded. "You're right. I know you're right. Still, I worry." She toyed with a thin gold chain around her neck and managed a weak smile.

"That's what makes you such a good mom," Jo told her. "Kevin's lucky to have you."

"Yes." Allison looked at her for a second. "Yes, he is." She stood up. "Thanks, Jo." Then she turned and strode out of the cafeteria.

"There you are! What are you doing? The egg is still out there, and so is our thief!" Fargo's voice reached Jo within seconds of Allison's departure, and an instant later the wiry little scientist was standing in front of her.

"I'm taking a break, Fargo," Jo told him sharply. "We've been on this thing almost nonstop since yesterday morning. So I'm having my coffee, and then I'm going back to work. Alone."

"What? But—"

"I hate to break it to you, but the Thunderbird theft isn't the only crime in Eureka." Jo drained the last of her coffee and rose to her feet. "I need to check in with Carter, see what else is going on, and help him handle it. That's my job, Fargo. Don't worry, I'll let you know if anything comes up about the Thunderbird."

"What am I supposed to do in the meantime?" he called after her as she tossed her empty cup in the trash and headed for the door.

"I'm sure you've got some work to do somewhere," Jo replied over her shoulder. "Start with that." She left before he could reply. Heading toward the parking lot, and her car, Jo found herself in a better mood than she'd been in since this whole mess had begun.

It was nice to be on her own again.

Nice—and quiet.

CHAPTᴇR 23

"You're doing this just to mess with me," Carter accused.

"I'm really not, honest." But Zane was grinning when he said it. Carter glanced at Russell, who laughed and shook her head, but he couldn't tell if that meant "don't ask me, I'm not getting involved" or "he really isn't," or even just "you boys!" Still, despite being a prankster, Zane generally took his work seriously, and threats to reality *very* seriously. And he'd said they needed Carter here at the lab while they tried the energy-burst plan a second time.

Though why they needed him to do this, he wasn't entirely sure.

"Can I at least put my arms down?" he complained. "I know da Vinci's man makes this look easy, but it really isn't!" He was standing with his feet apart and arms straight out at his sides, like he'd been caught in the middle of a jumping jack. Which, given the exercise's name and his own, he sort of had.

"I suppose," Zane agreed grudgingly. "Don't wander off that mark, though." There had been an X taped to the lab floor, right by the main console, and they'd positioned Carter at its center. "That's right where you were when you got zapped by the faulty wiring, judging by the security footage, and it's almost exactly dead center for the input arrays, so if having you here helps at all, this'll maximize the effect."

Carter nodded, then wondered if he was allowed to do that, either. To hell with it, he finally decided. He shifted his feet to a slightly more comfortable position, and put his hands in his pockets. Surely the fate of the universe—two universes!—couldn't be altered by the way he held his arms.

"Good to go," the other Dr. Russell reported through the speakers.

"Roger that." Zane and Russell checked a few readouts, scanned through a display on the main console's screen, and then gave a thumbs-up. "Let's do it. Hit the juice!"

Carter watched in the large overhead monitor as the other Dr. Russell flipped a switch and nodded. He could actually hear the thrum of her machinery through the speakers, and he could see the lights of her computer banks flickering behind her. He waited, squeezing his eyes shut and tensing slightly in case the energy did suddenly flow through to their world and decide to use him as a living battery.

But after a minute, he slowly opened one eye. He hadn't felt a thing.

"Did it work?" he asked softly, glancing around in case the otherworldly lightning was just lying in wait for him. Around here, he wouldn't be all that surprised.

But Zane and the Russells were all frowning. "No," Zane answered, pulling up two different readouts and comparing them. "Not at all. Same as last time." He sighed and rubbed at his jaw. "I must have done the math wrong."

"I double-checked your calculations," Russell pointed out. "We both did." Her double nodded. "Everything worked."

"But it isn't working." Zane was being surprisingly calm, Carter thought. "Absolutely nothing has happened. Just like before."

"So it's not me?" Carter asked, relieved to not be the problem for once.

"No, the readings didn't change from last time." Zane was still staring at the screen. "Having you here didn't make a bit of difference."

"Except for the whole 'other Eureka that exists because I wasn't here' thing," Carter corrected under his breath. He knew what Zane had meant, but the offhand comment still stung a bit. "Okay, well, if you're done trying to electrocute me . . ."

That got a ghost of a smile, at least. "For now."

"Great. I've got to get back to work, then. Ladies." Carter nodded at the two Russells, and they actually giggled a little bit. It reminded him of these two twins he'd dated in college, one of them a cheerleader and the other a political science major. They'd . . . He shook himself to drive that memory away. At least for now. "Let me know if anything changes."

"We will, Sheriff," Russell assured him. "Thank you." She waved quickly before turning to confer with Zane about the recent failure, and Carter took the opportunity to slip away. He still wasn't completely convinced he wouldn't get fried on the way out the door, so he breathed a little easier when he reached the GD lobby unscathed.

Then he saw a familiar face.

"Dr. Herrera!"

"That's Mayor Herrera," the tall, good-looking cloud scientist corrected. Then he noticed who had addressed him. "Oh, hello, Sheriff . . . Carter, is it? Director Stark mentioned you, but I don't believe we've met." He held out a strong, calloused, tanned hand. "Paulo Herrera."

"I know." Carter hesitated for a second, remembering Allison's concerns about contact across the realities, but then shook hands anyway. "Nice to meet you." He knew his version of Dr. Herrera, of course. The cloud scientist had run for mayor a little while back, going up against both Vincent and Zoe's boyfriend, Lucas, and had certainly produced a slick campaign, complete with tailored cloud images. All three of them had ultimately lost out to Henry, who had been a write-in, but Herrera at least hadn't seemed to hold a grudge. Apparently in the other Eureka the election had turned out differently.

"Right, right." This Herrera looked just as slick and self-assured in his hand-tailored suit, with his short dark hair and ready smile. "How's everything going on this end, then?" He put an arm around Carter and leaned in closer, lowering his voice. "Because I've been hearing stories from my constituents about being held against their will while they're here, and about unsuitable housing conditions."

"You've been hearing—?" Carter blinked. "Really." He straightened up and removed the other man's arm from his shoulder. "Well, Mr. Mayor, I'm sure we can answer all your concerns very easily. If you'll just follow me."

Herrera nodded and fell into step as Jack led the way to the forward conference room. "You understand why I'd be concerned," he offered as they walked. "I just want to make sure my people are being treated fairly."

"Your people are also my people," Carter assured him, though maybe with a bit more bite than he'd intended. "I am the sheriff of Eureka—at least, on this side. We are asking everyone who steps through from the other side to wait here, to minimize the chance of people encountering their own selves and also to keep people from getting upset by seeing another life that could've been theirs. It seemed best for everyone."

"I agree," Herrera assured him, smiling and showing all his teeth. "As long as you've set up suitable accommodations."

"Have a look." Carter nodded to Jo, who had been heading down the corridor toward them and had reached the conference room door first. She swiped her hand in front of the door's access panel, letting it read her DNA, and then tugged on the handle when it beeped and the light flickered to green.

Herrera stepped forward and glanced past her into the conference room. "Yes, this seems acceptable," he agreed after a moment.

"Take a closer look," Carter urged. "I insist." And he put a hand to the mayor's back and gently but firmly propelled him fully into the room.

"Wait, what—?" Anything else Herrera might have said was cut off as Carter slammed the door in his face. The light on the panel immediately darkened to red, and there was an audible click as it locked.

"He's not going to be very happy about that," Jo pointed out as they walked away. But a flicker of a smile touched her lips.

"Yeah, well, he can fire me if he wants," Carter offered with a grin of his own. "Or he could, if I even existed in his town. Guess he'll just have to settle for being annoyed and complaining to Stark, who'll complain to Allison, who'll tell me I should've been a little nicer." If that. He knew the smug, self-righteous Herrera wasn't exactly her favorite person, either.

"I doubt she'll bother," Jo replied, agreeing with his own assessment. Her half smile turned to a slight frown, though. "She's been acting a little weird lately."

"Well, she has seen her dead ex-husband, still very much alive and now remarried to her," Carter mentioned. He tried to keep his tone from getting too defensive. Allison could definitely take care of herself.

"I know, and that's got to be a huge shock," Jo agreed. "Apparently Zane and I aren't together over there, because Zane never came to Eureka, either. He's wandering around in that world somewhere, probably in prison, and that version of me has never even met him. Imagine me trying to explain that one if I ever meet her—I mean, me—I mean, the other me." The frown was still there, though. "But this is different. I can't put my finger on it, but . . . I was talking to Allison in the cafeteria just a little bit ago. And something about the way she was acting, the things she said . . . it just didn't feel right."

"She's just stressed." Carter sighed and glanced around. "We all are. And she doesn't like not having all the answers."

His deputy grinned at him. "Why does that sound familiar?"

Carter scuffed his feet on the polished floor. "Yeah, well, what can I say? I like knowing what's going on. All the time. Everywhere." They both laughed as they made their way out of the building. "So, speaking of what's going on, how's it going with the Thunderbird egg, anyway? Anything new?"

"Besides me wanting to kill Fargo, you mean? Which is

by no means new." Jo balled her hands into fists and threw
a few quick shadow-punches, scowling when her fists didn't
actually impact anything. "This whole thing is making me
crazy!"

"I know, but try not to take it all out on Fargo. We may
need him." Carter tried not to laugh. "Once we find the egg,
he can go back to working for Allison full-time, and you'll
have to console yourself with me as your only partner again."

"Gladly!" Jo's eyes narrowed and she glanced around the
parking lot. "And where is he, anyway? I told him I was going
to take care of other things, but I'm still expecting him to pop
up and beg to tag along."

"No idea." Carter patted her on the shoulder and turned
toward his Jeep while Jo continued on toward her car. "But
I'm sure wherever he is, he's getting himself into trouble."

"Where am I?" Fargo asked himself as he wandered.
He'd been walking back to his office after speaking with Jo
and must have taken a wrong turn, because he'd found himself in a corridor that didn't look at all familiar. Which was
strange because he knew all of GD backward and forward.
Still, it was possible they'd remodeled the hallway for some
reason and he'd just forgotten about it. He kept walking,
figuring he'd come across something familiar sooner or later,
but that hadn't happened yet. And it had to be getting late.
Allison would be wondering where he was.

At least, he hoped so.

He was starting to despair a bit when he turned a corner
and saw that the hallway widened up ahead. And was that—?
Yes, yes it was! Fargo increased his pace and soon stepped
out of the strange corridor and into the main lobby.

But something still wasn't quite right.

Fargo knew the lobby well. Very well. The circular archi-
tecture, the polished stone floor with the stylized sunburst in
the center, the steps leading up to corridors at various points
like spokes of a wheel, the large screens that showed a soothing water image, the glassed-in wall that fronted Allison's of-

fice, the towering ceiling broken by bands of light where the other floors lay, the spherical sculpture that hung suspended from two stories up, the GD logo mounted on the ceiling—he saw it every single day.

And this wasn't it.

Oh, at first glance it looked the same. But Fargo—for all that Carter and Jo and others gave him trouble for being clueless—noticed things. And there were things here that didn't add up.

Like the floor. It was the wrong shade.

And the sculpture in the center. The shape was right, but it wasn't gleaming Lucite. He squinted up at it. Bronze? It looked like bronze from here.

And the shimmering water image. It was still water, but more like the trickle of water down a window in the middle of a storm.

Something had happened. This wasn't the GD he knew.

"Let me guess. You're wondering what happened?" a voice asked. A voice that sounded awfully familiar.

Fargo jumped a little, then composed himself. "Well, yes," he admitted. He turned to face his questioner—and froze, his jaw dropping.

He was staring at himself.

Or a version of himself. A version that stood a bit straighter, looked a bit prouder, even seemed to have a bit more muscle to him. He certainly filled out his sheriff's uniform well, anyway.

The grin looked the same, though. Fargo saw it in the mirror all the time.

"Welcome to Eureka, Dr. Fargo," the sheriff told him.

"Thank you, Sheriff Fargo," Fargo replied with a matching grin. "It's a pleasure to be here."

CHAPTᵉR 24

"It's getting worse, isn't it?"

Carter nodded. "Sure seems that way."

He and Jo glanced back over their shoulders at the closed conference room doors behind them. They'd had to expand their "otherworldly waiting room" operation to a second conference room because the first was now filled to capacity. Oh, they could cram a few more people in, maybe, but only if they treated them like cattle. And these were honest Eureka citizens, respected scientists and researchers. It wasn't their fault they'd wound up in the wrong reality, and Carter didn't want to be any harsher toward them than he had to.

Which was already plenty harsh.

"I can't believe Seth Osborne tried to deck you." Jo laughed.

"Yeah, well, it wasn't all that funny at the time," Carter groused, rubbing the back of his neck. "Makes sense when you think about it, though. He's never been big on respecting authority, and I'm not even his sheriff, so why should he listen to me?" He'd had several run-ins with this world's Seth, a botanist who specialized in tailoring exotic plants—

often with disastrous consequences. More than once the big, burly scientist had come close throwing a punch at Carter, and each time Carter had intimidated or reasoned him down. This time, it hadn't worked quite as well.

"Did he actually land the punch?" Jo squinted at him, inspecting his face for bruising.

"No, but it was close." Fortunately, Carter'd had plenty of training in handling belligerent and violent individuals. He'd blocked the punch, twisted Seth's arm behind him, and handcuffed him before the big man knew what was happening. If that blow had landed, though, Carter had a feeling he would've been picking his teeth up off the floor.

"And all because you told him to stop working?" Jo shook her head. "You know, anywhere else people would be thrilled if the cops showed up and said, 'Okay, knock it off and go home for a while.'"

Carter laughed. She was right. Most workers would be delighted to have an excuse to take a break. But folks in Eureka were pretty driven, by and large. "Yeah, he told me his experiments were at a critical stage and he needed to monitor them closely. I tried explaining that his lab was in the other Eureka, so it wouldn't do him any good to head to a lab here, but he didn't believe me."

"So now he's locked up with the rest of our ghosts."

"Until he fades away." That was the one thing that had kept this situation from becoming completely unmanageable—nobody stuck around for too long. After a little while, anywhere from a minute to half an hour, the other faded out and apparently reappeared in his own world. The conference rooms were constantly changing in terms of who was there and who wasn't.

But it seemed to Carter that people were staying here longer and longer. And that couldn't be a good sign.

"How much longer do you think this'll go on?" Jo asked, leaning against the wall and crossing her arms over her chest.

"Not much longer." Carter sighed, looked around, and lowered his voice. "Either Zane and Dr. Russell will figure out what they've been doing wrong and fix it so they can push the two worlds apart again, or—"

"Or the two worlds overlap completely, and cancel each other out, wiping all of us off the face of the map," Jo finished for him. Then she stiffened slightly. "Wait, Zane's still working with Russell?"

"He sure is." Carter smiled slowly. "Tall, blond, gorgeous Dr. Russell. And a genius physicist to boot. They've got a lot in common, don't you think?" He chuckled as his deputy's eyes narrowed, then took a step back and raised his hands in surrender as she turned that murderous gaze in his direction. "Okay, okay, I surrender!"

"He can work with her all he wants," Jo ground out through clenched teeth. "I trust him." But her knuckles were turning white where her hands were clenched into fists.

"Relax, Jo," Carter told her gently, reaching out and taking one of her hands. She flinched at first, but then let him. "You've got nothing to worry about. Zane's crazy about you—and for good reason. Russell's just a colleague on a project, nothing more."

"You're sure?" There it was again, that brief glimpse at the Jo inside, the quiet, vulnerable little girl afraid to have her heart broken.

"Positive." And he was. He'd seen the way Zane looked at her. The young whiz kid was head over heels.

"Right, then." She pulled her hand away, and turned from Carter for a second, composing herself. When she swiveled back around, she punched him in the arm. Hard.

"Hey!"

"That's for teasing me," she warned. But her tone had changed back to its more typical "give Carter a hard time" snarkiness, and he knew everything was okay between them again.

He really needed to keep his sense of humor in check, though. It was always getting him into trouble.

"So."

"So."

"Sheriff, eh?"

"Yep. Executive assistant to the director of GD?"

"Yep."

Fargo nodded, and rocked back and forth on his heels. Sheriff Fargo did the same thing. They were still standing in GD's lobby, though they'd moved off to one side, and people gave them curious looks as they walked past.

"What's it like?" both of them asked at once, then laughed together. "After you! No, after you!"

Finally Sheriff Fargo held up a hand. "It's good," he admitted. "Crazy-busy most of the time, with things mutating or escaping or being stolen or getting broken, not to mention all the little squabbles and infractions you'd get in any town, but with Eureka-level tech added in. But it's good." He hooked his thumbs in his belt and puffed up a little bit. "I'm the law around here. People listen to me, and they do what I say."

"Must be nice," Fargo muttered. "Nobody listens to me until it's too late, usually. And nobody does what I tell them, even when I tell them the right thing to do!" He brightened a bit, thinking about his job. "It is good, though. I work for Allison Blake, and I'm involved in the day-to-day operations of GD, plus I've got a hand in almost every project going on here. I get to see everything, and talk to everyone, and I've offered suggestions on hundreds of different experiments. Plus, it never gets dull—in one day I'll help collate reports from a bio lab, order supplies for a pharmacology experiment, watch the test run of a new propulsion unit, study the latest medical tech developments, and balance the budget for five experiments. That's when I'm not helping Jo and Sheriff Carter solve something."

"Ah. Jo. I'd heard she was still deputy there, too." Sheriff Fargo smirked a little. Fargo studied him as best he could without openly staring. Was that a hint of stubble on his double's chin? "Is she still just as hot?"

"Amazingly so," Fargo agreed. "But in my world she's going out with a guy named Zane." He waited for a sign of recognition, but the sheriff shook his head.

"Never heard of him."

"Yeah? Well, you're lucky," Fargo groused, adjusting his glasses. "He's smart, really smart, and good-looking, like a dark-haired surfer. And he was a high-tech crook so he's got that bad-boy vibe. We didn't stand a chance." A thought struck him. "Wait, she's not seeing anybody in your world?" There was something . . . knowing about his double's smirk. "Are the two of you . . . ?"

"It's complicated," Sheriff Fargo replied, but his smirk widened slightly. "Jo and I, we work together, after all. Can't just date when we're colleagues, too." Now he was positively grinning. "But there's definitely interest there. No question about it."

Fargo frowned, considering this. Was his double telling the truth? Did he have the better job, the respect, the authority, and Jo as well? Or was he exaggerating to impress him? It's what *he* would do, after all. And there was something about that look, the way his other self wouldn't meet his eyes, the way his lips twitched like he wanted to say something else but didn't dare. No, Fargo decided finally. No, maybe there was some tension there, but he didn't believe his other self had won Jo's heart. He felt a wave of relief. At least the sheriff version of him didn't have *everything*.

And it wasn't like he was lonely himself these days. "I've got a girlfriend myself," he bragged. "Her name's Julia Golden. She's a researcher at GD." He smiled, thinking about her. "She's great." Though he had to admit that, much as he liked Julia, she wasn't the same as Jo. Far from it. Which didn't make Julia any less awesome in her own right, but sometimes Fargo wondered if he was just settling. Then he usually kicked himself.

"Really? Good for you!" His double seemed genuinely happy for him, and maybe a little bit jealous as well. That made Fargo feel a little better. "So, you help Jo and your sheriff—Carter, right?—out with cases?" Sheriff Fargo clearly wanted to change the subject. Fargo let him. No point in humiliating him by calling him on his lie. "You helping them with anything now?"

"Actually, yes." Fargo rubbed his hands together. "Jo and

I are working on a theft here at GD, in fact. In one of the bio labs. It involves a project called—"

"The Thunderbird," his double said at the same time he did. Then he grinned. "Nice! I'm working on the exact same thing!"

"Wait, you've got a Thunderbird project, too?" Fargo stared. "And it was stolen?"

"Yes indeed—both eggs got swiped, by someone who knew exactly what they were doing." Sheriff Fargo shook his head. "Shut down the security cam beforehand, disabled the door panels, shorted out the containment fields, took both eggs, and disappeared. By the time Dr. Korinko got in, they were long gone."

Fargo nodded. "Of course. That makes total sense! In my world, the thief only got away with one of the eggs," he explained. "I was in early and noticed the security alert about the containment fields. The thief shut down the security to the lab and blanked the cameras all the way there, but didn't think to disconnect the energy sensors, so they registered the change from the containment rupture. I hit the alarm and alerted Sheriff Carter and Jo, and they showed up in time to interrupt the thief. One of the eggs hatched prematurely, and they had to dissipate the fledgling Thunderbird before it could hurt anyone. But the thief got away with the other egg in the confusion." He left out the part where his attempts to contain the gases from the containment field had caused the hatching and provided the cover for the thief's escape. No need to go into all that right now.

But of course it was almost impossible to lie to himself, and his double had a knowing smile as he took all this in. "Good thing you were there to help" was all he said, however. Then he laughed and pushed the hat back on his head. Fargo had always wondered how he'd look in a hat. He wasn't entirely sure it worked, though it did add to the uniform's overall effect. He wondered if he should suggest a hat to Carter when he got back home. "So, you got any leads so far?"

Fargo shook his head. "Nothing. We talked to Korinko, but she's too genuinely upset to have taken it. We haven't caught Sean Boggs or Andee Wilkerson yet—"

"Don't bother," his other self interrupted. He looked frustrated, too. "We talked to them on our side. Neither of them had anything to do with it."

"Oh. Okay. Thanks." It occurred to Fargo that teaming up with himself could save both of them a lot of time. After all, it was the same case, right? "Then we inspected the lab, but it was clean, no traces of fingerprints or bootprints or DNA." Sheriff Fargo nodded. "We've tried tracking the Thunderbird's energy signature, but with no success. And there was an anomalous microstorm, but it turned out to be a high school kid working on his science project." Both of them snorted at once. "After that, we started looking into how the thief might fence the egg, if that was his intent. So we talked to Victor Arlan—"

"Victor Arlan?" Sheriff Fargo interrupted again. "Why?"

That brought Fargo up short. "What do you mean, why? Isn't he in prison here, too?"

"Prison? No, of course not—he retired from GD last year and moved to some tropical island somewhere."

"Oh." Fargo debated whether to tell his other self what Arlan had been up to with the Vault all those years. Would it do him any good now? Probably not. "Well, he had some . . . contacts in the black market. We talked to them, and put the word out that we'd be interested in buying the egg if it came up for sale. So far, though, it hasn't."

"Which means they may not be looking to sell it," Sheriff Fargo muttered, mainly to himself. Then again, talking to Fargo was talking to himself, in a way. "Or they may just be waiting until the heat dies down."

"But they won't have a whole lot of time," Fargo reminded him. "Even if they don't get caught, and they've got a containment field of their own to keep the egg stable, it'll hatch within the week. That's what Korinko told us."

"Right. So maybe they didn't steal it for the money." Sheriff Fargo rubbed his chin, and Fargo did likewise. Both of them chuckled at the synchronicity. Fargo realized it was like watching himself in a mirror. Only with different clothes. "Why take it, then?"

"Revenge?" Fargo suggested. "A prank? Diverting attention from something more serious?"

"Maybe so." His other self nodded approvingly, then smiled. "Hey, you'd make one heck of a sheriff!" They both laughed. This was fun! Finally, some intelligent conversation in Eureka, and with someone who really took him seriously!

"We'd wondered if the Thunderbird had caused our two worlds to draw together," Fargo mentioned, "since the timing seemed suspicious. But it turns out the impetus was—"

"Your sheriff—Carter, right?—getting a massive shock off the collected energy and becoming magnetized with energy from my world," Sheriff Fargo finished. "I heard." He frowned. "Huh. But even if the Thunderbird didn't cause the problem, maybe—"

"It contributed somehow?" Fargo finished. His other self didn't get angry at him for interrupting, either. He just nodded. "Especially since it exists on both sides?"

"It's worth looking into," his double agreed. Then he blinked at Fargo. "Why're you getting all . . . hazy?"

Fargo looked down at himself. Was he? He looked the same. But, glancing around, he realized that his other self and that world's GD lobby were getting a bit blurry around the edges. He must be returning to his own world.

"Looks like time's up," he said, and his words sounded strangely faint. "It was really great meeting you . . . me . . . you!"

"Same here," Sheriff Fargo replied. "We'll coordinate through the Drs. Russell, okay? Together we'll figure out who took our Thunderbird eggs and get them back." He gave a thumbs-up, and Fargo echoed it. Then everything wavered, and Fargo found himself standing in his own GD lobby again. He felt slightly dizzy.

"Whoa." He wobbled for a second, waving off the looks of the people passing by, then took a deep breath. That had been wild! And a bit depressing, to be honest, but also very cool.

Plus, he had new information to report to Jo and Sheriff Carter.

And a question to put to Dr. Russell.
He debated which to do first.

"We've got a problem," Allison reported as she ap-proached the conference room. Jo, Henry, and Carter all looked up. Henry had just stopped by with a take-out bag from Café Diem, and Carter and Jo were crouching down to give their knees a break, sipping their coffees after finishing a few of Vincent's excellent baked goods.

"What's up?" Carter's eyes automatically went to the short, heavyset Asian man behind her. "Dr. Kwan." When the occupational therapist nodded vaguely but didn't make eye contact, Carter frowned and directed a questioning look at Allison.

She nodded. "Yes, Dr. Kwan is from the other Eureka. He and I bumped into each other in the hallway, and when he looked confused I guessed as to the reason why."

"Wait, you bumped into each other?" Jo rose to her full height like she was on springs. Carter took a second longer to straighten up, his knees twinging in protest. "Literally?"

Allison nodded. Then she reached back and patted the man on the shoulder. "See?"

That was bad. Up until now they'd resisted touching any of their visitors directly. The other-Eureka residents had no problem sitting in their chairs, working on their computers, even eating their donuts and drinking their coffee, but more than once Carter had noticed someone's hand not quite touching a wall or a door. It was like they were mostly here but not fully.

Until now.

"We're still drawing closer together?" Henry asked Allison quietly as Jo ushered Dr. Kwan into the conference room. He went without arguing, or even saying a word, which might have been another difference between the worlds—their own Dr. Kwan never seemed to shut up.

"Must be," Allison agreed just as softly. "Which means Zane and the Russells haven't solved the problem yet."

Carter sighed. "Not good."

"No." She smiled but it didn't touch her eyes. "Not good."

"Dr. Russell?"

Fargo hesitated just inside the doorway. Russell was bent over the main console, with Zane right beside her, both of them poring over something scrolling past on the screen. The other Dr. Russell was doing almost exactly the same thing in her world, though she didn't have anyone else with her. Fargo hated to interrupt them right now, but if he and his counterpart were correct it could be important. Very important.

He waited a second, but no one glanced up. Should he call out again? Or just come back later, and hope to hell his question didn't wind up being the one thing that could have saved them?

And, if that was the case, that no one ever found out?

Then he saw a flicker of movement in the monitor. A figure stepped into the doorway, strode confidently across it, and headed down into the lab.

An extremely familiar figure.

Clad all in tan.

Right down to the hat.

Okay, then. Fargo mirrored his actions, and hurried his pace so he reached Russell and Zane at the same time his other self reached the other Dr. Russell. Sheriff Fargo met his gaze in the monitor and tipped his hat. Fargo nodded back.

"Dr. Russell," they both said together. "We have a question for you."

"Hm?" Russell—both Russells—glanced up. Then at their respective monitors. Then back again. "What is it, Fargo?" Russell asked. Her counterpart's response only varied because she said "Sheriff" instead of "Fargo." And Fargo didn't think he imagined the fact that her tone was less wearied and more genuinely attentive. Damn.

Zane, meanwhile, looked up, saw both Fargos, saw what the other Fargo was wearing, and did a double take. "You've got to be kidding me."

That, at least, amused Fargo to no end.

"The Thunderbird," Fargo continued, and this time his other self stayed quiet and let him talk. "We know it didn't trigger this event. But could it have contributed to it? It's an electromagnetic anomaly, after all. Could it have skewed your results somehow?"

Russell and Zane looked at each other. Then they both swiveled back toward the console. The other Russell was already punching in data on her end.

"Damn," Zane said softly after a minute, as new figures appeared onscreen. "You were right, Fargo." Fargo could sense how much it galled him to say that. Another point for him. "The Thunderbird's energy warped the input frequencies just a little bit. They added extra oomph."

"And they acted as another electromagnet," Russell added, indicating one spot on a graph. "They increased Carter's effective charge somehow."

"He got zapped by the first Thunderbird hatchling," Fargo explained. "Just a little while before he came in here. He must have still been carrying that charge when he got zapped again."

"And the frequencies meshed, and compounded," Zane agreed. "That's been throwing off all our numbers! We were basing them on Carter's getting charged once, not twice!" He grabbed the keyboard and started typing rapidly. "But we've got the Thunderbird's energy signature already in the system, and we know when Carter absorbed it, so we can calculate how much energy he absorbed then, and work out the rate of decay, and then factor that into the later encounter, and—" A new formula appeared on the screen, which then resolved into a new string of numbers. "Voilà! A revised target frequency!"

"Good catch, Fargo," Russell told him with a nod. "Both of you. That may have made all the difference." The two Fargos grinned at each other.

"Happy to help." Fargo turned to leave, but then stopped. "So," he asked, "what happens if the remaining Thunderbird egg hatches? It'll produce another anomaly like the first one, but this time without the bio lab's built-in shielding, there will be a significantly larger energy output."

Zane frowned. So did Russell. "It could throw another monkey wrench in our attempts," Zane answered. "Especially if it somehow distorts the energy the other Russell is feeding us, and alters it so it doesn't rebound from Carter anymore. The energy wavelengths have to match precisely. If they don't, they won't be deflected—they'll hit us full-on." He rubbed his chin. "Enough energy and we could wind up vaporizing Eureka before the two realities merge and flatten whatever's left."

Fargo gulped. "Great. Jo and I will make sure we get the egg back safely, then." He turned and hurried out.

But not before he saw the look on Zane's face when he mentioned that he'd be working with Jo again.

Score another one for the Fargonator!

CHAPTᵉR 25

"Where the hell've you been?" Jo demanded when Fargo emerged from one of the corridors and hurried over to her beside the conference room door. "I said get your other work done, not go on vacation!"

"I have been working," he assured her quickly. "And I've found out some stuff that'll help us, too." He thought about it for a second. "Or, at least, some stuff we don't have to worry about anymore."

"Like what, exactly?" She crossed her arms and tapped her foot, still scowling. Henry had gone back into town to watch for other strays, and Carter had gone with Allison to talk to Russell. Which left her here minding the conference room door.

"I've eliminated Dr. Boggs and Andee Wilkerson as suspects," Fargo announced proudly. He expected her to be impressed. Instead, the scowl just deepened.

"You what? You talked to them without me?" She shook her head, and he could tell she was trying to keep her voice level. "Fargo, you're not a trained investigator. You don't know how to question a suspect!"

"Maybe not here," he agreed, just a little hurt, "but the other me sure does."

"The other you?" She rolled her eyes. "Oh, right. Sheriff Fargo."

"Exactly. We talked. He's already spoken to both of them, and neither of them were involved."

"You talked? When?"

"Just a little bit ago. I wound up over there, and we ran into each other."

Now Jo didn't look pissed. She looked worried. "You were there? You got transported to that reality, instead of him being pulled over to here?"

"Well . . . yeah." Fargo stopped and thought about that for the first time. "Oh, crap. That hasn't happened before, has it?" Jo shook her head. "Which means . . ."

"Which means we have even less time than we thought," she finished. "All right, assuming I trust your other you's assessment of those two, what else?"

"Well . . ." Fargo took a deep breath. "It turns out the Thunderbird was partially responsible for our current dilemma." He recounted the recent conversation with Zane and the two Drs. Russell and his other self. It was starting to get confusing with so many people having their other selves around at the same time.

"So we've got to find it before it hatches, or it could kill us all anyway," Jo summarized after he'd finished. "Great. Just what we needed—more pressure."

"I know." He shrugged helplessly. "Keeps us focused though, right?" She didn't bother to answer. "So we know it wasn't one of the three working on the Thunderbird project, anyway. And we know whoever did take the egg hasn't tried to sell it yet. What do we do now?"

Jo shook her head, sending her ponytail flying. "I don't know," she admitted. "We still don't have anything else to go on." She growled and slammed a fist into the wall. Then she pushed off and headed for the front doors. "Come on."

"Where're we going?" Fargo asked as he trotted after her.

"When in doubt," she answered over her shoulder, "you

drive around and look for evidence. This is Eureka—half the time, it blows up in your face."

"Not literally, I hope," he muttered as he followed her out.

"Got it. Yeah, thanks. I'll let them know."

Carter hung up and turned to Allison, Zane, and Russell. They were conferring via the monitor with Stark and the other Russell. "That was Jo," he explained. "She's with Fargo. Apparently he and 'Sheriff Fargo' met each other recently."

"They did," Russell confirmed. "The two of them came into our labs to ask about the Thunderbird, and whether it could have been involved. That's how we figured out we had to reset the frequencies slightly."

"Right." Carter nodded and ran a hand over his head. "But did they mention how they met?" He got blank looks in return. "Fargo went there, to the other side. He was in Sheriff Fargo's Eureka."

That produced expressions of concern all around. "If our two worlds are close enough that people from here can wind up over there," Allison said, "we're right on the edge of the two realities overlapping completely."

"We're out of time," Stark agreed. "If we're ever going to push our worlds apart again, it's got to be soon."

"We've been trying," Zane argued. "Dr. Russell—your Russell—has fired off three sets of energy bursts since we reset the frequency. They should be perfectly calibrated to Carter's energy charge now, and their exact opposite. But nothing's happening." He indicated the monitor. "None of that energy is returning. Carter isn't deflecting it, and it's not pushing our worlds apart. If anything, it's drawing them even closer, even faster, and binding them tight."

"Why isn't it working?" Carter asked. "It's not the Thunderbird this time, right?" A thought occurred to him. "Could the other egg have hatched? Would that cause more problems?"

"It could," Russell replied, "but it would have to be somewhere nearby, or producing enormous amounts of energy, or both. It would have to be masking or warping either your

energy signature or the energy coming in from the inputs."
She scanned the readouts again. "We're not picking up any
interference, though. Everything's quiet. There's no reason it
shouldn't be working."

"You're absolutely sure the math is right this time?" Allison asked.

"We've triple- and quadruple-checked it," Zane told her.
"I'm absolutely sure."

"I checked them, too," Stark added. "And they look right.
They should be right."

"So we've got the math right," Carter said slowly. "And the
equipment's all set up. And I'm a living electromagnet." He
folded his arms and paced. "So what're we missing? What's
gone wrong?"

Then he had a bad, bad thought. "What if . . . what if
somebody has been messing with it?"

"Messing with it?" Stark stared at him. "This isn't a high
school science project, Sheriff. Even if someone could get
access, and had a reason to, they'd have to know exactly what
they were doing to affect the process."

Carter almost laughed—Nathan Stark was telling him he
was an idiot, though not in so many words. It was just like
old times. He sobered quickly, though. "I've seen some of
the high school science experiments around here," he pointed
out. "Those things are dangerous in their own right. And it's
easy to screw something up. You just have to change one
number and it'll do the trick. A lot easier than figuring out
how to do it right, believe me."

"That's certainly true," Allison confirmed. "But even so,
why would someone do that? Not to mention, how would
they get access? Once we realized the danger, Nathan and I
both put the project on restricted access. Nobody else can tap
into the files or the equipment without our direct approval."
Carter noticed the slight pause when she'd said Stark's name,
but he didn't say anything. She was dealing with it. And now
wasn't the time, anyway.

"Never mind who and how," he said, though the way his
gut was sinking he had the feeling he already had an answer,

and it was one he really wasn't going to like. "We can deal with that later. The first question is, did anything undergo any last-minute changes? Equipment placement, energy output, whatever. Anything that could have affected the results."

Zane and the two Russells were already tapping out commands. Carter, Allison, and Nathan hovered nearby, waiting impatiently.

"Holy—" Zane muttered finally. "You're right! Somebody did throw a monkey wrench! Look!" He called up a screen, which showed a long string of numbers. None of it made a single bit of sense to Carter. Allison was frowning at the screen—she was a genius herself, and she knew the project, but this really wasn't her field. Stark was scowling, however, and gestured to a line on his Dr. Russell's monitor.

"Exactly," she agreed. "It's in the energy output," she explained. "Someone altered the frequency."

Allison shook her head. "I thought you did that," she asked Zane, "when you realized the Thunderbird's contribution had altered Carter's initial charge, and distorted the later one as well?"

Zane nodded. "I did—that's right here." He pulled up the activity log and indicated an entry. "But somebody else changed it right after I did." He scanned back up. "And look, there was a change earlier, too—right after we reversed Carter's charge."

"I feel like a walking collect call," Carter muttered, which earned him a raised eyebrow from Allison and a chuckle from Zane. "Okay, so somebody has been deliberately interfering," he said, just to be sure he understood correctly. "It's sabotage, not faulty math."

"Definitely." Zane was scanning the procedure again. "Whoever did this has a pretty good grasp of what we were doing, too. He or she knew all they had to do was modify that frequency, and only by a hair. That's why we didn't notice it before—it looked right." He glanced at Carter. "How'd you know it wasn't?"

Carter shrugged. "Around here, it pays to be paranoid," he explained. "Besides, if you and Stark and both Russells say the math is right, it's got to be right. Same with the equipment. Which leaves either operator error, random outside influences—or sabotage."

"Okay, but who would want to sabotage this?" Russell asked. "If we fail, both our worlds, our entire realities, will be destroyed!"

"I can't tell you for certain who it was," Zane offered, "but I can tell you one thing—they're standing in this room. These rooms." He zoomed in on the activity log, and highlighted the entry showing the most recent change. The name field read "Director, GD."

"What?" That was Allison and Stark simultaneously. But Carter felt his stomach clench even more.

"Why would either of us do something like that?" Stark argued. "That's ridiculous! We've both been working to get this fixed!"

"I know," Zane agreed. "But you see what it says. Someone with director-level access reset the frequencies."

"But I didn't, and neither did Nathan," Allison countered.

"It had to be one of you," Russell said, a little hesitantly. "No one else has director-level access."

Carter hated to bring this up, but obviously it was important. "That's not entirely true," he corrected. He said it softly, but everyone turned to look at him.

"Explain, Sheriff," Stark demanded.

"You and Allison are the only two with director-level access," Carter stated. "But that doesn't mean it's just the two of you."

He saw the understanding wash across both Allison's and Stark's faces. And then Allison's phone rang.

"Hello?" she answered. "Elaine? What's wrong?" She listened for a second, and then suddenly sagged back against the console. "What? No, I— No, that's not possible." The phone fell from her hands to the floor.

Carter took a step closer, but stopped when she glanced up at him. He'd never seen such horror in her eyes before. Or such fear. "Kevin," she whispered.

"What happened?" Carter hurried to her side. "Allison, what about Kevin?"

"It was . . . that was his school," she explained quickly, through sudden tears. "They wanted to know why . . . why I hadn't told them ahead of time that I'd be taking him out of school early today."

Carter was already racing for the door.

"I'm coming with you!" Allison shouted, but her legs wobbled when she tried to stand.

"No, you stay here," Carter replied over his shoulder as he reached the doorway. "They need you here. I'll take care of this." He stopped and met her eyes. "I promise, Allison. I'll get him back."

She stared at him for a second, and he could see her two sides, GD director and mom, warring within her. Then common sense won out, and she nodded. That was all the permission he needed to bolt.

"Stupid, stupid, stupid!" Carter cursed as he ran down the corridor, waving his arms to warn people out of his path. He should have seen this coming! The other Allison's shock at learning Kevin was still alive. The way she'd clung to that locket, and eyed his Allison with such longing, such hunger. What Jo had said, about Allison's saying strange things to her in the cafeteria. The fact that she'd been around when they'd magnetized him or whatever had happened, but conveniently wasn't here now. And the fact that her alterations—because she was also Allison Blake, which meant the computer would have accepted her DNA and granted her director-level access—had only pulled the worlds closer together.

Close enough to touch. Close enough to wander back and forth.

Close enough to step over and claim the one thing she lacked. The one thing she had been desperate to get back. The one thing that was here and not there.

Her son.

Carter couldn't even find it in him to hate her, or to blame her. Not completely. If it had been him and Zoe—if he had lost Zoe, and learned she was still alive in the other Eureka—what would he have done to get her back? What wouldn't he have done?

Anything. Anything at all. He would have done whatever it took to get her back.

Even risked two whole realities just to find her again.

He just hoped he could find Allison and Kevin now.

Before it was too late for all of them.

CHAPTᵉR 26

"Look out!"

"I see it, I see it!" Jo jerked hard on the wheel, and her car leaped to one side, almost running up on the curb. But the truck in front of her continued on, its driver clearly not noticing that they had almost collided.

Which made sense, since it was only partially there.

They had been driving around town, desperately hoping to stumble across some clue as to the Thunderbird's whereabouts. Fargo was enjoying being out and about again, but Jo was getting more and more irritable. Which was probably for the best, because her nerves were wound wire-tight as a result. So when the air in front of them had wavered, a vague outline beginning to form and then rapidly fill in with color and depth, she had reacted instantly.

Now there was a rusty old pickup truck chugging along down the street, right where they would have been if she hadn't shifted her car out of the way.

"That was close," Fargo breathed after a second.

"Too close," Jo agreed. She hadn't pulled over, but her

hands were gripping the wheel tightly, and she took the next turn to put some distance between her and the truck.

"Do you recognize that truck?" Fargo asked, more to take both their minds off the near miss than because he was curious about who had nearly flattened them.

She nodded. "It's Big Ed's."

"Really?" Fargo twisted around to stare back the way they had come. "That was Big Ed?" "Big Ed" Fowler was a biochemist at GD. He was also the local bowling league's star player, and he'd been Fargo's secret weapon in the grudge match against their bowling rivals from Area 51. Big Ed was a former PBA champion, and the best bowler in town.

Or at least he had been, until he wound up dead. Devoured by an organism he had created to cleanly dispose of radiation by consuming it.

Now here he was, trundling down the street in his old truck, alive and well.

But in the wrong Eureka.

"Should we do something about him?" Fargo asked.

"Like what, Fargo?" Jo braked hard at a stop sign and turned to glare at him. "What would you like me to do? Write him a ticket for being in the wrong reality? Warn him to look both ways before he slips from one world to the next? Or maybe just invite him to your next bowling night, seeing as how the version of him from here got killed a little while back and now there's a vacancy!"

"Okay, okay!" Fargo raised both hands to protect his face—Jo's hands hadn't left the steering wheel yet, but he knew how fast she could move when she wanted. "I just figured we'd been reporting everyone else who showed up, and bringing them all back to GD, so shouldn't we take him there, too?"

She sighed. "I'm sorry," she admitted after a second. She removed the band holding her ponytail in place, shook her long dark hair loose, and then bound it back up again. "I'm just on edge, that's all. The worlds are drawing closer together, we still don't have any leads on the Thunderbird, and we almost got crushed by a dead man whose truck tried to materialize on top of us! None of which is your fault."

Fargo let out his breath. "That's okay. I'm pretty freaked, too." He thought about the almost-accident, and his brow furrowed. "And that was the first time we've seen anything as big as a truck come through. That means the worlds are really close together now."

Jo thought about that. "We could have other vehicles wandering across, couldn't we?" He nodded. "I'd better put out an alert, then," she decided. "Let everyone know to stay off the streets until we give the all-clear."

"*If* we give the all-clear," he muttered as she hit the gas and took off again, this time heading for the sheriff's office. If Zane and the two Russells couldn't sort out their equations in time, the worlds would overlap and a traffic jam would become the least of their problems. But he didn't say that part out loud.

It wasn't like he had to.

"We'll have to put the Thunderbird investigation on hold a little bit longer," Jo told him apologetically as she floored it and her car leaped forward. "Right now having cars and trucks appearing on the road is the more immediate threat."

He nodded. Having almost been the victim of one such appearance, how could he not agree? Privately, he just hoped whoever had stolen the Thunderbird egg was taking good care of it for now. The last thing they needed was for it to hatch right when the others were trying to separate the two worlds, and have all that energy throw off their efforts.

There would be time enough to go after the Thunderbird thief later.

If they survived that long.

Henry looked around.

This wasn't his Eureka, that much was clear. He'd been heading to Café Diem to get some lunch when everything around him had gone hazy, like he'd been wrapped in a sudden fog bank.

Which, in this town, wasn't impossible. Or even all that unusual.

When the world around him had cleared, Henry had noticed at once that it was different than it had been.

The most noticeable change was the lack of Café Diem. There was a small coffee shop in its place.

He remembered Jack telling him about that—it was what had first made him realize that Dr. Russell had succeeded in her attempt to visualize another reality, rather than just somehow showing their own downtown by mistake. Which meant he was now in that other world himself.

But what he should do now, and how he would get back, he hadn't a clue.

It actually felt a bit strange, and oddly humbling, Henry admitted to himself, not being in the know. He was usually the one Jack called upon to help him solve a problem. But in this case, it wasn't Jack's call. And while Allison had made use of his expertise many times over the years, with a problem of this nature Zane was just as well versed, if not better. Plus, it was Dr. Russell's own project, so naturally she was the first one they'd turn to for how to fix it.

He didn't blame them at all. Too many cooks could spoil the soup. With both Russell and Zane involved, they didn't really need him, and one more person might have wound up getting in the way.

But that didn't mean it didn't sting a little.

Plus, it meant that he didn't know exactly what was going on. He wasn't sure how close they were to finding a solution. And he'd heard that they were corralling the people who'd wandered across to his Eureka, keeping them all in one of GD's conference rooms so they wouldn't get into trouble.

But what was happening with the people who wound up over here instead?

Only one way to find out, he decided. He'd just have to ask.

Looking around, Henry smiled. There was Aaron Finn, crossing the street a dozen paces away. Tall and slim, the boyish-looking Finn was an astronomer. He'd won the high school science fair award at Tesla High, back in the day, and had been helpful a year or so ago when one of Tesla's current students had bitten off more than she could chew and endangered the entire town with her own project. Henry had always liked Finn. He was quiet, and unassuming, and very organized. He also worked at GD, like most of the town. He'd have heard what they were doing for their own otherworldly visitors.

"Aaron!" Henry called out. He headed toward the other man. "Hey, Aaron! Hold on a sec!"

Aaron Finn turned, scanning the area to see who had called him. But when his eyes hit upon Henry, he didn't react as expected. Instead he stopped dead, eyes going wide, face turning pale. Then he started backing up. Quickly.

"Aaron, slow down! I just had a quick question!" Henry sped up. What was going on here?

"Stay away from me!" Finn shouted, flailing. He turned and began running away in earnest. "You stay away!"

Henry chased after him for a step or two before giving up. What was going on? Why was Aaron Finn, of all people, running from him? And why did the mild-mannered astronomer looked so horrified?

Henry turned away, and spotted Bill Fielding. "Hey, Bill!" Fielding was a gravitation expert. He'd designed a zero-gravity birthing chamber for Lexi Carter when she'd still been in town and pregnant. Of course, it had turned out that Fielding had gotten some unorthodox help with his research—from Carter's sentient house S.A.R.A.H., of all things—and had almost destroyed them all, but that was par for the course around here. Henry had never had any problems with Fielding, and they'd always gotten along fine.

Which made Fielding's reaction all the more surprising.

"Ah!" The curly-haired researcher shouted when he recognized Henry. "No! What are you doing here? They locked you up!" Then Fielding took to his heels and ran like a startled rabbit.

"What is going on around here?" Henry asked out loud. He turned in a slow circle, arms held out. "Why won't anybody talk to me?"

Something shifted off to one side, and he caught the motion from the corner of his eye. But before he could turn to see what it was, something small and solid slammed into him right below the arms, and Henry was thrown off his feet.

He landed with a solid thud, fortunately on the stretch of grass beside the sidewalk, and let out an *oof!* as the air was knocked out of him. He groaned a second time as whatever had hit him landed on top of him, twisting him onto his stomach and shoving him down into the grass and dirt.

"What the hell?" he managed to gasp, spitting out bits of lawn.

"That's what I'd like to know," a familiar, rage-filled voice snapped just behind his ear. Henry started to relax a little at the sound, but that was hard to do when his arms were wrenched back behind him.

And even harder when he felt the cold steel of handcuffs clamping down on first one and then the other wrist.

"Jo?" he asked, trying to turn his head to look at her. But a firm hand shoved his face back into the dirt before he was finally hauled back to his feet. "Jo, what are you doing? It's me!"

"I know who it is, thank you very much," Deputy Jo Lupo replied sharply, glaring at him as she yanked him down the street toward the sheriff's office. "And I don't know how you escaped prison, but it was stupid of you to come back here. You're going right back there as soon as I can arrange transport."

"Prison?" Then Henry groaned. Of course! He'd heard from Jack that, in this world, Kevin hadn't survived. The Artifact had killed him. In their own world, he'd saved Kevin's life, but only by faking an emergency that forced GD's total evacuation and tricked Allison into using the executive director's emergency bunker. He'd needed her and Kevin down there so he could send Kevin through the Subatomic Reconstructive Transport, or SRT, and have the teleportation device reconstruct the boy, atom by atom. That way it would strip away the Artifact's influence, and sever the link that was killing Kevin.

Except that he hadn't accounted for all the changes the Artifact had wrought in Kevin during the past few months.

If Carter and Stark hadn't forced their way past all of GD's security measures to reach the bunker in time to warn him, he would have doomed Kevin just as surely.

Afterward, General Mansfield had had Henry arrested for creating a false panic and risking people's lives just to save one young boy. Eva Thorne had pardoned him a month or two later, after he'd helped them solve another crisis.

Clearly, in this world, that last bit had never happened.

No wonder everyone had recoiled from him! They thought he was an escaped convict!

"That's not me, Jo," he told her as she dragged him down the street. "That's the other Henry Deacon. I'm from the parallel Eureka."

"Sure you are," she grated between her teeth. "And why should I believe that?"

"Which is more likely?" he asked her, letting her guide him toward the sheriff's office. No sense struggling—he knew Jo well enough to know she'd have no qualms about knocking him out and carrying him back that way, if she had to. "That I escaped a maximum-security federal prison and made my way back to Eureka without you hearing anything about it, or that I slipped over from another reality where I'm a free man?"

She frowned but didn't stop moving. "Maybe," she admitted after a second. "But that doesn't change the fact that I need to lock you up." The grin she gave him was as sharp as a knife. "If you're telling the truth, you'll fade back to your own world soon enough, no harm done. If you're lying, though, you'll be safe in jail until MPs can come to retrieve you."

Henry sighed. He couldn't fault her logic, really. But he didn't relish spending time in a jail cell for any reason.

And he really hated the idea of missing out on still more of the action.

He just hoped his friends were having better luck—and a better day—than he was.

Allison struggled to breathe.

Her heart hammered in her chest, and she could hear her

own pulse thundering in her ears. Her fingers and toes tingled, and she felt lightheaded. Her eyes were beginning to blur, and not just from the tears—her vision narrowed, going dark at the edges, and her throat ached and burned.

Then she gasped.

The sudden burst of air shot through her like a lightning bolt, crackling with clarity. She could feel everything again, and her senses cleared. But still her mind focused on one thing, and one thing only.

Kevin.

How could she not have realized? She'd seen the look her other self had given her, heard the catch in her voice when she'd asked about him. And she knew how hard it had been for her to see Nathan again, alive and well and forever out of reach. How much worse would that have been if it had been Kevin instead? He was her son, and her world revolved around him. She'd thought before about how, in a way, she had been the luckier of the two of them, her and the other Allison. She could find love again—one stubborn part, buried deep, suggested that perhaps she already had—but she could never have another firstborn son. Even if she had another child after Jenna, and it was a boy, it wouldn't be the same. It wouldn't be Kevin.

So of course her other self had lost control when she'd learned Kevin was still alive on this side. And of course she'd decided that she must get him back.

Allison understood. In the same situation, she would have done the same thing.

After all, she already had.

But now she risked losing him. And if that happened, she wasn't sure she could survive.

Of course, if she didn't do something now to correct the damage her other self had caused, she might not survive anyway. None of them would.

"We need to reset the frequencies," Allison rasped, her throat still hoarse from the recent shock. She was still propping herself up against the console, she realized, and levered herself to a standing position, then took a deep, slow breath and straightened up properly.

"Trying," Zane replied over his shoulder, his fingers dancing across the keyboard. "But the changes were locked in."

Allison reached past him and typed in a command. Then she pressed her finger to a small scanner set to one side, and winced slightly as a tiny needle pierced the flesh and drew a single drop of blood.

"Identity confirmed: Allison Blake, Director, GD," the screen flashed in one corner. "Access granted."

"Try it now," she commanded. Zane nodded and, retrieving the keyboard from her, canceled the lockdown.

"I've got access again," he confirmed. He pulled up the frequency diagram and figures. Then he called up the ones they'd built off their previous calculations. "One digit off, that's all it took." He shook his head. "Clever." His fingers massaged the keys. "I'm resetting it now." The top diagram shifted. Now it matched the lower one exactly. "Okay, we're all set."

The other Eureka's Dr. Russell nodded in the monitor. "I've got it," she told them. "Configuring new energy packets now." She tapped in more commands. "A minute, maybe two, and we'll be good to try again."

There was a strange shimmer in the air right beside Allison, and the tiny hairs on her arms tingled. She glanced over and frowned. The disturbance was faint, as if the air itself were rippling, and was only a little wider than she was, but arcing a foot or more above her head. Then she glanced back at the overhead screen—and gasped.

Nathan was starting to fade from view.

Realizing what that meant, Allison took a step back. And just in time, too, as the shimmer darkened. There were details beginning to appear within it—a human form, tall and broad-shouldered, in a dark suit. Darker blotches at the top and just below that—hair and a beard. She couldn't see the eyes yet, but she knew them all too well.

Nathan Stark was returning to Eureka. Her Eureka. But not her Nathan Stark. Not exactly.

A tiny, tiny part of Allison smiled and nodded. "You can steal Kevin from me," it said, sad and gleeful simultaneously. "But I get Nathan back in return."

She stamped that part down and threw it aside. This wasn't a game. These were real people, people she loved. People they both loved. She wasn't going to treat them like pieces on a checkerboard.

"It looks like we're running out of time," Nathan stated, holding up his hands to study them as they wavered between the two worlds. His words echoed strangely, heard both in the speakers and from inches away simultaneously, both not quite with his full resonance but vibrating from the strange doubling.

"Damn, that's not good," Zane agreed, starting as he swiveled back to watch Nathan's dramatic appearance. "We're dead center for the overlap—the pivot, essentially. If people are starting to merge here, our realties are almost finished overlapping. We've got an hour, maybe less, before they collide completely—and squash everything in both worlds flat as a pancake."

"Sending the energy burst now!" the other Russell reported. She stabbed a button, and the lights on her data banks and other equipment flashed as her system fired off the reconfigured energy.

Everyone waited. Allison realized she was holding her breath. So was Nathan, she noticed—he was almost completely on their side now, with just a shimmer remaining behind the other Dr. Russell. A few more seconds, and he'd be here in the flesh. Her hand was already reaching out to touch him, and she forced herself to withdraw it. Now was not the time, and she didn't want to open that door, anyway. Not until she knew what was going to happen with Kevin, with her, with Nathan—with all of them.

So they waited.

"Yes!" The whisper came from her side, and Allison turned back to Nathan again. He still had his hands up in front of him. But was it her imagination, or were they less solid than they'd been a second ago? She squinted at the monitor. Had the afterimage behind Russell gotten darker?

Another second passed, then two, and Allison nodded even though a little piece of her heart was breaking all over again. Nathan's presence behind the other Russell was definitely gaining solidity once more, even as he was turning translucent beside her. He was returning to his own Eureka.

It was working.

"We've stopped the overlap!" Dr. Russell announced. "We've achieved stasis!"

Allison had never thought she'd be so happy to hear that nothing was happening.

"Fire another energy burst," she and Nathan told the other Russell at the same time, and they smiled at each other in the monitor. Allison looked away first. She didn't want him to see the fresh tears that had sprung up. He was solidly back in his own world now, not a trace of him remaining here, but she thought she could almost feel his presence still beside her. It ached.

"Second burst," the other Russell confirmed, entering the commands and hitting the activation button. The wait felt less tense this time, like they already knew what the outcome would be. But Allison held her breath anyway.

"We've got movement!" Zane reported what felt like hours later, but had probably only been seconds. "Our realities are shifting apart again!"

"Yes!" Dr. Russell turned and held out a hand, then laughed as Zane slapped it instead. "We did it!"

"We still have a ways to go," Nathan warned in the monitor. Yet he was smiling. "But it's definitely a start. We'll have to take the rest of the separation slowly, to keep from tearing anything apart by wrenching it loose. Nice and easy. Another energy burst, Dr. Russell, but not for a few minutes, please." He met Allison's eyes again, and she saw the understanding there, and the compassion he kept hidden from most people but had never been able to disguise from her.

He was giving her time.

Time for Carter to find Nathan's Allison. Time to find Kevin.

Time to bring him back home.

She just hoped it would be enough, because they couldn't delay too long. They still had to combat the inertia that had built up over the past two days, as the worlds drifted together. If they let up the pressure for too long, they ran the risk of that inertia overpowering the new push apart. Their worlds could swing back toward one another. And if that happened, they probably wouldn't be able to pry them apart a second time.

Their realities would collide completely, destroying everyone and everything.

Allison appreciated the gesture Nathan was making. But they both knew they couldn't risk their entire realities just for the sake of her son. Better for Kevin to be trapped on the other side and alive than for all of them to die.

She hoped it wouldn't come to that.

There was nothing she could do about it, though.

It was all up to Carter, now.

CHAPTᵉR 27

"Come on, come on!" Carter hammered the horn with the heel of one hand, the other still gripping the wheel tightly as he tried to maneuver around a small silvery car that had swerved onto the road right in front of him. He cut into the opposite lane and sped up, racing past the smaller vehicle and then switching back into his proper lane again ahead of it.

But when he glanced in his rearview mirror to make sure the little car wasn't too close behind, it was gone.

"What the hell?"

His attention was jerked back to the front by a flicker of movement ahead and off to the side. He was approaching an intersection, a minor one of two roads with stop signs on the other lane, and a sporty red sedan was sitting there revving its engine, clearly waiting the customary few seconds before peeling out again.

It would sail right across Carter's path, and there wasn't enough distance for him to brake in time to let it get past, and too much space for him to speed up and hope to scoot by before it reached him.

The sedan was going to wind up smashing full into him.

He braced for impact, clenching his jaw and squeezing his eyes half-shut. His whole body tensed, and his other hand curled around the steering wheel as well, arms locked in place.

But the collision never came.

Surprised, Carter glanced around. He was crossing the intersection now, but the red sedan had disappeared.

"Okay, welcome to the phantom highway," he muttered as he sped on past.

At the next corner, Carter slowed and took a sharp right—

—and almost rammed a rusty green pickup truck as it barreled on by.

"Watch where you're going!" he shouted, rolling down his Jeep window so he could stick his head out. "You had a stop sign, you know!"

But something nagged at the back of his mind. He checked the rearview again.

There was no stop sign.

"I'm losing my mind," he told himself. "Clearly."

But there was another explanation, he realized.

The overlapping realities.

He was seeing—and almost running into—vehicles from the other Eureka. They were wandering over into his world, or maybe he was wandering into theirs. He knew there was a stop sign back there, but when he'd looked it hadn't been there. Had the sign vanished into that other town, or had he? There probably wasn't any way to tell. What it meant was that this race across town was going to be a thousand times more difficult. Normally he just had to watch for cars that didn't get out of his way fast enough, and oncoming traffic that couldn't see his lights and hear his sirens in time.

Now he had to worry about drivers who would never see him coming because they were in a whole other world.

Just then his phone chirped. He fished it out with one hand and held it to his ear.

"Carter."

"Carter, it's Jo." His deputy sounded frazzled, which was rare for her. He could also hear background noises—the rush of wind and the rumble of an engine—that told him she was in her car. Great minds thought alike. "We've got problems."

"Tell me about it." He hit the brakes and his Jeep fishtailed as he tried not to rear-end an old-fashioned wood-paneled station wagon that had not been in front him ten seconds ago.

"Cars and other vehicles are sliding into our Eureka from the parallel world," she reported. The way she said it so calmly almost made it sound like a normal occurrence, like saying that a streetlight was down or that someone had been caught speeding for the third time in a week. "Driving right now is extremely dangerous."

"Yeah, I think I figured that out." He swerved to the left to avoid a tall, powerfully built biker in a blue spandex biking suit on a black and blue racing bike, and sped up to get past him. The biker was still there when Carter drew alongside, but now the biker was wearing red and his bike was red and gray. The man himself looked the same, however, and he nodded to Carter as the Jeep pulled past.

"Are you on the road right now?"

"Allison—the other Allison—took Kevin," he explained. "I've got to get him back."

"Damn." There was something more than just shock and anger in his deputy's voice. "It's my fault," she added a second later.

"What?"

"She came to talk to me in the cafeteria," Jo explained. "I didn't realize it was the other Allison. But she was talking about Kevin, and how worried she was about him. I said . . . I said something about his school, and how they were there for him." Her words were heavy, her voice dull. "I told her where to find him, Carter."

"You couldn't have known," he assured her. "None of us realized until it was too late. And she'd have found out from someone else. This isn't your fault."

"Maybe." Jo's voice had turned brisk and businesslike again. "Do you need any help?"

"No, I think I've got this," he replied slowly, after considering her offer carefully. "I don't want to spook her. Where are you, anyway?"

"Almost back to the office." He could hear the sound of squealing brakes, and someone yelling. Was that Fargo? "I'm going to issue a city-wide alert, tell everyone to stay in their homes and off the streets."

"Good." That had been his thought as well. The streets were dangerous right now, and the more people they could get off them, the better. Which led to another idea. "Have Allison get in touch with Sheriff Fargo—she can have Russell talk to their Russell, if necessary. If he issues the same alert on his side, that should cut down on traffic considerably."

"I'm on it." He could hear the pause. "Are you okay? You sure you can get Kevin back on your own?"

"No," Carter admitted. "I'm not sure. But I've got to do it anyway."

"Good luck."

"Thanks. Oh, and don't forget about the Thunderbird. Now would be a perfect time to get it out of Eureka—with everything that's going on, he could walk right by us, balancing the Thunderbird egg on the tip of his nose, and we'd never even notice."

"Got it." Jo hung up, and Carter slipped his phone back into his pocket. Even if Jo reached the office a few minutes from now, and put out the alert immediately, and everyone got off the streets as they'd been told, that was still ten to fifteen minutes before the streets were clear. And he couldn't be sure "Sheriff" Fargo would even receive, much less follow, his advice in issuing the same order. In which case there could still be plenty of traffic, only it would all be from the other side.

Where he wouldn't be able to see it coming.

Carter sighed. This was going to be an extremely stressful drive.

After what seemed like an eternity, Carter pulled up to Allison's house. Her sleek sedan was missing from the driveway, but there was a stylish hybrid station wagon in its place. Which made sense. He suspected Allison would have switched to driving something like that herself, if not for her duties at GD.

Which, of course, wasn't a problem for the other Allison.

As he got out of his Jeep and walked along the drive to the front door, Carter studied the place. He knew Allison's house well, better than almost any other dwelling in Eureka beyond his own. The exterior looked the same as he remembered it, a split-level ranch made of redwood and stone with a sloping roof and large windows. The yard was more trees than grass, and the house blended in among the trunks and foliage nicely, giving it a welcoming, rustic look.

He skirted the station wagon, and one hand brushed up against it. That made him stop for a second, and he rapped his knuckles against the car's side panel. The high-tech plastic produced a dull echo.

So he was in the other Eureka now, his whole body in one reality. Swell.

He trekked up the steps and along the winding path to the front door, and let himself in. This was Eureka—most people didn't bother to lock their doors. They had other ways of keeping people out.

A security panel beeped as he stepped into the entryway, but as Carter watched, the blinking red light wavered, then turned a steady green. Strange. Allison had programmed him into her security system, of course, but that was back in his Eureka. On this side he didn't even exist, so why would he have been granted access?

Carefully he shut the door behind him and edged his way down the hall. The walls were lined with pictures: Allison and Stark, Kevin, Jenna, both adults with one kid and then with the other. The story those images told tore at his heart. There weren't any pictures of Allison and Stark with both Kevin and Jenna, because Kevin had died before Jenna was born.

And in his world, it was Stark who'd died before he could ever meet his little girl.

"Hello?" Carter called out as he walked. He didn't want to

startle Allison if she was here. And he was guessing she was. It was her haven, her safe place, her sanctuary.

Plus, her car was outside, and it had still been warm when he'd felt it.

He peeked into rooms as he passed. The family room was empty. So were the dining room and the kitchen. Carter sighed. That meant they had to be upstairs.

He started to climb the steps, then stopped and looked around again. His eyes narrowed, and he rubbed a hand across his head.

Okay, that was weird.

When he had first moved to Eureka, Allison's kitchen had been more modern, with sleek appliances of brushed steel, counters of smooth granite, and a backsplash of a mottled, bump-textured blue metal. She'd remodeled a year or two back, changing the kitchen to suit the rest of the house better, replacing the steel and granite and blue with light wood grains and sandstone and creamy tile. It was a warmer, earthier kitchen, filled with browns and reds, very comforting.

The kitchen counter matched what he remembered, right down to the high-backed barstools set along it and the slightly wilted plant balanced precariously near the counter's edge.

But just beyond that, next to the stove, the counter was still sleek gray granite, and the wall behind it was a rich, mottled blue.

Carter shook his head. "Oh, this can't be good."

He headed up the stairs, taking them two at a time. If he were in his own world, he knew that Kevin's room would be the first door on the left. Opposite it was the hall bathroom. Jenna's was the next door on the right, and opposite that was Allison's own bedroom, which had a private bath attached. He was guessing her room—now hers and Stark's, a thought he tried not to examine too closely—was still in the same place, and so was Jenna's. Kevin's was probably a home office, unless this world's Allison had kept it as a shrine to her dead son. He'd seen plenty of grieving parents react that way. It wasn't healthy, but sometimes it was necessary for them to keep those reminders for a while.

Since they weren't downstairs, he was guessing he'd find Allison and Kevin in Kevin's room, or what was left of it.

Reaching the top of the stairs, Carter saw that the door to that first room was closed. He tried the handle. It wasn't locked.

Gently, he eased it open. "Allison?" he said softly. "Kevin?"

There wasn't an answer, but he thought he heard movement from within.

Carefully he opened the door. This was Eureka, and even if Allison wasn't the GD director here, her husband was. Which meant she had access to all sorts of home-protection devices. He really didn't want to have his face melted off, or to find himself frozen solid, or to be turned into a puddle of goo.

But no one attacked him.

Slowly, he eased the door open enough to see inside. It was Kevin's room, all right. But Carter frowned. There was a poster up on the wall right above the bed. It was for the movie *Inception*. He had taken his world's Kevin to the movie himself, and they had both loved it. Carter had bought him the poster a few weeks later. But that movie hadn't even been written when everything with the Artifact went down!

Something shifted in the dim light of the room, and he squinted, trying to see through the gloom. Why weren't the lights on? Then he saw the problem. Kevin was a mathematical and mechanical genius, and he was always tinkering with things—he related to machinery and to numbers far better than to people, most of the time. At one point, he'd rewired his room, altering its lighting system so it ran on bioelectricity and responded to his electrical impulses. The lights literally changed with his mood, and cycled down into darkness as he drifted off to sleep.

But it had taken him a while to work out all the details. Carter hadn't remembered the exact timeline, but evidently Kevin had started the process before he'd encountered the Artifact—and finished it afterward.

There were exposed wires hanging from the ceiling and poking out of the walls in places. Clearly this world's Kevin never had the chance to finish what he'd started.

But even in the dark Carter could still make out that poster, staring back at him.

And he could see the two figures huddled on the bed, one of them stretched out and the other sitting up with the first one's head in her lap. Allison was stroking Kevin's head gently, cradling him to her like he was a baby again instead of the tall, slender teenager he'd become.

"He got so tall," she whispered, looking up at Carter but not really seeing him. "I never thought he'd be so tall."

"I know." Carter stepped into the room, slowly, and edged toward the bed. "But you know he doesn't belong here. Not anymore."

Allison's eyes focused on him as he inched closer. "You're the sheriff," she said, half-accusingly. "Carter, right?"

"That's right. And in my world, I'm good friends with Allison—and with Kevin." He was a few feet from the bed still, but he wasn't sure what he could do about it, really. Allison had Kevin's head on her lap and one arm around him. If he had to, he could shove her out of the way and grab Kevin off the bed, but he wasn't entirely sure that would work. Plus, he had a hard time imagining doing that, even if it wasn't really his Allison.

"You can't have him," this Allison insisted, tightening her grip on the boy. "He's mine, and I won't give him up. Not again. I can't."

Carter lowered his hands and moved forward to perch on the edge of the bed. "But he's not," he pointed out gently. "Not really. And you know that."

"I lost him once," Allison argued. "And now I've got a second chance. I won't let him go."

"Think about what you're doing," Carter urged her. "And about what it means to everyone else. Sure, you could keep Kevin here until we all die, or until they reverse whatever you did and the worlds separate and he can't go home. You'd have him back, plus you'd still have Jenna, and Stark." He studied her face. "But think about what that would do to my Allison. She's already lost Stark—on their wedding day, no less." He saw this Allison gulp just thinking about it, and continued to press his point. "She almost lost Kevin, the same as you. We managed to save him just in time. But now you're stealing him away from her. She has to live with losing Stark, and now you want to take Kevin away from her, too. Is that really fair?"

Carter leaned in so she was forced to meet his eyes. "Is that something you can do to someone else, when you know how much it hurts to lose one of them, let alone both? Is it something you can do to yourself? Put yourself in her shoes. She is you, after all. How would you feel if she did the same thing to you?"

Slowly Allison's eyes filled with tears, and her hands shook where they clasped Kevin's shoulders. "I wouldn't want to live," she admitted softly, her words thick with grief. "I couldn't bear it." She took a deep, shuddering breath. "And I couldn't bear to inflict that kind of pain on someone else. Especially myself."

Gently, Carter leaned in and lifted her hand off Kevin's arm. Then he held out a hand to the boy, and Kevin grasped it and pulled himself upright. Carter rose from the bed and stepped away from it, toward the center of the room, and Kevin followed him.

Allison watched them retreat from her, eyes mirror-bright, but she made no move to stop them.

"I'm sorry," she whispered. Carter wasn't sure if the apology was to him, to Kevin, or to Allison, but he answered for all of them.

"I know. I probably would have done the same thing, in your place." He led Kevin out of the room that was half his and half his younger self's, and closed the door gently behind them. He could hear the sobs rising from the bed they had just vacated. He could give her some privacy, if nothing else.

Guiding Kevin by the shoulder, Carter followed the boy down the steps and into the kitchen again. Once they had reached that floor he pulled out his phone and called his Allison. Time to tell her the good news. He was bringing her son back to her.

But when he tried to dial her, all he got was static. Carter frowned at the phone. They were smartphones Henry had designed for Eureka years ago. The clever little devices were powered by a central grid and completely wireless. They provided perfectly clear audio and video anywhere within city limits, and for a few miles beyond. He shouldn't be getting any kind of static on it, and it shouldn't have any trouble connecting. Section Five, GD's top-security military projects level, was shielded to prevent phone signals, but Russell's lab wasn't in Section Five. He should be able to raise Allison without a problem.

Unless . . .

Quickly Carter scanned the house's interior. And what he saw made his stomach clench. The kitchen counter was granite now, just like the counter by the stove. The plant was gone, replaced by an elegant abstract sculpture that practically screamed Stark's influence. As did the floating seats that hovered in place of the barstools.

The kitchen was a seamless whole. It had been half and half before, half his world and half this one, because the two realities had been so close to overlapping completely. But now it was all one—and the wrong one.

Allison and Zane and the Russells must have fixed the problem. They'd gotten the worlds to start shifting apart again.

But he and Kevin were trapped on the wrong side!

CHAPTᵉR 28

"That should take care of that, at least." Jo hung up and tucked her phone back into her pocket. She could have issued an alert from anywhere, of course—all of Eureka's smartphones were linked together, and she and Carter and Henry had special access that let them broadcast to all phones simultaneously for exactly this kind of emergency. It was both scary and reassuring that Henry had expected major crises that would require contacting the whole town at once.

But Jo hadn't wanted to try sending the alert while driving, especially not under such hazardous conditions. She'd also wanted to see the situation firsthand, which had required going out in the thick of it. And she thought and functioned best here, at work. It was her safe haven, and had been since she'd first signed on as Eureka's deputy sheriff.

Besides, the office had a whole array of equipment housed within its walls, including systems set up to enhance the power of an all-phones broadcast. Sending it from here meant the signal would reach absolutely everyone, even those in heavily shielded areas. The only place the alert couldn't penetrate was GD's Section Five, but anyone working down there was most likely obsessed with whatever project they were on, and probably wasn't going to be driving anytime soon.

"No more disappearing, reappearing drivers?" Fargo asked. He was sitting in Carter's chair again, with his feet up on the desk, and he was tossing Carter's baseball back and forth. Or at least he was trying—he was missing the catch about half the time, and he'd already fallen out of the chair twice while scrambling back for the ball and overbalancing. He'd flipped the entire chair over only once so far, which was surprisingly good, all things considered.

Jo was doing her level best to ignore those minor mishaps. She could see they embarrassed him enough as it was. No sense in making it worse by noticing them.

She didn't have to ignore his question, however. "I can't be sure," she admitted. "All I can do is tell everyone here not to drive if at all possible. And hopefully the other Eureka's sheriff did the same thing. If he did, and people listen, there shouldn't be any cars on the road in either reality, so no, no more disappearing and reappearing vehicles."

Fargo was now grinning from ear to ear, however. "'The other Eureka's sheriff'?" he repeated. "Don't you mean Sheriff Fargo? As in, me?"

"Not you," she snapped, stomping across the office and snatching the baseball in midair before he could flail after it yet again. "You are not the sheriff, and you never will be. That is a different reality, and clearly one where everything is completely messed up." She still couldn't believe it. No Carter, and did she become sheriff in his absence? Of course not, because that would have meant there was justice in the world. No, instead they had somehow hired Fargo to do the job! What was next, putting Seth Osborne in charge of GD and Larry the obnoxious office assistant taking over as mayor?

"It's still me," Fargo corrected, grinning just as widely. "Just a slightly different version, with a wildly different career path." He leaned forward and propped his elbows up on the desk, steepling his fingers in front of him. "And he seemed to be doing a darned good job as sheriff, from what I saw."

"Which means what? No gang warfare or burnt-out buildings or stacks of corpses lying about?" Jo shook her head. As if Fargo needed another reason to be stuck up about himself.

"I'm just saying, he seemed to have everything under control," Fargo stated smugly. He leaned back again and crossed his hands behind his head. "Which means I could do the same thing here. This chair could be mine, and you could work for me."

Jo shoved his feet off the desk, causing Fargo to topple over, chair and all. "Never," she told him softly, biting the word off. "I will never work for you."

Fargo started to say something else, when his eyes flicked past her and widened. Jo glanced in that direction herself, wondering what he'd seen, and then half jumped, her gun already leaving her holster as she adjusted her stance to face that way properly.

Toward the cell.

It wasn't a very big cell, just a little nook in the back of the office, with brick walls on two sides and bars comprising the other two. A cot sat against the back wall. There wasn't much room in there, which is why she couldn't possibly miss the shimmer that filled much of the space, rippling the air just above and in front of the cot.

The rippling distorted her view of the cot and the wall, darkening them and filling the space with strange shadows.

Then those shadows thickened.

They took on substance.

And, as Jo watched, they gained detail.

Now she was staring at a body perched on the cot. A man. African-American, average height, slender, wearing a stained tan coverall with a patch over the left breast that read "mechanic."

Jo lowered her gun. "Henry?"

Henry glanced up at her. "Oh, thank god," he said happily, sighing and seeming to relax a bit. "Jo, let me out of here, would you?"

"What're you doing in my jail cell?" she asked, stepping toward the barred door, but Fargo got there first and blocked her path. "Fargo, get out of the way."

"Hang on a sec, Jo," he pleaded. "Look, think about this. How do we know that's really Henry? Our Henry?"

Jo started to reply with something sarcastic, then stopped. Fargo had a point. They were dealing with alternate realities, after all. They all had doubles there—well, all except Carter and Zane, at least. But those doubles weren't exactly the same. So what if this was the other Henry? What if there was a good reason he'd been locked up on that side?

"It is me," Henry told them, standing up and stepping closer to the bars but not touching them. "I promise you, I'm the real Henry. And I know I'm in my world because you"—he looked at Fargo—"are clearly not the sheriff here."

"Why should we take your word for it?" Fargo demanded. "If you're the other Henry, you could have heard about this world and the differences between here and there. So you'd know I wasn't sheriff here." He crossed his arms over his chest. "Prove that you belong here."

Henry sighed. "I can't prove it, Fargo," he explained. "Most of the things that make me who I am happened to the other Henry as well. Right down to breaking into the SRT to try saving Kevin's life." He looked down at his feet. "But in that world, Carter wasn't there to help, and Nathan Stark didn't reach that Henry in time. Kevin died. I—the other me—got sent to prison. But over there, I didn't get paroled by Eva Thorne." He frowned. "Actually, I'm not entirely sure Eva came to Eureka. She might not have. But I'm in prison over there." He grimaced and rubbed at his wrists—Jo could see mild abrasions, in the exact shape of handcuffs. "As I found out the hard way, when people mistook me for an escaped felon and Jo—the other Jo—tackled me and handcuffed me."

Jo smiled. Good to know she was still a badass, even over there.

She studied Henry for a minute. Then she made her decision. "Get out of the way, Fargo," she announced. "I'm letting him out."

"That could be a huge mistake," Fargo warned, but he quickly slid aside when she took a menacing step toward him. "I'm just saying, better safe than sorry."

"Your counterpart said much the same thing," Henry commented, stepping back so Jo could unlock the cell door and swing it open. "I told him I was from here and he said, 'If that's the case, you'll wind up slipping back to your own reality before too long. But if you are from this world and you did escape prison somehow, I want you back behind bars as soon as possible.'" He nodded his thanks to Jo as he emerged from the cell and into the office proper. "Which I completely understand and agree with." He glanced around. "Where's Jack?"

"Heading toward Allison's—the other Allison's—last I heard." Jo explained the situation.

"Wow." Henry scratched his head. "I can't even imagine what that's like." Though something in his eyes told Jo he could imagine it, at least a little bit. She knew what he'd gone through with Kim. It wasn't exactly the same, but it was similar. "I hope he can get Kevin back safely."

"Me, too," Jo agreed. Fargo nodded behind her. He might be obnoxious most of the time, but at least Fargo's heart was in the right place. It was a large part of why Jo, Carter, and others were friends with him.

"Well, I'd better get back to my garage and make sure nothing's disappeared—or appeared." Henry pulled his hat out of his back pocket and slipped it onto his head. "Let me know if you need me though, okay?" Jo nodded, and Henry headed for the door. After he'd left she dropped into her desk chair and scowled at the empty jail cell.

"Regretting letting him go?" Fargo asked. "I did say it was a bad idea."

"It's not that." Jo waved the comment away like a particularly annoying fly. "I'm thinking about the Thunderbird."

"Ah." Fargo came over and perched on the edge of her desk, a move that was eerily reminiscent of Carter. "That."

"Yes, that." She frowned at him. "Carter was right. This would be the perfect time for the thief to sneak the egg out of town. We're so busy watching for cars and trucks to materialize that we'd probably never even see him. And even if we spotted him, we'd have a hard time pursuing him." She pounded one fist on the desk. "It's when I'd make a break for it, if I were him."

"So we should go back out and drive around some more, in hopes of spotting him?" Fargo asked. "Or patrol the town's border, to keep him from slipping past?"

But Jo shook her head. "Neither of those will work," she admitted. "We've got too much ground to cover. If he wants to slip by us, he probably will." She bared her teeth and came very close to growling. "He could be long gone by now, and we'd never even know it."

Fargo was thinking furiously. "Maybe not." He pushed his glasses back up to the bridge of his nose. "You told everyone not to drive, right? Because of 'unstable conditions' and 'atmospheric disturbances.'"

Jo shrugged. "I figured it was suitably vague but still completely accurate. So what?"

"So we can assume this thief knows Eureka pretty well." Fargo hopped off the desk and started pacing in front of it. "He knew GD well enough to bypass its security. He knew the containment fields well enough to cut through them, too. He's probably a local, which means he has a standard-issue Eureka smartphone."

Jo nodded. "Okay, so he's got a phone. So what?"

"So that means he heard your alert." Fargo grinned. "About atmospheric conditions. The Thunderbird egg's at a critical stage right now—it's so close to birth. And he obviously knows what it is and what it can do. But that means he also knows how unstable it is right before birth—and how too much electromagnetic radiation nearby could cause it to hatch prematurely. Just like last time."

Jo nodded, seeing his train of thought. "So now would actually be a terrible time to sneak the egg out." She pushed back from her desk and stood. "He needs to keep it safe and cool so it won't hatch before it's ready. If he can wait until after all of this is taken care of, then he can sneak past while everybody's recovering and checking for damage and comparing stories."

"Exactly!" Fargo pounded his fist down on her desk—and winced. "Which means the Thunderbird egg is still in Eureka, and will be at least until you give the all-clear."

This time it was Jo who grinned, tight and nasty. "It would be a shame if I forgot to sound the all-clear for a few hours," she pointed out, her voice just as sharp as her expression. "Maybe just long enough for him to slip up and reveal himself."

Fargo grinned back at her. And deep inside, Jo was forced to admit to herself that maybe working with him isn't as terrible as all that.

At least, not all the time.

"Damn it!"

Carter raced back upstairs, taking the steps two at a time. Kevin followed quietly behind him. He was never completely sure how much the teenager understood of what was going on around him, but right now all that mattered was that he stay close to Carter.

"What?" Allison looked up as Carter banged open the door to Kevin's room. He didn't have time for subtlety. "I thought you were taking him back."

"I was," Carter agreed. "But I may be too late. The worlds have started to slip apart again. And we're still here."

She wiped the tears from her eyes and nodded, focusing on the matter at hand. "Won't the two of you just fade away and wind up back in your own world? That's what happened to me when I found myself over there instead."

"Maybe, but I don't know for certain." Carter frowned. "And we have no idea how long before that happens. If it's too long, the worlds could be too far apart for us to get back at all." He saw the hope wash across her face, though she was decent enough to try to hide it. "I've got a daughter of my own," he explained quietly. "Zoe. She just started college."

That put an end to Allison's hopeful expression. "What can I do to help?"

"Call Dr. Russell," he told her. "Maybe she's got some idea."

He headed back downstairs—better to be closer to the door in case they needed to make a run for it—and Kevin followed. So did Allison. She had her phone out as she walked.

"Dr. Russell?" she said after a second. "It's Allison Blake-Stark." Carter hoped she didn't see him wince at that one. "I've got Sheriff Carter here with me. Yes, from the other Eureka." She sighed just a little bit. "Yes, and Kevin, too. But the worlds are starting to shift apart again, aren't they? The worlds were so close he slipped through before, but now he and Kevin are on this side and he's not sure how to get them back home again."

She listened for a moment, and Carter watched her face intently. But after a few seconds she frowned, and the mild expression hit him like a freight train. "Oh. No, I understand. Well, if you do think of anything, please let me know. Thanks." The look she gave Carter was filled with remorse. "I'm sorry, Sheriff. She said they can't reverse the process without tearing both worlds apart or squashing them together all over again. And she has no idea how to get you back to your world, because she never expected anyone to cross over in the first place."

Carter sighed. He'd been afraid of that. Having people from one reality appear in the other had been a fluke, an accident brought about by the larger accident of the worlds shifting toward each other. Now that they'd corrected the bigger problem, the smaller one was probably taken care of as well. Which was great as far as the people in their proper reality were concerned.

But it meant he and Kevin could be stranded here for good.

He bunched his hands into fists and pounded them on the kitchen counter. No, he wouldn't accept that. He belonged back in his own Eureka, and Kevin with him. Allison was waiting for them. So was Zoe, even if she didn't know it yet. There had to be a way to get back home.

He turned away from the counter and his foot slipped—the floor was different from the one he remembered. His hands shot out to stop his fall, and one grasped the counter's edge. The other brushed the sculpture that stood there—and twitched as the contact gave him a mild shock.

Ouch!

"What the hell is it with me and shocks lately?" Carter muttered as he shook his hand out, trying to get rid of the tingling sensation. "Did I swallow a balloon or something?"

Then he thought of something.

"Call Russell back," he told Allison. "And hand me the phone." She did, and he got another minor jolt as he took the little device from her. "Thanks."

"Hello?" Dr. Russell was saying on the other end.

"Hey, it's Sheriff Carter," he told her, holding the phone to his ear. "Listen, I'm trying to figure this out. I was the door between our two worlds, right? That's why most of the early appearances from your world to mine happened right after I'd been someplace?"

"That's right," she agreed.

"So shouldn't I still be a door?" he asked. "The realities are not completely apart yet, right?"

"Not completely, no. They're still linked, though that link is getting more and more tenuous." She thought about it. "But yes, you should be still be the focal point for that link."

"Okay. So there's got to be some way to jump back to my own world," Carter insisted. "I'm the doorway—there has to be a way for me to use that to get me and Kevin home." He glanced at the screen, and the pretty blond researcher shown in it. "I'm still getting shocks from everything. What does that mean?"

"You are?" She frowned. "You were magnetized to attract energy from here," she said after a second, "and that's what pulled our worlds together. The other me and Zane reversed that charge so you'd push us apart instead." She paused. "You may still have a mild charge," she decided finally. "It shouldn't be much by now, but your body's electrical field may still be a little higher than normal. That's why you're getting shocked."

Carter thought about magnets. "And I'm still negatively charged in relation to here, right? Which means I should be positively charged toward home. My body should attract energy from my own Eureka—and vice versa."

"Yes," she said slowly. "But your physical mass is anchoring you here. You can't simply trust the charge to pull you back home across that gap. Especially since it's getting wider, and would take more energy to cross it."

"What if I got more energy?" he asked her. His mind was racing. "What if I got a really big zap? What would that do?"

Russell considered. "It might shake you loose from here," she finally admitted. "It would have to be a massive charge, but yes, it could amp up your magnetic charge and pull you through the link." She frowned again. "But there's no guarantee it would get you all the way back home," she warned. "You could be stuck between our two worlds, in the space between dimensions. That's pure energy, and you couldn't survive that for very long."

Carter nodded. "I'd need something to pull me back the rest of the way," he agreed. "Something to latch on to me, or my remaining energy charge, and drag me back to Eureka. My Eureka." He wracked his brain. There was something there, he just couldn't quite grasp it. "Something to basically suck the energy back down and get me home."

Then he had it.

"I need you to do something for me," he told Russell. "Fast as you can." He glanced outside and saw that the driveway was empty past Allison's station wagon. He might be here, but his Jeep was apparently back home. Fortunately, he didn't have far to go. Unfortunately, he had to hurry. "Allison, I need to borrow your car."

She didn't argue. She just tossed him the keys.

"Did you get all that?" he asked Russell as he headed for the door, guiding Kevin by the shoulder.

"I did," Russell assured him. "And you're right, it could work." The worry on her pretty face told him it could also *not* work—and what would probably happen if it failed.

"You could just stay here," Allison told him quickly, following them to the door. Her eyes went to Kevin, and she started to reach out, but stopped herself. "I know you'd be trapped, and I'm sorry, but at least you'd be alive and safe. Both of you."

"I've got to try." Carter grabbed her hand and forced her gaze to move to him. "We don't belong here. You know that. If there's any way for us to get back home, I've got to take it."

She nodded.

"Okay," he told Russell as he yanked the door open. "Let them know as quick as you can, and fingers crossed."

"Good luck," Russell called out as he tossed the phone back to Allison and raced outside to her station wagon. A minute later, with Kevin belted into the front passenger seat, Carter floored it and took off in reverse, barreling out of the driveway. Then he jammed the car into drive, his foot still slammed down on the accelerator, and they shot forward, toward their only chance at returning to their own world.

Carter didn't have to look in the rearview to know that Allison had followed them out to the driveway and was watching them go.

CHAPTER 29

Allison was struggling to remain calm.

It wasn't working.

Every minute that Carter was gone—thirty-seven so far—meant one more minute that the worlds were gliding apart. And that he didn't have Kevin back.

Where was he?

She knew it was ridiculous to pin so much hope on one person. But Carter had always come through for her before. Always. Every time they'd been in danger, every time she'd needed him, he'd been there.

A part of her brain took great pleasure in pointing that out. Because how many people could you say that about, really? How many people were always there for you, and always came through?

Not very many at all.

So where was he now?

She stared at her phone, trying to will it to ring by sheer desperation alone. She knew he'd call her the minute he had Kevin. She didn't even have to ask. It was understood.

But the phone continued to lie dead and silent in her hand.

Movement on the screen tugged at the corner of her sight, but Allison didn't look up. The phone had her full attention. And through it, Carter. Wherever he was.

"Allison."

Zane's voice was soft, but there was something in its tone that made her look up. She belatedly realized what it was. There was an urgency that she'd rarely heard from him before. Most of the time, Zane treated everything like it was one big joke. The world was silly, and he was happy to play along, hamming it up and goofing off and trusting his genius to get him through unscathed.

He wasn't joking now.

Glancing up, she saw the other Dr. Russell leaning into her microphone. Judging by her expression, the pretty blond researcher was sharing something important.

But all Allison heard was static.

"Damn!" That was Zane, as he checked the controls and readouts. "We must have drifted just far enough apart to lose audio!" The quick glance he shot Allison wasn't lost on her.

If they were too far apart to have sound transfer anymore, what were the chances people could make it back across?

And her phone was still silent.

Russell was gesturing at her counterpart, indicating her ear and shaking her head. Her double caught on and leaned back, looking frustrated. Then she bolted from her chair and ran toward the back of the lab. A minute later she was back, dragging the whiteboard. They'd forgotten all about those after the two Russells had managed to set up the mikes, but no one had thought to remove them.

Which now turned out to be a good thing.

Everyone watched as the other Dr. Russell scrawled something on the whiteboard. "Man, I hope we can read her writing," Zane muttered. It looked like typical scientist scribbling, all but illegible.

"I can read it," their own Russell promised, her lips quirked in a half smile. "I've been deciphering my own notes for years."

But nobody needed to translate the first word. And Allison felt relief buoy her up, even as a sense of dread washed over her.

The first word Russell wrote was *Carter.*

"Carter is okay," their Russell read off to them, squinting at the monitor. "He has Kevin. They're both safe."

Allison wanted to cry. But she knew "safe" was a far cry from "home." Especially since their safety was being conveyed to them via whiteboard from another dimension!

"Worlds too far apart to slip back across," was the next line, and Allison felt her phone digging into her palm as her hands clenched. That was exactly what she'd been afraid of. She couldn't lose Kevin. She just couldn't!

And, if she was being honest with herself, she couldn't bear to lose Carter, either.

But Russell was still writing. "Carter has an idea." Allison couldn't help it—she laughed. Of course he did. Carter always had an idea. For an average guy surrounded by geniuses, it was sometimes amazing just how many good ideas he had. Crazy ones, but then Eureka was a crazy place. And most of his plans wound up working.

Which was why she knew she could count on him, and why the relief was starting to outweigh the dread.

As Russell wrote down the details, however, even Allison gaped. And Zane shook his head.

"He's certifiable," Zane claimed, staring at the instructions again as if reading them a second time would somehow change them so they made more sense. "He's completely mad."

"Will it work?" Allison asked him quietly.

Zane considered it. "Maybe," he admitted finally. "It could. I can't be sure." He shook his head again. "But who would even think of that?"

"Carter would." Allison felt more laughter bubbling up inside her, some of it verging on hysteria, and forced it back down. She'd have time to laugh later. Assuming Carter's plan worked.

But she had a good feeling about it.

It was Carter, after all. And he'd never let her down before.

Her phone was still in her hand, and she opened her fingers, wincing at the belated pain from where it had pressed into her flesh. But she didn't hesitate to raise it and switch it on. Time was of the essence here.

Dialing the number, Allison lifted the phone to her ear. "Hello?" she said as the call connected. "Dr. Savile?"

"Listen to me, Kevin," Carter said as he sped down the street. "I'm going to try to get you back home to your mom, okay?" He didn't bother trying to explain that the woman they'd just left behind wasn't her, or at least not exactly.

Kevin nodded. "That wasn't her," he said, gesturing back behind them. They'd already gone several blocks, but Carter wouldn't have been at all surprised to learn that Allison was still standing there, staring after them. He probably would have been, in her shoes. "It was a quantum variant."

"That's right. But I'm going to get you back to your real mom, okay?" It always amazed Carter just how Kevin's mind worked. The teenager was often oblivious to the world around him, and sometimes didn't seem to understand things as basic as checking for cars before stepping out into the street, but then he could perform amazingly complex math in his head, and sometimes had surprising insight into people and events. Like now.

Kevin nodded. "I'd like to go home," he admitted, glancing out the window as they raced along. "This is an interesting variation, but I don't feel comfortable here."

"Me either," Carter assured him. "Me either."

They drove the rest of the way in silence, with Carter concentrating on the road and Kevin staring at the almost-familiar homes and streets that were whizzing past. Fortunately, it seemed that Jo's alert—and Fargo's, here—had convinced people to stay off the roads, and the streets were almost completely empty.

They skidded on two tires as Carter yanked the wheel, forcing Allison's station wagon into a hard right onto Silver Road, and he held his breath. It should be right about—there!

He almost shouted with relief when the little stuccoed house came into view. True, it was a dusty blue rather than an alarming orange, but there was no doubt it was the same home.

He just hoped it belonged to the same person.

Carter sped up the driveway and then slammed on the brakes, rocking the car to a stop just shy of the garage door. He was kicking open his door and yanking off his seat belt before the engine had even finished shuddering. "Come on, let's go," he urged, but Kevin was already following his lead and stepping out of the car.

The front door opened as they stepped onto the walk, and a man emerged from the house. "Sheriff Carter?" He was average height and stocky, bald, and with a neat brown beard.

"Dr. Savile?" Carter let himself relax a little—but just a little—when the man nodded and extended his hand. "Boy, am I glad to see you!"

Savile smiled. "So I heard. Though I don't know if I should feel the same way, after being told that you want me to deliberately overload my heat sink, which could set me back months of research." He didn't look upset, however. If anything, there was a gleam in his eye, and Carter had the sudden sense that Savile was the kind of man who enjoyed breaking the rules occasionally.

And, while normally as sheriff he had to take a stand against that sort of thing, right now Carter was all for it.

"Come on inside." Savile ushered them both in, and Carter allowed himself to be guided through the short front hall and into a large, studio-style living room. The furniture—all ultra-modern, blond wood Scandinavian-style pieces, Carter noticed—had been shoved to the sides, and in the center of the floor sat a ceramic and metal box about the size of a large cooler.

"That's it?" Carter eyed the thing warily. He'd expected something significantly larger, and with a lot more wires and dials and switches. Something more high-tech looking. This thing looked like a snazzy way to hold a few beers when going on a picnic.

"That's it." Savile's pride as he admired his handiwork

was unmistakable. "The basic concept of an ambient heat sink was the easy part, in a way. Getting it to be this portable was a lot trickier." He knelt in front of the device, flipped open a panel along one side, and began fiddling with something in there. "I've been storing energy for several days while testing its capacity," he explained. "So there should be more than enough of a charge for your purposes." He grinned over his shoulder. "Assuming it doesn't fry you to a crisp, of course."

Carter shuddered. "I'm trying not think about that."

Savile laughed and shrugged. "Well, all we need to do"—he yanked out a wire as he talked—"is disconnect the buffer system." He tossed the wire aside, leaned back on his feet, and wiped his hands on his slacks. "Which I just did." Then he rose to his feet again and retreated a few paces. "I've got the heat sink set up to be run by remote, so I can trigger it from a safe distance. You'll need to be touching it, however." He glanced from Carter to Kevin, the question clear on his face.

"Kevin, come over here," Carter instructed. The teen did so without question. "We're going to stand right next to that thing, okay? I'm going to touch it, and it's going to give me a shock. I want you to grab my hand as soon as that happens. Can you do that?"

The boy nodded. "You're hoping to break the gravitational bonds of this reality, and supercharge the pull between yourself and our own world," he stated calmly. Then he smiled. "I like it!"

"Well, that makes one of us, at least." But Carter couldn't help smiling back at him. "Okay, let's do this." He nodded to Savile, who produced a small silvery remote from his pocket and aimed it at the heat sink. He waited like that, poised, while Carter and Kevin approached the device.

Carter took a deep breath. This was it. Either this would work, or they'd be stuck here forever—or he'd be burned to a cinder and wouldn't care much either way.

But the longer he waited, the worse their chances became.

So he reached out and set his hand palm-down on top of the heat sink.

There was a soft thrum as Savile activated it, and Carter could feel it vibrate under his hand. The vibrations increased, shaking him along with the device, and it heated up as well, almost burning his flesh. He maintained the contact, however, and squeezed his eyes shut as the noise increased, going from a hum to a whine to a screech.

Then there was a violent flash of light, blinding even through his eyelids, and his whole body jerked as a massive surge of energy poured into him from his hand.

Ba-zoom!

He felt like he'd been struck by lightning—not once but a thousand times. Every inch of him was taut and crackling. His mouth was dry as a bone. His eyes burned. His nostrils ached, and there was a faint, acrid smell of charred flesh. His whole body was spasming, and he was having trouble breathing as his lungs quivered and flailed.

Then he felt Kevin's hand on his other arm.

The boy's touch was soothing, his skin cool compared to Carter's own. He discovered he could breathe again, and drew in a great gasping breath.

Then he noticed that the heat sink under his other hand didn't seem as hot as it had a second ago.

Or as solid.

Cracking one eye open, Carter saw that the world around him seemed to be wavering. It was like a fine, shimmering curtain had been drawn over Savile's living room, and it was wafting in an invisible breeze, causing the outlines of everything around him to flicker and blur.

Everything except Kevin. He was still solid and real.

Twisting slightly, Carter took his hand from the heat sink, which felt filmy and rubbery now anyway, and threw his arm around Kevin's shoulder. He wrapped his other arm around the boy as well, holding him tight.

"Here we go," he whispered.

Then all the color and shadow faded from the world around them.

Carter blinked. There were swirls surrounding him and

Kevin, but he couldn't make out any details. Or any colors, really. Just faint flickers of motion and depth.

He didn't feel like he was burning up anymore, either. But his body was still tingling with energy.

And that was a good thing.

He'd gotten them loose from the other Eureka. He didn't need Kevin to tell him that they were essentially adrift now, floating in the void between the two realities.

Now they just needed to get back home.

Carter really hoped Russell had gotten his message to her double, and to his own Allison.

He hoped his plan would work.

He hoped he didn't have to take another breath. He had a feeling there wasn't exactly any air around them.

And he hoped this hadn't been a huge, colossal mistake.

But most of all, he hoped Kevin would be all right.

And that they would both see his mom again, real soon.

Really, really soon.

"Now!" Allison shouted.

Dr. Savile nodded and hit a button on his remote. His ambient heat sink sat in the middle of his living room, and Allison watched, hands clasped almost in prayer, as the small device began to hum. She could feel the room around her growing colder as the device drew all of the heat from the air, and the large studio darkened as the object absorbed the visible light as well.

Then they waited.

"I'm getting a massive energy spike," Savile reported after a minute, studying the tiny screen inset in his remote. "A ton of energy just entered the heat sink's operating range."

Allison crossed her fingers.

"Drawing it in now," Savile announced, fiddling with his remote. They could both hear the increased pitch of the heat sink's whine. "It's pushing the limits of the heat sink's capacity." He frowned. "I hope it doesn't overload."

Allison tried not to think about what would happen if it did. Would Carter and Kevin be tossed back into the other Eureka if that happened? Or would they just dissipate, lost energy scattered to the four winds?

She tried really hard not to think about that.

And they waited, shivering as the temperature plummeted, squinting as the shadows lengthened.

Was that a shadow right next to the heat sink? Was it flickering slightly?

Allison strained to see better, taking a half step forward.

Yes, it was definitely shifting!

She took another step.

Now she could see that shadow elongating, stretching, growing.

And it was lightening as well. The shadow had been blue-gray, but now it was changing color, becoming paler and also brighter, the hue mutating along with the shade—

—veering toward something like tan. And red. And a splotch of blue.

Carter had been wearing his sheriff's uniform, of course.

And Kevin had picked out a red T-shirt and jeans this morning.

Allison blinked away tears and stepped a little closer. It was definitely more than shadows now. There was a shape there, a large writhing form, and she could make out more details. A dark blotch, topped by a swath of black. A lighter patch, with just a touch of darker color above.

Heads.

Two heads.

Carter's—and her son's.

There was a faint sound, like an onrushing of air, and then she heard a thump as the two of them landed on the floor.

"Shut it off!" she shouted over her shoulder, but Savile was already in motion. He had the remote raised like a gun, and aimed right at the heat sink. With a push the device switched off, its hum fading slowly, along with the glow that had sprung up around it. As it released its hold on the energy around them, the room's temperature rose again slightly, as did the light.

She could see clearly again.

And she rushed to Carter's and Kevin's sides and seized them both in a fierce hug.

"You did it," she whispered to Carter, squeezing him tight. "You did it." Then she concentrated on Kevin. "I love you, baby."

For once, he responded. "I love you, too, Mom." And he hugged her back.

Carter shuddered and took a deep breath. Then he blinked and glanced around. "Guess it worked, huh?" He gave her a weak grin. "Talk about a wild ride!"

Allison slapped him on the arm, then rose to her feet and helped pull first him and then Kevin up. "Only you would think jumping from one reality without any guarantee you'd reach a second one was fun," she retorted.

"Naw, Jo would have loved it," Carter answered. He staggered and stretched. Then he shivered. "Geez, can we get out of here? It's freezing!"

The relief overcame Allison finally, and she laughed. "Absolutely."

With a wave of thanks to Dr. Savile, she led the two most important men in her life out of the room.

CHAPTᵉR 30

"We're out of time," Jo stated, rising to her feet and moving out from behind her desk. "The two Eurekas are almost completely apart again. The danger's past. I should sound the all-clear and let people take to the road."

Fargo, still occupying Carter's chair, leaned forward and rested his arms on the desk. "But if you do that, the Thunderbird thief will know this is the time to try sneaking the egg past us."

"I know." Jo paced, arms crossed, brow furrowed. "I can hold off on letting everyone know, but not for too long. We need to catch this guy, but we also need to maintain order, and having everyone panic for a few extra hours doesn't really help that much."

"So we've got a small window of opportunity," Fargo insisted, standing up and leaning on the edge of Carter's desk. "How do we catch this guy?"

"I don't know!" Her answer was a low rasp, almost a growl, and Jo scowled and increased the fervor of her steps, making each one a stomp. "We don't have anything to go on! He could be anywhere!" She shook her head. "If Carter was here, he'd have some crazy idea that would sound completely ridiculous but would wind up working perfectly. Or he'd stumble into the answer without even realizing it." She stopped suddenly, her back going rigid. "But I'm not Carter," she admitted. "And I don't know how to do what he does. Not that part of it, anyway."

"Me either," Fargo told her. "And my other self's the sheriff in his Eureka! He must have figured it out—too bad I never had the chance to ask him!"

But as Fargo puzzled over that one, a thought occurred to him. Had his other self really learned how to act like Carter? Or had he just found a way to be sheriff on his own terms?

After all, Fargo reasoned, he was smart. Even for Eureka he was smart. And unlike most Eurekans, he was scientifically omnivorous—he didn't stick to just one discipline, but knew a little bit about all of them. It meant that he might not have gotten as far in any one field as he could have, but he had a decent grounding in all of them. Which was why he could help Allison keep track of everything, and why he could often help Carter—and Jo—get up to speed on any problems at GD.

So maybe his other self had used that background, and that inherent flexibility, in his approach to being sheriff. Maybe he hadn't tried to make himself more like someone else, but had found a way to make the role more Fargo-like instead.

And if the other Fargo could do that, so could he.

"Okay," he said half to himself as he stood and started pacing in front of Carter's desk. "What do we know, exactly?"

After staring at him for a second, Jo nodded. "We know someone took the Thunderbird egg," she started, but then she stopped and shook her head. "No, that's not really the start of things, is it? We can go back further than that."

This time Fargo was the one who nodded. "Right. We know someone knew about or found out about the Thunderbird project. We know they decided to steal it. And we know they broke into the Thunderbird bio lab and tried to make off with both eggs."

Just then, Jo's phone chimed. She glanced at the readout, and her face lit up. Fargo suppressed a groan. There was only one person who made her beam like that. Sure enough, she answered with a cheerful, "Zane! What's the good word?"

She listened for a second, and broke out into a sigh and a big smile. "Really? Excellent! Thanks!" Then, remembering she wasn't alone and she spoke away from the phone. "Carter made it back somehow. He and Kevin are both fine."

Fargo slumped a little with relief. He actually liked Carter, and certainly appreciated the care he took of the town and its residents. And he liked Kevin, too. The fact that they'd somehow pulled off a safe return was good news indeed.

Jo was still listening, and Fargo saw her eyes widen. "Hang on a sec," she told Zane, and pushed a button on her phone. "Okay, say that last part again."

"I said, now I can get back to finishing upgrading GD's security systems," Zane repeated, his voice coming through over the phone's built-in speakerphone. "I'm not really sure why it's necessary, though."

"Because somebody broke into GD, and got into the Thunderbird lab, and stole the Thunderbird egg," Fargo replied, hating the fact that his voice always got a bit whinier when he was dealing with Zane.

"Oh, hey, is that Fargo?" Zane asked. "Hey, Fargo. Well, yeah, but the thing is, I don't know how they managed that. I've rewritten the algorithms for the security protocols, but they were actually pretty tight to start. They're better now, of course, but even so—it would take one hell of a thief to bust into this place."

"Someone like you, you mean?" Jo asked dryly.

"Hey, if you've got it, flaunt it, right?" her boyfriend replied with a chuckle. "But seriously, this place had top-notch security to start. I could have gotten in, but not a lot of other people could claim that."

Jo glanced over at Fargo, and he knew exactly what she was thinking. "The thief came from within," he said, and she nodded.

"It makes sense." Jo held up fingers as she ticked off points. "He knew about the Thunderbird project, including where it was. He knew how to get into the building. He knew how the containment fields worked. And he knew enough about GD's security to short out the cameras in that immediate area."

"Yeah, I'd guess it was an inside job, too," Zane offered. "Listen, I've gotta go. Catch you later, JoJo. Fargo, behave yourself." Then he was gone.

"I always behave," Fargo muttered to himself, but he quickly forced his irritation aside to concentrate. They were getting somewhere here, finally. "Okay, so it's somebody in GD. We could comb the personnel files, but that would take forever."

Jo put her hands behind her head and stretched, forcing Fargo to try not to stare. Too much. "If it's a GD employee," she said, "what're the chances he stole the egg to sell it?"

Fargo considered that. "Not good," he answered after a second. "There are plenty of other projects that could fetch more money on the black market, and a lot of those are more portable, and much easier to handle."

"Right. So maybe it wasn't stolen for money." Jo smiled. "Which means the thief may not be trying to smuggle it out after all."

"So, what, he wanted it as a pet?" Fargo asked. "I can see it now. Some GD employee heard about the Thunderbird and thought, 'Hey, that's what I need around the house—an electromagnetically charged entity that looks like a Native American mythological creature. I'll never have to worry about static cling again!'"

Then he froze as the words he'd just uttered burst into his brain.

"That's it!" he shouted. "Of course!"

"What's it?" Jo was staring at him. "Fargo, have you totally lost your mind?"

"Not at all!" He grabbed her by the shoulders. "Listen, think about what I just said! The Thunderbird's a small, sentient storm, right? A ball of electromagnetism, tied to a biological entity. Basically a big bundle of charged ions with wings, claws, and a brain." Jo nodded. "So whoever stole it has been in close proximity to the egg—which carries the same properties—and to the one that hatched."

Jo pursed her lips. "Static cling," she said finally.

"Exactly!" Fargo shook her enthusiastically. "Static cling! Whoever he is, he's carrying a static charge from the Thunderbird!"

"But you covered the whole area with that voltmeter you built," Jo reminded him, brushing his hands from her shoulders and taking a step back to put a little distance between them. "You didn't find anything."

"Because the readings were too faint to register," Fargo explained. He grinned. "But that's not the only way to check for something like that." He turned and strode for the door.

"Where exactly are we going?" Jo asked. But Fargo noticed that she didn't argue, and that she'd fallen into step beside him.

"Back to GD," he answered. "To the scene of the crime. I'll need you to distract the security guards once we get there, and give me a few minutes to adjust some things. Then you should sound the all-clear." He glanced at his watch. It was a little after five o'clock. Perfect. "With any luck, we'll have our culprit in hand before dinner."

He couldn't help grinning as they headed toward Jo's car. This was how it was done, Fargo-style!

"Are you sure you're okay?" Allison asked Kevin for the hundredth time as they walked along the corridor toward the extradimensional visualization lab. He nodded but didn't answer otherwise. After that short burst of conversation on the way to Dr. Savile's, the boy had returned to his usual nonconversational self. But Allison was clearly thrilled to have him back anyway.

Carter brushed past a pair of scientists, and glanced over at Allison. "Place is pretty busy," he mentioned. "I'd have thought everybody'd be home instead, given the recent danger."

"Jo warned people to stay off the streets," Allison explained, "but we never issued a state of emergency. There wasn't much point—either the worlds were going to collide or they weren't, no matter where people were. So everyone's here as usual. And Jo hasn't told them they can drive again, so nobody's left for the day yet."

"She'll take care of it," Carter assured her. He did wonder why she hadn't yet, but he had complete faith in his deputy. Though she did have Fargo with her, he remembered, and that could put a crimp in anyone's plans.

They'd reached the door to the lab, and Carter opened the door—and then turned around and blocked the doorway. "Maybe we shouldn't," he suggested.

Allison glanced over his shoulder, and he felt as much as saw her stiffen. She paused for a second, but then she raised her chin. "I need to."

He considered that. "Yeah, I guess you do," he agreed. "But maybe we should keep Kevin in back, and find something to distract him. I'm not sure he needs to see her right now."

Allison nodded. She pulled a handheld video game out of her purse and offered it to her son, who grinned and snatched it from her hands. Within seconds he was playing something, and had completely shut out the outside world.

Satisfied, Carter stepped aside and let Allison enter first. Then he followed, guiding Kevin by the shoulder. He led the teenager off to the side and settled him into one of the chairs arranged along the back wall. Kevin never even glanced up.

Which was good, because it meant that he didn't see the woman who was sort of his mother, and the man who had once been his stepfather and had almost become so again, visible on the overhead screen.

Carter followed Allison down to the center of the room, and stood a few paces from her—near enough for moral support but far enough to give her some space. Then he waited.

Stark nodded at him, and he nodded back. The other Allison smiled sadly. Her eyes flickered to Kevin, and teared up, but her smile widened.

They'd wheeled the whiteboards back over, Carter noticed, and now the other Allison went to the one on their side. She took up the marker and wrote, *I'm glad you both made it back safely. I'm so sorry.*

"It's okay," Carter said. Then he realized she couldn't hear him. But she understood his nod and his smile, at least.

His Allison had taken their own marker and replied on their whiteboard, *It's okay. I understand.* The two Allisons nodded at each other.

Stark watched all of this without speaking. He had his arm around his Allison, but he was watching Carter's Allison as well. There was something in that look, Carter thought. Regret, and sympathy, and apology. But something else, too. Desire, maybe. Or perhaps just a recognition of her desire.

Carter turned to study Allison, and almost wished he hadn't. He could see the emotions playing across her face and in her eyes. Anger, certainly, but sorrow as well. And grief. Seeing Stark there had been hard for her, he knew. And almost losing Kevin had been far worse.

Now, though, she smiled at Stark. It wasn't a flirtatious smile, or a look of longing. It was sad, and sweet. It was something Carter had seen all too many times in his days as a federal marshal, usually when someone came in to identify a body.

It was a look of farewell.

"Our worlds are almost back into their original positions," Russell reported, studying her screens. "The rate of movement has slowed significantly. Inertia should kick in once we're back in place, and that'll be the end of it." She smiled. "Viewing only from now on."

"Sounds good to me," Carter agreed. "I don't think I could take another trip like that." He patted his head. "It's going to take forever for my hair to recover, as it is."

Allison laughed. She nodded to both Stark and her other self, and to the other Russell as well. "Let me know when it's over," she told their Dr. Russell, and then turned away. "I'm going to get Kevin home."

Carter followed them back into the hall.

"Hey, Allison," he said softly, reaching out to touch her lightly on the arm. She stopped and swiveled back to face him. "Are you okay?"

"I will be," she told him honestly. "I'm still a bit of a mess right now, Jack. But I'll be okay—thanks to you." The smile she gave him more than made up for everything he'd been through. It practically lit up the dim hallway.

"I'm impressed you could forgive her so easily," he admitted. "I don't know that I could have."

"Oh, I'm still furious," Allison told him, her smile tightening for a second before turning sad. "But obviously I understand why she did it. And clearly, in another world, I would do the exact same thing. I don't want her to beat herself up about it—she's gone through enough as it is." She shrugged.

"And seeing Stark again?"

"That was hard." She sighed. "Very hard." Then she brightened. "But it was good, too. Before, I didn't get to say good-bye, really. Now I have. That helps."

She reached out and hugged Carter, then gave him a quick kiss on the cheek. "Thank you for bringing Kevin back to me," she told him again.

"Anytime." He watched her lead her son away, and thought about everything that had happened. Allison was always so calm and cool, so in control of herself and the situation around her. She had to be, in order to run GD the way she did. So it was rare to see her lose control of herself. In a way, it was a little refreshing. And a little frightening. Her emotions ran deep, much deeper than she let on. Carter wondered what it would be like to be the recipient of those emotions.

He touched his cheek where she'd kissed him. Maybe someday he'd find out.

Then, whistling softly, he followed in the direction she had taken, aiming for the central lobby and the main entrance. Time to leave the other reality behind and get back to the work of handling this one.

CHAPTER 31

"**Explain to me again what you're going to do,**" Jo insisted as she pulled into the GD parking lot and swerved into a space near the front door. "Just so I know when both Allison and Carter tell us to knock it off."

"I'm going to rewire the security gates," Fargo explained, undoing his seat belt and hopping out of the car as soon as she'd shut the engine off. "Just a little bit."

"And what will it do once you've done that, exactly?" Jo kept pace effortlessly as he jogged across the small plaza, around the GD sculpture centered there, and toward the building's main entrance.

"It'll administer a mild shock to everyone who passes through it."

He reached for the door, but Jo thrust out an arm, slamming her palm into the door and pinning it shut. "Define *mild*."

"Like the one you get from static," Fargo assured her. "Nothing more, I promise." At least, that was what he was aiming for. The exact voltage would depend on a number of factors, including the distance the individual had walked to get there and what sort of footwear they were wearing. But he decided not to mention that.

"And the point of this, besides it being an amusing little prank?" She still held the door shut tight.

Fargo sighed. "Look, the Thunderbird generates electricity, right? And the thief has been in contact with the egg since stealing it. Plus, he could still be carrying a charge from the one that hatched." Jo nodded. "Well, that means he's already got charged ions clinging to him. When he walks through the security gate, they'll absorb the extra charge."

"And he'll be the only one who doesn't receive a shock." Jo stepped back and lowered her arm. "Clever, Fargo." She actually gave him a small, if grudging, smile. "Strange, and potentially irritating, but clever."

"Thanks."

"So why don't we just tell Allison what we're doing, and do it officially?" was Jo's next question as they stepped inside.

"Because we can't rule out the possibility that one of the guards is involved," Fargo pointed out, turning toward her and keeping his voice down so the guards in question wouldn't hear him. They were only a handful of paces away from the security gates now.

"Right." To his surprise, she nodded. "Okay, we'll do it your way." Then she stepped around him and marched toward the guards. "Take me to the security station, right now!" she demanded.

Both guards started, and saluted as she approached. They were military, after all—GD (and all of Eureka, really) was part of the Department of Defense, and soldiers were used for all security details. The only exceptions were the town-appointed sheriff and deputy, and even those positions required the DoD's approval.

To their credit, neither of the guards questioned Jo. They just jumped up and fell in behind her as she cleared the gates and moved quickly away, in the direction of the security master station. Which was off a corridor and well out of view.

One of the guards did pause, however, to reach for the phone beside his station. Fargo cringed. He had to be calling this in and asking for someone to take over. Which would ruin any chance he had of getting his hands on the machines.

But Jo had noticed as well. "No time for that!" she snapped. "You'll be back before you know it, and we need to move now! Let's go!"

Again, the soldier reacted instinctively. He let his hand drop, saluted again, and rushed to keep up with her and his fellow guard. Within seconds they were down the corridor and out of sight.

Leaving Fargo alone at the security station.

"Right." He rubbed his hands together and stepped over to the gate. "Let's have a look inside you, shall we?"

Down the hall, Jo stormed into the security center control room. "I need a full diagnostic, right now!" she demanded.

"Deputy Lupo!" The security officer in charge jumped to his feet and saluted. "I'm sorry, ma'am, but we'll need to—"

"Now!" Jo insisted, moving forward until she was right in his face. "Before everyone starts filing out for the evening! Otherwise we're screwed!"

In the face of her superior authority—and her bluster—the officer did the only thing he could. "Yes, ma'am!" He saluted again, then turned back to his console. Using the key around his neck, he opened a particular panel and hit a series of buttons on a small keypad. All around the small room, the monitors went dark. Then they began scrolling numbers faster than the eye could follow.

"We'll have a full diagnostic in ten minutes," he informed Jo. "Systems will be back up and running in eight."

Jo nodded. "Let's hope that's fast enough," she grated, and folded her arms over her chest, feigning impatience.

But inside, she was hoping eight minutes would be enough to let Fargo do what he had planned.

Otherwise they could be facing a whole lot of questions. And she wasn't sure Allison—or Carter—would like all of their answers.

* * *

"So?" Jo asked as she rejoined Fargo not far from the security gate. He was leaning against the wall, looking very pleased with himself.

"Piece of cake," he replied smugly. "All I had to do was change the scanners' frequency so they're emitting straight electricity instead of X-rays, deactivate the safety buffers, and reconfigure the sensors so they can still broadcast but they can't receive. And voilà! An instant electrical net!"

"Is it dangerous?" she asked him quietly, eyeing the altered security gate.

"Not at all," Fargo assured her.

"Good." She moved away from the wall and headed toward the door. "Because we're going to be the first ones through it."

"What? Why?" Fargo stayed where he was and stared at her, a look of horror flickering across his face.

"We need to be near the doors so we can see each person as he or she walks through," Jo pointed out. "And so we can grab the thief after he's through the gate and before he can make it outside. If we stay on this side, we'll have to charge through after him, and that might give him enough time to get away." She glanced back over her shoulder. "If you did this right, it shouldn't hurt too much. And you did get it right, didn't you?"

"Of course." He pushed off and trotted after her. "But that doesn't mean we have to test it on ourselves!"

But Jo was already stepping through the gate.

Zap!

There was a blue flash as she passed under the archway, and a faint crackling sound. Fargo thought he saw her brow furrow slightly, but she didn't pause or falter, and a second later she was on the other side. She beckoned him to follow.

"Great. If I'd known, I'd have set it to reconfigure itself after I went through," he muttered as he approached the gate itself. He paused just in front of it for a second. Then, squeezing his eyes shut, he took another step forward.

Zot!

"Ow! Gosh darn it! That stings!" The guards looked on, confused but chuckling, as Fargo danced from foot to foot, trying to shake off the stinging in his hands and arms. He rejoined Jo, who looked up at his head and grinned. That made him reach up to feel. Sure enough, all of his hair was standing on end.

"Why didn't this happen to you?" he grumbled at her, trying to pat his hair back down into some semblance of normality.

She just shrugged. "You're the one who set it up—you tell me." Her grin faded as she got back down to business. "The shock worked fine, though. We should be able to see clearly if anyone isn't affected."

Then she raised her phone. "Time to let everyone know they're free to go. And then we watch, and we wait."

Fargo nodded. He just hoped he didn't have to go back through that thing. He'd always admired Albert Einstein, but that didn't mean he wanted the great man's hairstyle.

Twenty minutes later, people started emerging from the corridors and converging on the main lobby. From there they filed through the security gates and then outside to reclaim their vehicles and head home for the day.

"Ouch!" said the first person to exit, their resident sleep and dream expert, Dr. Suenos. "What was that?"

"Sorry, the machines are acting up a little today," Fargo called out from his spot along the wall between the gate and the front door. "We'll get them recalibrated before the morning."

"Ow! Hey, what's the big idea?" Dr. Bubay, one of GD's seismic chemists, demanded as he got zapped.

"Technical difficulties," Jo advised. "Don't worry about it."

"Ooh, that was nice—sorta like a massage," Taggart commented as he passed through the gate. He wriggled a bit and grinned at Jo. "Jo. Fargo."

"Hey, Taggart." Jo gave him a nod and a smile but followed them with her "not right now, I'm working" glare. The lanky Australian took the hint and kept moving.

Dr. Korinko was one of the next ones through. "Have you found the egg yet?" she asked as she approached them. She was still wringing her hands a bit from the shock, and the ends of her hair were rising from the static. Jo and Fargo exchanged a glance. Definitely not her, then.

"We're still working on it," Jo replied. "But we think we'll have an answer very soon."

"How soon?" Korinko demanded. "That egg can't have much longer before it hatches!"

"I know, and we're working as fast as we can," Jo assured her. "I promise you."

Fargo was only half listening to the conversation. The other half of his attention was on the gate, and on the people who passed through it.

Zap!

Zot!

Crackle.

Nothing.

Nothing?

He looked up, studying the person who'd just cleared the cordon and who was now approaching them. The man was average height, a few inches taller than Fargo but just as wiry, with tight blond curls and a boyish face.

"Dr. Wilder," Fargo called out as the man approached him. "Can we speak to you for a moment?"

Jo glanced up at the request, then at Fargo. Her eyes narrowed when he nodded.

"I'm a little busy," Wilder replied. He checked his watch. "Can it wait until tomorrow?"

"I don't think so," Jo answered. "Now would be best." Her tone indicated that it wasn't a request.

"What's this all about?" Wilder asked as he slowed to a stop a few feet from them. He nodded at Dr. Korinko. "Hey, Anna."

Korinko nodded back, the expression on her face showing how puzzled she was. "Dan."

"Any idea what's going on here?" he asked her, ignoring Fargo and Jo for the moment.

"What's going on is that you broke into her lab, trashed it, and made off with one of the Thunderbird eggs," Fargo jumped in. He leaned in toward Wilder but stopped when he felt his hair twitch and his skin tighten. Even from a few feet away he could feel the charge the other man was carrying.

"What are you talking about?" Korinko asked. She looked at Jo. "Dan's a biogeneticist like me," she explained. "He wasn't on the Thunderbird project with us."

"But his lab is nearby, isn't it?" Jo asked. She vaguely remembered seeing him in the hall at one point. "And he knew what you were working on. Plus, his lab has the exact same security systems as yours, right down to the containment fields. He'd know how to disable them. And he could easily smuggle the egg back to his lab after all the confusion following the theft, and then remove it later when nobody was looking."

"This is ridiculous!" Wilder claimed. "I didn't steal anything! Why would I? Anna and Sean are friends of mine, not to mention colleagues. I'd never jeopardize their work like that!"

"I don't know why," Fargo admitted. "But you're definitely the thief." He gave Wilder his best tough-guy smile. "And I can prove it."

"Oh yeah?" Unfortunately, judging by the biogeneticist's smug look, he wasn't impressed. "Fine." Wilder put his hands on his hips. "Go ahead."

But Fargo was ready for that. He reached behind his back and whipped out—his voltmeter.

"That's it?" Wilder laughed. "Give me a break. What're you gonna do, detect lies?"

"No, I'm going to measure your electrical charge," Fargo answered. He waved the voltmeter in front of Wilder, letting the device scan him fully. Then he checked the readout. "Aha!"

Jo leaned in to study the small screen. "Which means what, exactly?" she asked.

"He's got a lot of energy around him right now," Fargo explained, indicating the numbers. "A lot more than he should from just a simple shock. And check out the frequency! That's an exact match for the hatched Thunderbird!" He glared at Wilder. "He's our thief!"

"Good enough for me." Jo reached for her handcuffs. "You're under arrest, Mr. Wilder. You have the right—"

But Wilder didn't wait to hear the rest of his rights. He turned instead, and bolted back the way he'd come. Back into GD.

Back through the security gate.

"No!" Fargo lunged and caught Jo by the wrist as she started to go after the man. "Don't! He's carrying a double charge now, on top of the energy he already had from the Thunderbird! It could stun you or worse if you touch him!"

"Then I won't touch him," Jo insisted, pulling loose. But as she flew toward the gate, she saw that Wilder was already halfway across the lobby—

—and rapidly approaching a familiar tan-clothed figure who'd just emerged from one of the hallways.

"Carter!" Her friend and boss looked up at her shout. "That's our Thunderbird thief! Stop him!"

Carter frowned, looked around, spotted Wilder sprinting toward him, and nodded. He dropped into a half crouch, arms out, ready to tackle the fugitive biogeneticist.

"But don't touch him!" Fargo yelled. "He's electrified!"

That made Carter freeze, before hitting Fargo with an all-too-familiar "you couldn't make this easy, could you?" look. Wilder had heard the warning as well, and now he broke into a grin and slowed his pace, deliberately aiming straight for the wary sheriff.

"Better get out of my way, Sheriff," Wilder taunted. "I'd hate for anyone to get hurt."

Carter twisted his head from side to side, sweeping the area for anything that could help with this dilemma. Then he spotted it.

Dodging past Wilder, he ran over to the security station. He snatched something from the desk there, then turned and raced back. As he neared Wilder, Carter held up his recently acquired prize.

A water bottle.

"No!" Wilder threw up his arms as Carter's arm swung forward in a sharp arc. The open bottle sprayed its contents across the room—and doused Wilder completely.

ZOT!!!

All the energy that had built up around the biogeneticist discharged at once. The flash was blindingly bright, and the sound explosive. Wilder was blown off his feet, and landed heavily on the floor, soaking wet but thoroughly wiped clean of any electrical charge.

Carter wasted no time. He dropped to his knees, flipped Wilder over onto his stomach, and handcuffed the man's hands behind him.

"Well," Carter announced, looking around. "Guess we all know what he'll be charged with."

CHAPTER 32

Jo had dodged around the security gate while Carter was splashing Wilder—no sense getting shocked twice!—and reached him a few seconds after the takedown. She helped Carter haul the thief to his feet, and glared up at him.

"Okay, mister," she growled, getting in his face. "You're caught and you know it. You might as well talk."

Fargo and Dr. Korinko were right behind her. "Is it true, Dan?" Korinko asked. "Are you really the one who took the Thunderbird egg?"

Dan shook himself and water went flying. For a second it looked like he was going to deny the accusation, even now. But then he hung his head.

"I'm sorry, Anna. I never meant for all of this to happen."

"So you did take it," Fargo accused. "Where is it? What've you done with it?"

"It's at my studio," Wilder admitted. "It's perfectly safe."

"Why did you do this?" Korinko asked. "We were friends. Colleagues. You know how long Sean and I had worked on this."

"Worked on creating a creature, a beautiful majestic creature, only to cage it forever!" Wilder snapped. "You had re-created the Thunderbird of legend, and why? To sell it to some third-world country so they could grow yams? You were defiling centuries of history with crass commercialism! I had to do something."

Carter shook his head. "So you stole the Thunderbird—so you could set it free?"

"Of course." Wilder glared at them. "I've dedicated my life to reintroducing species to the wild. How could I stand by and watch something as awe-inspiring as the Thunderbird be subjected to a life of servitude?"

"Servitude?" Korinko stared at him. "It could help repopulate the deserts, Dan! It could bring life back to whole sections of the world where nothing has grown in centuries! It would roam free through those areas, bringing storms just by its presence! We weren't going to cage it—we were going to set it loose under controlled conditions. Exactly the same way you do with the extinct species you've reverse-engineered."

Wilder gaped, and then slumped. "Really?" He shook his head. "I heard—I thought—there was talk about corporate sponsors, and preorders, so I assumed . . ."

"Never assume," Fargo pointed out smugly. "You make an ass out of you and me." Carter and Jo both rolled their eyes. Wilder glared. "What? It's an old saying!"

"And an accurate one, if cheeseball," Carter admitted. He eyed his captive. "You didn't stop to talk to them about their plans, and so you jumped to conclusions. And created a whole big mess as a result."

"I didn't mean to," Wilder argued. "I just wanted to set the Thunderbirds loose so they could live their lives in peace."

"They will." Carter tugged on the man's handcuffed wrists. "You, on the other hand, are another story."

"I'll take my punishment," Wilder announced, raising his chin. "I deserve it. But you need to retrieve the remaining egg from my studio. I've got it in a containment field, and it's stable, but I don't know for how much longer." He looked down at his feet, embarrassed. "That's why I was in such a hurry. I needed to get back and check on it."

"And if you hadn't, you might have been able to talk your

way out of all this, instead of panicking," Jo noted. She shook her head. "Good for us, bad for you."

"Tell me where the studio is, and we'll retrieve the egg," Carter instructed. But Wilder shook his head.

"I need to show you," he claimed. "I've got the site secured—you could break in, but that might disturb the egg and force it to hatch prematurely."

"Please," Korinko pleaded. "I need that egg back intact."

Carter considered. "All right," he said finally. "But don't try anything."

He started to lead Wilder out, but Jo stopped him. "I know you're the one who actually grabbed him," she said quietly, "but Fargo and I were the ones who caught him."

"You're right," Carter agreed. "It's your collar, Jo—yours and Fargo's." He stepped back and let Jo reach in and grab Wilder's wrists instead. "You two go retrieve the egg. I'll meet you back at the office."

Jo smiled. "Thanks, Carter." Then she nudged Wilder with her foot. "Let's go."

Fargo lingered, unsure what to do now that they'd caught their man. But as she passed him, Jo paused and raised an eyebrow.

"Are you coming, or what?"

With a grin, Fargo stepped in beside her, and together they guided their culprit out through the gates and toward the parking lot.

Zot!

"Ouch!"

"How did it go?" Carter called out as Jo and Fargo led Wilder into the sheriff's office an hour later.

"Great," Fargo replied, falling back so Jo could take Wilder over to the jail cell. He'd been in there once or twice himself, and liked to keep a safe distance from it, just in case. "The egg was right where he said it was, and he'd maintained the containment field perfectly. We took the egg back to Dr. Korinko, and she confirmed that it'd been expertly cared for and was still viable." He grinned. "She and Dr. Boggs should be the proud parents of a baby Thunderbird inside of the week."

"I'll have to think of a suitable baby gift," Carter replied, leaning back in his chair. "Maybe a pair of asbestos booties." He laughed, and Fargo laughed with him to be polite.

Jo finished locking Wilder in and joined them by Carter's desk. "All squared away," she reported. "I'll fill out the paperwork in a little bit, so the DoD can charge him formally." She glanced at the prisoner over her shoulder, then lowered her voice. "It may get ugly. Breaking and entering, destroying government property, sabotage, theft, endangerment—Wilder could go away for a long time."

Carter tilted his head to the side to study the biogeneticist, who was sitting slumped on the cell's cot. "He did take care of the second egg," he pointed out quietly. "And led you to it without a problem once we'd caught him. That might help a little." But he knew it wouldn't help much. The DoD was very serious about security in Eureka, and especially at GD. They tended to throw the book at anyone who violated the rules, and particularly anyone who destroyed property or research or endangered personnel. Wilder was going to be looking at a lot of prison time.

Still, Carter couldn't feel too sorry for the man. He might have meant well, but he had still put all of them at risk. And his little stunt had contributed to the problem with the other Eureka, which had put the entire world in danger. That sort of recklessness deserved a hefty sentence.

"Good work, both of you," he told Jo and Fargo, switching mental gears. "I'm impressed."

"Fargo's the one who deserves all the credit," Jo insisted. "It was his idea to electrify the security gates to catch the thief."

Fargo shuffled his feet and watched them intently to hide his blush. "Aw, it was nothing."

"No, you did good, Fargo," Carter told him. "Really good." He smiled. "But I'm not surprised."

"Neither am I," Jo agreed, favoring Fargo with a smile of her own. "I knew you could do it."

"Thanks." Fargo couldn't meet their eyes, but he felt a warm flush of pleasure at the compliments. And he realized something, too. He'd been jealous of his other self for being sheriff in that version of Eureka, but more importantly, for having everyone's respect. But it turned out he had respect, too.

Sure, they teased him a lot. And he was sort of the unofficial town scapegoat, who got blamed first whenever anything went wrong. And Allison often gave him the world's most boring assignments, like overseeing inventory or double-checking vacation day requests. But he was useful. He was the one Carter and even Jo went to whenever they needed help with something technical.

Well, after Henry.

And maybe Zane.

But they still asked him for help a lot.

And so did Allison. She relied on him, and she wouldn't trust him with the small stuff if she didn't think he could handle it, and if she didn't know she could count on him.

So maybe he'd always had the respect he'd been looking for.

Sure, it wasn't the same thing as being sheriff. Or director of GD, but at least it was something.

"By the way," Carter mentioned, fixing Fargo with a look. "Allison called while you two were on your way back here. You're going to need to fix whatever you did to the security gate before tomorrow morning. Nobody wants to start their day by getting electrocuted."

Fargo sighed. Well, maybe respect was something you had to work toward, one tiny bit at a time.

"Everything seems back to normal," Henry commented as Carter joined him at their usual table at Café Diem.

"Seems that way," Carter agreed, leaning back and smiling as Vincent brought out his order, a bacon double cheeseburger and waffle fries. "For now, anyway."

"The realities are stable, though, right?" Henry had a turkey club, and took a healthy bite after asking that.

"Yeah, that's all good." Carter munched on a fry. "Russell says they won't shift again as long as the arrays function properly, and there's no reason they won't. She and Zane beefed up the breakers and cutouts so even if there's another energy surge, they won't be able to reset those systems."

Henry nodded. "Good. One visit to another reality was enough for me, I think."

That got a laugh out of Carter. "Yeah, I heard about your little visit to the jail. Not eager to repeat it?"

Henry chuckled. "Do I look like Otis Campbell to you? No, thanks—once was enough."

"Hey, you'd make a good Otis!" Carter argued, remembering the old TV show character. "Which would make me Andy Taylor, and Jo could be Barney Fife." He laughed again as his imagination filled out the rest of the cast. "Zoe would have to be Opie; she'd love that. And Aunt Bee—"

"Would be S.A.R.A.H.," Henry finished for him. "That does sound about right, actually. Nice one, Jack." He sobered a bit. "But it was an interesting experience, seeing what the town was like, how it was different, what had changed and what had stayed the same."

Carter nodded. "Yeah, that was wild." He leaned back in his chair and took a big sip from his chocolate milkshake. "You know, there've been plenty of times where I've thought that Jo could handle this whole place just fine without me. And more than a few times when I've come close to calling it quits."

"And once where you were fired, at least for a little while," his friend pointed out.

"Exactly. But seeing that other Eureka . . ." Carter shook his head. "It was actually encouraging, in a way, to see just how much of a difference I've made in this town." He glanced around, his eyes serious. "You never know how many lives you touch, sometimes. What sort of influence you've had on the people around you. How the world wouldn't be the same place if you'd just done a few things differently."

"'I took the one less traveled by,'" Henry replied, clearly quoting something. "'And that has made all the difference.'"

Carter smiled and scanned Café Diem again, thinking about this town and its people. His town. His people. A place, and a job, he wouldn't trade for anything.

"It definitely has," he agreed. "It definitely has."